Dear Reader:

What can I say about the incredible Allison Hobbs except that I am extremely proud of her; she continues to perfect her writing style with each title. *Lipstick Hustla* is no exception. Misty, the freaky and engaging young hustler from *Double Dippin'* and *Big Juicy Lips* is back with a vengeance. This time, instead of only pimping out one or two men, she has acquired an entire stable of muscular, well-endowed men to service her growing clientele. Both men and women gladly cough up big dollars to spend some quality time with her "man servants." Misty continues to be the ruler of her own world and she brandishes an iron fist as she does it. Nobody messes with Misty.

But...there is one man that Misty can no longer claim as her own: Brick. After using Brick like a piece of trash for many years, pimping him out to male clients, Brick is now married to Misty's very own mother and about to become a new father. This is almost too much for Misty to handle; not that she has a voice in the matter. *Lipstick Hustla* is like visiting an old friend; one that you often wonder whatever happened to them. Misty is one of the most memorable characters in recent history; a woman who knows what she wants, demands it, and accepts nothing less. I am sure that you will enjoy this book as much as I enjoyed editing it. Also, make sure you check out the entire Allison Hobbs collection; especially *Stealing Candy*, which came out a few months before this one. It is a true eye-opener about the sex trafficking of teens, a topic that unfortunately has started to land on the news on a practically daily basis.

As always, thanks for supporting me and the Strebor Books family. We work extremely hard to bring you well-written, stimulating books that reach outside of the box. If you would like to email me, you can contact me at Zane@eroticanoir.com.

Blessings,

Zane

Zane
Publisher
Strebor Books International
www.simonandschuster.com

ZANE PRESENTS

A NOVEL

LIPSTICK HUSTLA

ZANE PRESENTS

A NOVEL

LIPSTICK HUSTLA

ALLISON HOBBS

SBI

STREBOR BOOKS

NEW YORK LONDON TORONTO SYDNEY

Strebor Books
P.O. Box 6505
Largo, MD 20792
http://www.streborbooks.com

ISBN 978-1-59309-283-2
ISBN 978-1-4391-6910-0 (e-book)
LCCN 2010934202

First Strebor Books trade paperback edition October 2010

Cover design: www.mariondesigns.com
Cover photograph: © Keith Saunders/Marion Designs

10 9 8 7 6 5 4 3 2 1

Manufactured in the United States of America

For information regarding special discounts for bulk purchases,
please contact Simon & Schuster Special Sales at 1-866-506-1949
or business@simonandschuster.com

The Simon & Schuster Speakers Bureau can bring authors to your
live event. For more information or to book an event, contact the
Simon & Schuster Speakers Bureau at 1-866-248-3049 or visit our
website at www.simonspeakers.com.

This book is dedicated to my son,
"Korky" Carl Johnson
You Make Me Smile

CHAPTER 1

Traveling at a high rate of speed in a thirty-mile-per-hour zone, Misty checked the rear-view mirror. There was no sign of a police car trailing behind her on the desolate, dark road. She switched her gaze to the left and then the right—no cops hiding in the shadows either.

Smiling with pleasure, she accelerated the Lamborghini. With a tingling thrill, she watched the needle of the speedometer jump from eighty to one-hundred-twenty almost instantly.

Adrenaline pumped as she handled the sleek, fast car. Whipping down the asphalt road, Misty owned the night!

But there was no time to bask in her glory. She had a big problem.

That goddamned Troy wasn't worth shit. She'd given him a simple assignment: take good care of Smash Hitz.

Having celebrity clients of Smash Hitz' magnitude had contributed in building Misty's empire. She was known for her professionalism and discretion, and the stars who were listed in her little black book didn't have to worry about Mediatakeout.com or Bossip.com putting their freaky preferences on blast.

What the hell was Troy thinking when he stole that man's signature bling? Fucking moron!

Smash Hitz had called Misty at two in the morning, waking her from a deep sleep.

"Hey, Smash, what's good?" she had answered. Though she was half asleep, she managed to speak in the sweet voice that was reserved for VIP clientele.

The call had taken her by surprise; she assumed the rapper had already left town and was on his way to the next city on his tour.

Misty had sent Troy to the mansion Smash was rent-ing, in-structing him to relieve the rapper's depraved urges. According to Troy, he'd left Smash Hitz wearing a satisfied smile.

So why was Smash calling? Did he want some more of Troy? Did he want to take her worker on the road with him? Hmm. She'd have to charge Smash up for that kind of extended service.

Smash must be insatiable, Misty decided. Fuck it though; she wasn't turning down good money. Smash had bank. As far as she was concerned, he had carte blanche to get his freak on with Troy and any sex slinger on her payroll for as long as he wanted.

Picturing mega bucks and other perks, she injected a smile into her voice as she rephrased her question. "So what's crackin', Smash?"

"Bring me my shit, and I ain't saying what it is," the rapper demanded in the countrified, gravelly voice that had brought him fortune and fame.

"What shit?" Misty murmured. She cut a suspicious eye at Troy, who was lying in bed next to her. Smash didn't sound like he was in the mood for more sex service. In fact, he sounded furious. *What did Troy do?*

"I ain't got all night, either," Smash Hitz growled.

Misty kicked Troy, trying to wake him up.

Troy didn't stir. He'd had a long night. Tending to Smash Hitz had been easy, but satisfying Misty's demanding coochie had required putting in some work.

After blowing her back out for over two-and-a-half hours, Troy had to finish Misty off with his tongue. *Nigga had to go deep diving to make me cum.* She smiled in remembrance, and then scowled, recalling that she had to coddle the incredibly wealthy rap artist who was on the other end of the phone.

"Did you say you want me to bring something to you?" She laughed nervously, like the request had to be a joke. *I hope this rappin' asshole don't think I'm getting out of my bed at this hour of the night.*

"Look, I'ma 'bout to jet outta here, but I want you to come through. So get your pretty lil' self over here, ASAP."

"Why? Did something happen with Troy?" She shot a hot glance at Troy's sprawled-out, lanky ass.

"You and me gotta have a serious talk about your slimy business practices."

She gasped. "My business is—"

"Save your breath, mamacita. We gon' have a sit-down. After you hand over my shit, then I'ma give you a chance to lay out all the reasons why I should keep fuckin' with your thievin' ass."

Misty flinched at the insult. "Mr. Hitz, I am *not* a thief. I would never steal from my clients and put my reputation at stake. I'm sorry about this confusion." She could flip the script and get professional whenever the situation demanded it.

"Ain't no confusion. Bring me my shit back."

There was no reasoning with this psycho mufucka. Misty took a deep, calming breath. "Okay, I'll be there shortly." Though she tried to keep it professional, her words came out sounding like a flunky. She groaned in humiliation.

She glared at Troy. She would kill Troy if he fucked up her relationship with Smash. *What kind of hellish trouble has this ashy asshole gotten me into?* Her angry eyes roamed down Troy's thighs. As expected, his kneecaps were as ashy as ever.

Earlier that night, Misty had insisted that Troy slather himself with gobs of her most expensive lotion, but obviously the effects of the deep-penetrating moisturizer had worn off.

His long, snake-like, good-fucking dick tended to be on the ashy-side, too. But many of Troy's regular customers liked the crustiness that clung to his skin.

With the phone pressed against her ear, she squinted menacingly at Troy, who was snoring in his sleep while she had to put up with Smash Hitz' bad attitude.

I'ma fuck you up, Troy. Them Z's you catchin' are about to come to an end.

Having to listen to Smash's gruff-sounding voice, making outrageous demands, was really getting on her nerves.

"Matter of fact…" Smash Hitz continued in his slow, Southern drawl, "I ain't gon' be satisfied 'til I see your lip prints on both cheeks of my ass."

What the fuck! All of Misty's sex slingers were inked with the image of her lips on their forearm. This design informed her clients that she'd sampled the goods and the worker was stamped with her kiss of approval.

Though Misty was extremely flattered that a rap icon like Smash Hitz wanted to wear her tattoo on his butt cheeks, she considered the request peculiar as hell and somewhat disturbing.

Despite the fact that her insignia would be hidden inside the seat of Smash's pants, Misty didn't like the idea of him wearing her lip prints on his ass.

Frowning, she wondered if she was being overly sensitive about her trademark, and then shook her head.

Nah! Smash Hitz' request is straight-up disrespectful.

The wealthy rap artist had purchased everything money could buy; now he wanted to get tatted with her personal symbol. That was crazy. Her workers had fucked and sucked with the amazing skill and expertise that was required in order to flaunt her design on their arm. She didn't take her brand lightly.

Sure, Smash had bought her the Lambo, but she had damn sure earned every dollar he'd spent. He was her most difficult client, making her work extra hard for the money he paid her.

Misty's mind raced, trying to think of a polite way to tell this egotistical lunatic that she couldn't have her tattoo disrespected like that. Not even by Smash Hitz.

"So lemme get this right. You wanna wear my tattoo on your ass?" she inquired, trying her best to conceal her repulsion.

"Hell no! I want the real thing," he said, sounding completely irrational.

"I'm confused."

"Lemme help you get your mind right." Smash paused. "Thanks to me, you doin' big things and you wanna stay in business for awhile…am I right?"

"Of course." Misty seethed. Smash was holding something over her head and she wished he'd get to the damn point.

"Then you gon' have to make it your business to get over here and kiss my ass."

Kiss his ass! Smash Hitz had lost his damn mind. She didn't appreciate being spoken to like she was some desperate video vixen.

Smash had it twisted. She called her own shots. He had a lot of fuckin' nerve, talking to her like she was some stank-ass hoe or one of his muthafuckin' groupies.

She was the head bitch in charge of her organization, and she didn't lick, suck, or fuck unless she wanted to. She damn sure didn't kiss anyone's ass—under any circumstances.

Though she was heated, Misty managed to keep a civil tone. "What's going on, Smash? I don't understand."

"Let's get it crackin'. Put on some bright red lipstick. When you get to the crib, I want you to bow down and pucker up!" The next sound she heard was the dial tone.

"Troy!" Misty yelled, bringing Troy out of his blissful sleep. "What did you take from Smash Hitz?"

"I aint take nothing from him," Troy replied, recoiling as he rubbed his eyes.

Infuriated, she could feel her face turning red with rage.

"Stop lying! You stole something from Smash or he wouldn't be calling me in the middle of the goddamn night." She was ready to throw a fit and break a lamp over Troy's head, but she needed to conserve her strength.

Instead of swinging on Troy, Misty screamed in fury, alerting her personal bodyguards. She could hear their pounding footsteps running toward her bedroom door.

"I'm telling the truth, Misty," Troy said in a choked voice, his eyes flicking to the set of double doors that barged open.

Nitro and Tank, two heavily muscled men, entered the bedroom with their guns drawn.

"You okay, Misty?" Tank asked.

Nitro glared at Troy. "Did that punk put his hands on you?"

"No. This sleazy hoe stole some shit off a VIP client, but he's denying it."

"You want us to get the truth out of him?"

"I didn't take nothing!" Troy shouted as if the volume of his voice would make his words sound sincere.

Tank and Nitro kept their guns aimed at Troy's head.

Troy raised a shaky right hand. "My hand to God, Misty. I ain't take nothing from Smash Hitz. I swear on everything I love."

Surprise registered in Nitro's and Tank's eyes. Neither man realized that the famous rap star was one of Misty's clients.

Misty felt like slapping the shit out of Troy for divulging the confidentiality of such a high-profile patron, but she didn't want to risk marring her fresh manicure or spraining her wrist in the process.

"Put your weapons away," Misty instructed.

Reluctantly, the security duo obeyed, tucking their guns inside of their waistbands.

"Beat the truth out of that ass," she snarled, nodding at Troy.

With the savage demeanor of killer Rottweilers, the two men rushed Troy, growling as they easily took the lightweight down. They delivered brutal kicks and stomps as Troy lay curled on her plush carpet.

"That's enough!" Misty ordered.

Tank and Nitro froze in action.

Groaning, Troy lifted himself up.

"What did you take from Smash?" Misty yelled, her face twisted in rage.

"His chain," Troy mumbled, his eyes lowered in shame.

Contrite, Troy stole a glance at Misty, trying to gauge how she was handling his admission.

Breathing hard, she seethed in silence, which didn't bode well for Troy.

"Did you take anything else?" Tank barked, flexing up and balling his fists like he was ready to break a couple of bones.

"No!" Troy scooted backward. The two muscled men stepped closer, hovering above Troy, poised to resume beating some more truth out of him.

Misty felt sick. She covered her mouth in shock, and then uncovered it. "You took Smash's chain? The one with his big-ass, diamond logo?" Her voice was high-pitched and raspy with alarm.

"I only borrowed it. I was gon' show it to some of my homies in my 'hood and then—"

"Where is it?" She spoke through clenched teeth.

Troy swallowed. "I was going to send it back to him—you know, on some anonymous shit."

"You stole his fuckin' signature bling!" Misty bent over and covered her face. Recovering quickly, she stood erect. "You've always been an idiot, but even a moron like you should know that fucking with that man's jewelry is a deadly mistake. Do you think I'ma let some lil' nothing mufucka like you destroy everything I've struggled to put together?"

Not knowing what to say or do, Troy shrugged.

"Young blood needs his head cracked open," Tank said, frowning and swaying as if he were having a difficult time restraining himself.

"He's gonna be dealt with, but not right now. I gotta make a run. When I get back, though…" She shook her head. "I'ma miss that ashy dick you been slinging, but I'm gon' have to flat-line your punk ass."

"Come on, Misty. Be easy, baby."

She shook her head. "You need to start saying prayers for your mother."

"Why?" Troy asked, confused and agitated. "What my mom got to do with this?"

Repeating words that had once been spoken to her, Misty said in an icy tone, "When you come up missing, your mother is gon' be shedding a river of tears."

"You ain't gotta go hard like that. I said I'm sorry."

"How long have I been feeding *and* fucking you? Huh, Troy? How long?" she yelled.

"Round 'bout two years or more." He looked down at the floor.

"You were wearing a dingy white T-shirt when I met you. Your elbows and arms…your entire body looked like you'd been rolling around in a white powder. You told me to call you Cash Money," she said sneeringly. "But all I saw was Ashy Cashy."

"Ashy Cashy?" Nitro and Tank said at the same time and exchanged disgusted frowns.

"Yeah, that used to be his working name," Misty enlightened. "He got a real long, ashy dick. And his stupid ass got the nerve to know how to work it."

The bodyguards screwed up their faces like they'd been given too much information.

Turning her attention back to Troy, Misty said, "Don't you realize I only send pretty mufuckas to handle business with my VIP clientele? But since you've been down with me since day one, I decided to let you in on some celebrity action." She shook her head grimly. "And look at how you repay me."

"I'm...so...sorry," Troy said, putting space between each word, hoping to express the depth of his sincerity.

"Fuck you!"

"You not tryna hear this, but I really love you, Misty."

"Hell no, she ain't tryna hear that. Man, shut the fuck up!" Nitro exploded.

"You got two seconds to tell me where you hid Smash's shit." Misty hissed.

"In my room." Troy finally caved. "Under the bed. His chain is inside the box my Polo boots came in."

With his gun pointed, Nitro kept Troy in his field of vision, while Tank stalked off to search Troy's bedroom.

Five minutes later, Tank handed Misty the famous, iced-out medallion that was an integral part of the Smash Hitz brand.

CHAPTER 2

Gliding down the desolate road, Misty concentrated on what ploy she would use to get out of kissing Smash Hitz' ass. The thought of it made her nauseous.

Perhaps it wasn't a good idea to meet with the dick-sucking freak in person. It might make better sense to FedEx his gaudy neckpiece.

Over the phone, and at a safe distance, she could placate him with the offer of a couple of freebies. Maybe she could get Smash to agree to experimenting with a new erotic pleasure...a big burly mofo wearing lipstick and leaving his lip prints on Smash's ass, his dick...or even on his muthafuckin' big, bald head! Wherever the fuck.

Unfortunately, Smash Hitz wasn't a reasonable man. He had it in his mind that Misty had orchestrated the robbery. He was making her take responsibility for setting him up with a thief.

Misty was laced up with fly gear. Both wrists, her neck, and her ears were frozen with pink ice. Rocking a new pair of Giuseppe Zanotis on her pretty feet, Misty looked like a five-star chick.

She hoped her divalicious image would give Smash a change of heart. He should take advantage of her beauty and use her for arm candy on his next walk down the red carpet. She was a stunner when they'd attended the Grammys together. Why would he want to force his gorgeous decoy down on her knees like a dirty hoe? Why would he insist that she kiss his stank ass? Smash was the craziest mofo Misty had ever met. If he didn't have bank, she would have cussed him out a long time ago.

But Smash was tight-fisted. Everybody recognized that. Being on the safe side, she'd brought lots of cash. Just in case she had to reimburse Smash, she had his money stacked inside of her Louis Vuitton bag.

What would be worse, she wondered…putting her lips on his butt cheeks or giving back his cake?

Both options made her want to throw up, but given a chance, she'd return the money before putting her gorgeous face anywhere near Smash's faggoty ass.

She thought about Troy and sucked her teeth. In some countries, they cut people's hands off for stealing. But Troy deserved far worse. Only death was good enough for a kleptomaniac, who had put her livelihood at risk.

She checked the time. Damn, she had to hurry up. If Smash left the mansion before she returned his medallion, there would be hell to pay.

Misty didn't even want to imagine losing her current lifestyle and the dynasty she'd fought to build. But if Smash

Hitz decided to put her on his shit list, she'd be black-balled for the rest of her life.

First, he'd replace her with another fake girlfriend... use another hot chick to play his decoy. There'd be no more Grammys or any other award shows for Misty. She'd be barred from the lavish annual White Party, dis-invited to exclusive listening parties, banned from popular hot spots, and unwelcome at all big-baller events.

One word from Smash and Misty's treasured black book wouldn't be worth shit.

Time was of the essence. She'd wasted too much time fucking around, getting the truth out of Troy. That skinny-ass, ashy-behind, long-dick mofo was definitely going to be dealt with.

Picking up speed, she hurtled down the dark high-way, rushing to catch Smash Hitz, and wondering if she could make peace with the idea of kissing his ass cheeks. She had to do what she had to do. *Damn!*

Taking her mind off of her troubles, she concentrated on the music that poured from the speakers.

Ugh. Alicia Keys was singing one of her heart-wrench-ing love songs, reminding Misty of the two men she'd truly loved and lost. She didn't want to go there. This was not the time to entertain thoughts of love, weak-ness, or failure. She had to totally disengage from her feminine side if she intended to win this toe-to-toe with Smash Hitz.

As Alicia Keys wailed, Misty changed to another CD.

Smash Hitz' coarse voice filled the interior of Misty's whip. *Ew!* She didn't wanna hear that nigga spittin' until they had worked out their differences.

Kanye came on next. *Nah!* Misty wasn't feeling him right now, either. He needed to do something about that lesbian trick. How he gon' just hand a hoe a career in the fashion industry? Shit didn't even make any sense.

That Amazon woman towered over Kanye, while Misty, on the other hand, was perfectly petite and a beautiful, exotic stunner. Misty was a much better fit for Kanye. Kanye West didn't have Smash's long money, but he'd be a nice replacement if Smash Hitz decided to dump her.

Peeved at Kanye for not being available, Misty clicked to another musical selection. Trey Songz. She smiled as she listened to his vocals. Yeah, that sexy nigga could beat the pussy up until Kanye came to his senses.

Suddenly, Misty heard an odd, knocking noise beneath the music. The racket seemed to be coming from her car.

The smooth glide of the Lambo became slightly bumpy, which was odd, being that the super car was in pristine condition.

A strange flapping sound jolted her.

What the fuck is going on?

Decreasing her speed, she turned the music off, and focused on the source of the disturbing noise. The flapping noise increased in volume. Then the Lambo started vibrating and shaking, making her fear that she might lose control of the car.

Shit! Beyond irritated, she pulled over to the side of

the dark road, her expensive Lamborghini wobbling and thumping like a beat-up hooptie.

Clutching the steering wheel, with the Lamborghini leaning to the side, Misty sat and fumed for a few moments. *I gotta fucking flat tire. How the fuck that happen?*

What the hell was she supposed to do now? A call for road assistance could take up to an hour or more.

What was she thinking when she decided to take this drive to no-man's, muthafuckin' land all by herself? She should have had Tank or Nitro chauffeur her to Smash's hidden-in-the-sticks crib.

But no… She wanted show off the way she wheeled her whip.

She also wanted to win some cool points for using discretion and handling her business solo.

She pressed a switch and the door pushed up. Black-Berry in hand, she stepped out the car and walked around to the passenger side. Misty sucked her teeth in disgust. The front tire looked like it had exploded.

As she poised her finger to call for help, she saw headlights bearing down on her.

A stroke of luck! Feeling fortunate, she rushed around her car, waving her arms, flagging down the car that was approaching.

Intending to sweet-talk the motorist into driving her to Smash's mansion, Misty stepped out into the road so that she could be seen.

The car suddenly picked up speed and was heading for Misty at a crazy, high rate of speed.

"Fucking lunatic!" Misty yelled as she attempted to scurry back to the shoulder.

But her timing was off and she had misjudged the intention of the driver.

Unbeknownst to Misty, the driver had locked in on her position and was careening toward her. Misty never made it to the safety of the shoulder.

Upon impact, she was catapulted through the air for what seemed like an eternity. Flung so high and for so long, she actually had time to acknowledge that the sensation of flying was somewhat pleasant.

She floated through the air for a few more seconds and then came crashing down, hitting the ground with a horrible crunch. She lay still for a few seconds, taking in the astonishing reality that she had survived.

She was alive and conscious. *Thank God!* Now she needed to confirm that she was still able-bodied. She tried to maneuver her legs, but they were hopelessly crumpled beneath her.

In a panic, Misty struggled to prop herself up, but her arm was limp and useless.

The car that had hit her sat in the dark with its lights out. The engine purred like a satisfied cat after capturing its prey.

Misty had never felt so vulnerable in her life. Lying on her stomach, her cheek on the ground, she faced the direction of the car. Her eyes were wide open as she panted intensely.

Headlights clicked on suddenly, illuminating her broken body…exposing her vulnerability.

I know this better not be no hit-and-run bullshit. That drunk-drivin' mufucka better get out of that car and help me!

Finally the car door opened and then slammed closed. Expecting to hear heavy footsteps rushing toward her, she was surprised when she recognized the sauntering cadence of stilettos clicking on asphalt.

With squinted eyes trained on the direction of the clicking sounds, she was finally able to discern a pair of shapely, stallion-like, sepia-toned legs.

A woman moved slowly toward her. She had a swagger in her walk that made Misty furious. It didn't improve her attitude when she noticed that the stilettos were new Louboutins.

Hurry up, bitch! Walking all slow like you da shit.

The woman grew closer. Misty blinked in shock when she noticed that a tire iron was dangling at the stranger's side.

Misty wondered what the woman thought she could do with a tire iron. Was she going to waste time attempting to pry the busted tire away from the rim? Incensed, Misty frowned excessively.

Fuck a flat tire! This no-driving bitch better get on her goddamn cell and send for a muthafuckin' ambulance.

The woman stopped and stood over Misty.

"Thanks," Misty forced herself to murmur, though she really wanted to cuss the woman out.

Keeping angry thoughts to herself, Misty focused on her only free limb and reached up a beseeching hand to the tall, silent stranger. She'd cuss her out and whip her ass later.

Right now, she needed to find out which limbs could function and which couldn't. Her right arm seemed okay, but her left arm and both legs were questionable. Maybe with this bitch's help, Misty would be able to stand up on her feet and try to walk.

Instead of feeling the remorseful, helping hand of a stupid and reckless driver, Misty felt the excruciating blow from the tire iron as it collided with the side of her face.

Dazed, she could hear the crunching sound and searing pain of two molars tearing away from her gums. She opened her mouth to scream but the sound was stifled as she gagged and choked on blood that was pooled inside her mouth.

Beginning to comprehend her dilemma, Misty closed her eyes and lay lifeless. *If I lay still and play dead, I might get out of this bullshit.*

Smash Hitz had to be behind this. The self-proclaimed gangsta wasn't nothing but a straight-up bitch, sending a woman to handle his beef.

But why would Smash send somebody to fuck her up before she delivered the goods? His oversized, goddamn medallion was in her car, wrapped in gold tissue paper and tucked inside her Louis Vuitton bag.

She could hear the clack of the stilettos as the female assailant strolled to the direction of the purring engine.

Misty listened intently as the car door opened and the woman got back inside the car. She felt a tremendous sense of relief when she heard tires squealing, realizing that the henchwoman was speedily leaving the scene.

Misty used the last bit of her waning strength to try to lift herself up again.

But when the car suddenly veered in Misty's direction, she had only a few seconds to reassess the situation.

She wasn't going to make it. The Amazon was a hired assassin. *She's gonna fuckin' kill me!*

So this is how it ends for me? Goin' down like some helpless, punk-ass bitch. Can't move. Can't even try to fight this slut. This is so fuckin' fucked up.

Tires rolled over Misty's back. At the sound of bones breaking, she submerged into peaceful, painless oblivion.

CHAPTER 3

One Year Ago

Too damn old to be giving birth, it would have served Misty's mother right if she'd gone into a seizure while pushing out Brick's baby.

Brick's baby! Misty doubted if she'd ever get used to that expression. If she wasn't such a strong woman… such a survivor, she would have probably ended up in a nut house for having to deal with the cold reality that her own mother had taken her man.

Brick wasn't just any man. He was Misty's good, faithful, freak-in-the sheets, money-making man.

It was the ultimate sin for her cut-throat mother to take Misty's breadwinner, and then turn around and marry him, as if legalizing such a foul betrayal made it acceptable behavior.

She would never honor Brick's union with her mother. Never! Their marriage wasn't nothing but a sham.

And that baby…Umph! Little Baron would probably end up being a retard or something. How could a child conceived by a pre-menopausal bitch and a damn-near illiterate mufucka be alright? Something had to be wrong with him. Time would tell.

Misty wondered who Brick thought he was fooling. He still loved her. That's why he was sitting on her mother's hospital bed, letting Misty rub on his arm.

Troy sat in a chair by the window. When Misty caught him scoping her move, she gave Troy the evil eye.

Like a good boy, Troy looked the other way. He picked up his cell and started playing some stupid game.

She watched the rise and fall of her mother's chest. She was out cold. Delivering a baby had worn her ass out.

"Brick," Misty whispered. "I miss you." She lowered her hand to his thigh. It was hard like concrete, turning her on. And making her mad at the same time. This nigga had some nerve to start sculpting his body after he hooked up with her haggard-looking mother.

But she pushed her resentment aside and began caressing motions that ventured closer to the inseam of his jeans.

Faking it like he didn't want her touching him, Brick inched closer to his unconscious wife, hugging on her as if for dear life.

"With your scar gone, and your body all ripped and everything, we could make a fortune together. You gotta be bored with this family bullshit. Don't you wanna get back with me? You know you miss the life."

Brick glanced at his wife and then cut an eye at the bassinette where his infant son lay sleeping.

"Let's talk outside," Brick said in a hushed tone. "I don't wanna wake them up."

Now, that's what I'm talking about! Misty stood, finger-combing her long hair, while Brick rearranged the blanket that covered the baby.

"Come on," Brick said in a whisper and began walking toward the door.

"I'll be right back, Troy," Misty said, her eyes dancing with delight. She gave Troy the thumbs-up sign, indicating that it was a wrap. Brick would be helping him handle the work load real soon.

"Let's go to the lounge," Brick said and walked ahead of Misty. The slight swag in his walk made Misty raise a brow. He was walking way ahead of her, which she considered the height of disrespect.

After being with her ancient mother, he should have been ecstatic to be walking side by side with a gorgeous diva.

Brick smiled and spoke to a few nurses as he passed by their station. Misty saw the nurses gushing and smiling... licking their lips like Brick was raw meat.

Then it dawned on her. Brick had game. He was putting on a show for those nurse bitches, trying to keep up the pretense that he was a faithful husband and a loving father. Misty made sure she put on her mean grill when she got close to the nurses' station.

Fuck them whores. Don't be worrying about what those bitches think, she wanted to tell Brick when she entered the visitor's lounge. But she held her tongue.

For appearances, she'd go along with this farce, but not for long. Brick was her man. He always was. Always would be.

Brick sat down. He leaned back in the chair and smiled at Misty.

Oh, goddamn! Brick had turned into a fine-ass mufucka. He looked so fuckin' good, she was ready to give him some "welcome back home" coochie right there in the visitor's lounge.

It took all her willpower not to hop out of her seat, straddle him, and start fucking the shit out of the sexy, new and improved Brick.

But she remained calm and focused. Giving him only a flicker of a smile, Misty got down to business.

"Brick, I want to apologize for everything. I didn't treat you right, but I've learned my lesson. I realize it's gonna be real hard for you to hurt my mother. You dread having to tell her you gotta bounce."

He gave her a wide-eyed look.

She took a deep breath and nodded her head reassuringly. "I'll be standing by your side when you break the news. I gotchu. We'll tell her together…make her understand that it's not personal. But you and me…shit, we go back to childhood. My mother doesn't understand how we do."

"Oh, she understands," Brick said, shifting his position, meeting Misty eye-to-eye.

"What do you mean?"

"Before she went to sleep, she told me to be careful. She loves you, Misty, but she knows she can't trust you."

Misty scowled. "So you still gon' put that dried-up bitch before me?"

Brick made a snorting sound. He dropped his head for a few seconds, composing himself. When he raised his head, his expression was serious.

"Thomasina is my wife. I love her. But I'm wasting my breath trying to school you on how I feel when you don't have the slightest idea of what love means."

Now teary-eyed, Misty said, "That's not true. I've always loved you, Brick."

"No, Misty. You love *you*. I ain't mad at you, though. Keep doing you."

Tears streaming down her cheeks, Misty shook her head in denial. "You feel sorry for my mother because she's all old and needy."

"Truth is your mother don't need me…I need her. And she ain't old. She's only in her forties. Thomasina is all woman. But you wouldn't know nothing about that."

"I'm not a woman?"

"Nah, you ain't nothing but a spoiled little girl."

Misty sighed.

"Thomasina gave me back everything that I let you take from me. My self-esteem, my pride, and my manhood. And she risked her life for me…giving me something that I never thought I'd have. A son. *My* son. So tell me, Misty, what did you ever do for me?"

Shocked speechless, Misty opened her mouth and closed it several times, but she couldn't find any words.

Trying to get sympathy, Misty sniffled.

"Your mother might love your selfish ass, but that don't

mean I have to. If you keep creepin' up on me like this, I'ma have to do something about it."

"I know you're not threatening me, Brick."

"Bring some trouble to my home and I'ma end up having to console my grieving wife."

Misty looked at him quizzically. "Whatchu mean?"

"When her daughter come up missing, my lady gon' be shedding a river of tears. That's not a threat, Misty. It's a warning."

"Why you coming at me like this?"

"I didn't have to give you a heads-up. But I did on the strength of what you said—we go back to childhood." Brick gave Misty a smirking smile.

With unmistakable swagger, Brick began making an exit.

He stopped and looked over his shoulder. "I'll tell your man hoe to meet you in the lounge."

Slumped in the chair, Misty frantically wiped her eyes. She couldn't let Troy see her crying like a little child. But the tears kept falling. She couldn't hold them back.

Brick's icy words had ripped her heart from her chest.

CHAPTER 4

Hiding her red eyes behind a pair of luxury sunglasses, Misty stood at the elevator bank with Troy at her side.

Inside the car, Troy waited patiently while Misty fiddled with the ignition, turning it off and on, trying to get the old, temperamental Pontiac to start.

"Come on, you piece of shit!" she yelled at the car.

The ignition finally kicked in, and Misty quickly reversed out of the parking spot. Lips drawn tight, she drove toward her and Troy's studio apartment.

"You going the wrong way," Troy informed her.

"What?"

"We going to the Red Lobster on the Boulevard, right?"

"Oh," she said absently and turned the car around. Steering toward the expressway, she couldn't take her mind off of Brick. She flinched as she thought about the cold tone he'd used and his sneering expression. Acting like he was better than her. Just because the mufucka had some work done on his face, and had pumped some iron didn't give him a new identity. Her mother was blowing up his head, calling him Baron and shit. But he was still Brick—a dumb-ass nobody.

Brick didn't have one ounce of gratitude, biting the damn hand that had fed him for most of his sorry life. *I made that mufucka. Taught him everything he knew. Slimy bastard.*

"So what ya boy say? Is he joining the team or what?"

Misty let out a sigh. "No. Not yet."

Troy frowned. "I thought you said—"

Misty hit the brakes and pulled over to the curb, the car idling loudly. "Fuck what you thought. Do you run shit?"

"Nah, I'm just saying…"

"I have a headache, Troy. I don't feel like driving way out to the Boulevard to get you some damn crab legs and shit."

"Come on, man. You promised."

"We don't have the money, Troy!"

"Damn! The shrimp and snow crab special only costs sixteen ninety-nine. We can't afford that?"

"No! We're broke! It ain't gon' kill you to grub on some Burger King until you can hustle up some more dough."

"Me? You said I could get a week off."

"Things changed. My gear wasn't cheap. We only have a couple dollars left."

"Why you go for broke? You spent everything I made on your gear?"

"I was trying to pull Brick away from my mother. I had to look the part."

"So what's up? When is Brick gon' be ready to start?"

She gathered her breath to cuss Troy out for asking so many questions, but then slowly exhaled. No point in taking out her rage on her one and only worker. Gritting her teeth, she pushed the gear into drive and merged into traffic.

"Brick is anxious to get back with me, but he can't right now. My mom had some complications and he needs to help take care of the baby until she can pull herself together," Misty lied.

"How long is that gon' take?"

"A few weeks. So you gon' have to make some sacrifices."

"Come on, Misty. You promised—"

"You gotta man-up, Troy! You bitching over seafood when we got bigger issues to deal with. The way I'm racking my brain, it feels like my head is about to explode. With all this mental maneuvering, I could be on the verge of giving myself an aneurysm or something. How you gon' live if something happens to me?"

Troy shrugged.

"What you do is easy. Humping mufuckas don't require no brain cells."

She made a sharp right turn and watched Troy out of the corner of her eye. He looked upset when she rolled into the Burger King parking lot.

Not being able to feed her worker a decent meal didn't sit well with her. She had banked on pulling Brick, but had failed.

Feeling like a failure made her mad.

Wearing her mean mug, she threw a twenty-dollar bill at Troy. "Don't try to keep the fucking change, nigga."

Troy looked hurt. "I ain't never stole nothing from you. It ain't even like that."

"Whatever," she muttered. Through the window, Misty could see the long lines of waiting customers inside the fast-food restaurant. She gave Troy the evil eye. "We ain't got all day for you to be fucking around in there."

She could have used the drive-thru to pick up his food, but Misty needed some time to be alone with her thoughts.

"Hurry up," she said in a nasty tone.

Troy took forever getting his long, gangly body out of the car. "You want anything?" he asked with a half-hearted smile.

"Hell, no! I'll starve before I eat that crap. Get your grub and then I gotta take you back to the crib so you can rest up. I want you to make a good impression on your client tonight."

She didn't have anyone lined up, but planned to scroll through her short list of clients and offer Troy's services at half-price. *Gotta do what I gotta do.*

"Tonight?" Troy's voice cracked.

"Yeah. Ain't no time to be sitting around bullshittin'."

Shit didn't pan out the way I thought it would so we gotta take it on the chin and keep it moving."

"That's messed up. You said I could get some time off."

"Look, nigga, we in a slump. Things keep going downhill like this, I'ma have to disguise you in a ski mask and strap your ass with a gun. What would you rather do? Risk your life robbing niggas or sling that ashy dick?"

"I guess I gotta keep slingin'," Troy mumbled.

"That's what I thought."

Troy walked away with his shoulders hunched up, hands in his pockets. His slow stride pointed out his hurt feelings.

Misty couldn't help feeling a little sorry for Troy. Damn shame she couldn't give the lanky nigga a decent meal. But money was low. She had to stretch out her last dollars until she could wrangle up a paying customer.

Getting back on her feet was taking longer than she'd expected. She'd been making ends meet by sending Troy out to her old clientele. Luckily she'd kept their phone numbers in her old cell.

Most of them were Brick's former regulars and they kept asking when they could see him again. She'd been promising that the website, updated with new, illicit pictures of Brick, would be up and running soon. But she didn't even have a computer at this point. Putting together her fabulous outfit had broken the bank.

CHAPTER 5
Present Day

Every now and then, Misty was able to get Troy some help. But no one stuck around for very long. What was wrong with young men today? A bunch of undependable, lazy asses who wanted something for nothing. After getting paid for one job, they usually disappeared for a few weeks, coming back when they got good and damn ready. Asking for more work when they needed some money.

That wasn't how Misty ran her business. She was getting real sick of the way none of her workers were taking her seriously.

It was critical that she hustle up two or three more dick slingers—some brawny muthafuckers. Puny-ass Troy had stuck by her side, but he was starting to buckle under the pressure. She doubted if he could hold down the fort by himself much longer.

Misty closed her eyes, thinking about all the good times she and Brick had shared in the past. He'd been by her side through the worst of times. It didn't make sense for him to be so cold-hearted and leave her hanging when she needed him the most.

Misty took off her shades and pulled down the visor to check out her reflection. Her eyes looked a little bloodshot from crying at the hospital, but she was still as gorgeous as ever. How Brick could choose her tore-down mother over her was beyond comprehension.

Damn, Brick. Why couldn't you at least help me out with a few jobs? It didn't appear that her mother would be going back to her job anytime soon. She shook her head. *That frontin'-ass nigga knows damn well he could use some extra dough.*

She put on some lipstick and admired her image. Fire Engine Red looked good with her olive-colored skin. She let out a long sigh, wishing she could press her lips against Brick's. *Damn, I miss him. I want that nigga back.*

On some real shit, if Brick wanted to demote her to side-jawn status, she'd do it in a heartbeat. She'd throw away her pride and accept her mother's sloppy seconds. Well…at least for a minute. She'd act like she was satisfied with the jump-off role until she could figure out a way to get Thomasina's tired ass out of the picture. Now how hard could that be?

She'd even get some therapy for her shopping addiction. She'd do whatever it took to get her man back.

But in the meantime, she needed some paper. She and Troy had been in survival mode for long enough. Brick was acting like a hater. *Haters are motivators.* It was time to go hard.

In the side mirror, Misty caught a glimpse of something interesting. A dude that was extra tall with a nice build. But he looked out of place; like he wasn't sure of himself. He had lighter skin than Misty preferred, but he had a real cute face. He looked like a knock-off version of the actor Jason Momoa.

Dude was obviously from out of town. Philly niggas had a certain way about themselves that distinguished them from all others.

Scrutinizing him, she noticed that his gear was corny and not up to par. There was no swag in his walk. Nothing about him was 'hood. He was heading toward the entrance of the restaurant, brows furrowed, deep in thought.

He looks like he got issues. She hoped that whatever his problems were, they worked to her advantage.

Misty honked her horn, startling him. He looked in her direction, squinting as if trying to figure out if he knew her.

His hesitancy confirmed that he had issues. A real nigga would be rushing over to the car, trying to find out what was up. She wondered if he was gay. It didn't matter, considering the tastes of her clientele.

"I don't bite!" she yelled in a friendly tone. "Come over here and let me holla at you for a minute!"

Taking hesitant steps, the light-skinned dude crossed the parking lot, face frowned up in confusion.

Misty started strategizing. Thoughts swam through her mind as she tried to think of what she should say. *I need to pull this yellow nigga. I can tell by his clothes that his money ain't right. How should I play this? Oh, fuck it. I ain't got time to piece together no long story. My flow is tight; I'ma have to freestyle.*

"Are you having car trouble?" the stranger asked, glancing at her older-model car. He didn't sound like he was from the 'hood.

"Um…no." Her eyes prowled his physique. Muscles rippled up and down his arms. He had well-developed, hairy legs with thick-ass calves bulging out. Even better, he was a straight sucker, willing to assist a damsel in distress.

Another plus was the desperate look in his eyes. Without a doubt, he was going through some sort of turmoil. And on closer inspection, Misty noticed that his clothes were more unsightly than she'd realized. His T-shirt bore a faded image of a dolphin. *Corny.* When she glanced down at his feet, she couldn't help from frowning in disgust. He was rocking a pair of off-brand, dusty-ass kicks.

"My name is Misty," she introduced, keeping her eyes on his face, which was so much more appealing than his wardrobe.

"Sailor," he replied.

"Sailor? That's your real name?" She wrinkled her nose in disapproval.

"Yeah, that's what my mom named me," he said, his light skin turning a little red.

"Are you black?"

Embarrassed by the inquisition, he squirmed. "No, not really."

She ignored his discomfort and didn't let up. "What do you mean, 'not really'? Either you're black or you're not. I'm mixed. My father is Hispanic but I still consider myself as being black."

"I'm not black."

Misty sighed. "You don't look totally white."

"Uh. Yeah, I know. My mother's white. My dad is... well, I never met him, but he's from Alaska."

"Your pops is an Eskimo?"

He chuckled uneasily. "You could say that. He's a native Alaskan."

In Misty's opinion, Sailor was all messed up. Half-white and half-Eskimo was a fucked-up combination. No wonder he seemed to have low self-esteem, even though he was fine as hell. *Perfect. She'd have him slinging dick in no time!*

"I'm not having car trouble, but I appreciate the fact that you were willing to help me. Most dudes from Philly wouldn't stop to help; they wouldn't want to get their hands dirty."

"I'm not from Philly."

"I didn't think so. You don't sound like you're from Philly. So where are you from?"

"Wisconsin. Oconomowoc, Wisconsin."

"Oco-where?"

"Oconomowoc," he repeated.

"Umph. I can't pronounce that shit and I'm not gon' try."

He laughed uncomfortably.

"I called you over here because I was wondering if you might be interested in making some extra cash?" she said, getting right to the point.

"I've been looking for employment, but I have to be honest with you. I don't have any ID."

"Not a problem," Misty said.

"Great! What kind of work are you talking about?"

"Body work," she said with a coy smile.

"Huh?"

"I provide escorts for desperate housewives." Misty figured she'd expose the truth of the matter after she had this cornball hooked.

"Do I need a suit?" Looking troubled, he glanced down at his shabby clothes.

"Nah, you wouldn't be taking the women out in public or anything like that. They only need to be escorted from the front door to the bedroom." Misty laughed.

"Bedroom? Are you asking me to be a male prostitute?"

"I like the word *escort*. Sounds better, don't you think? You get paid to play. Can you think of an easier way to make fast money?"

"How fast? I'm sort of…well, I'm in a tight jam."

A desperado…that's whassup! "I could probably get you some work tonight, but uh…you're going to have to rock some gear that's more appealing than what you're wearing. The casual look is aiight and everything, but sometimes the female clients like to get their freak on in five-star hotels. You can't stroll up in the Four Seasons looking like you're homeless. Feel me?"

He nodded and then tightly cradled his chin, looking a little distressed. "There's a problem with my clothes right now. All I have is what I'm wearing."

Misty rolled her eyes. *Like I don't know that already!*

CHAPTER 6

Misty caught a glimpse of Troy ambling out of the restaurant, carrying a big bag. When Troy noticed the man standing by the car, he froze. Misty stuck her hand out the window and did a secret hand wave, motioning for Troy to back up.

On point, Troy whirled around and went back into the restaurant.

"Where are your clothes?"

He exhaled. "I was staying around the corner on Armat Street—at the Caring House. You know, that place that takes kids off the street?"

"Whoa! Kids? You're not of legal age?" Misty wasn't trying to pimp out an under-aged minor.

"I'm nineteen. Be twenty next month. Caring House takes in young adults up to age twenty-two."

She smiled with relief. Dude was living in some type of group home situation. Shit sounded dire. "So what's your story? Why'd you have to be taken off the streets?" she asked, though she really didn't care.

"It's a long story, but I got kicked out of Caring House…" He looked down regretfully.

"You got evicted and they kept your clothes?"

"No, I got kicked out for fighting. But I didn't start it."

Misty didn't give a damn about his stupid fight. "Uh-huh. So, where's your gear?"

"Uncle Marshall claims I owe him back rent. He's keeping my duffel bag, my ID…and everything until I come up with six-hundred dollars."

"You have family here in Philly?"

"Uncle Marshall's not family. He's an older man; a friend. Everybody calls him Uncle Marshall."

"Some friend."

"Yeah," Sailor said, shaking his head.

"We can get that six-hundred dollars in a couple days."

"Oh, yeah?"

"But look…being that you gotta wear…no offense… but being that you have to go see the client wearing those tacky clothes, I'm going to have to send you to a married couple who won't mind your attire."

"A married couple. That's weird." Sailor shook his head.

"Their money is green like everybody else's, so I don't discriminate. The husband likes to see his wife getting freaked by black dudes."

"Gross!"

"Matter of opinion. They got bank and that's all that matters. I can't pass you off as black, but they might be able to work with that Eskimo twist."

Sailor nodded, but he didn't look happy. He silently mulled over Misty's words.

"I never ran into so many freaky people until I got stranded in Philly…" He paused as if waiting for Misty to show some interest in his situation.

"Oh yeah," Misty said absently. She had no intention of listening to his life story or his trials and tribulations with Uncle Marshall. She didn't care how Sailor got stranded and she didn't give two shits about his opinion of Philadelphians. Her mind was on money. *Horny Hubby and his wife will pay my full price if I build up this half-Eskimo's fuck game.*

She had no intention of telling Sailor the whole truth about the appointment she intended to make with the horny couple. What he didn't know wouldn't hurt him. He'd find out soon enough that Horny Hubby could only handle the voyeur role for only so long. As soon as wifey started moaning, Horny Hubby took that as his cue to get in on the action.

"Where'd you say you're staying?" Misty asked Sailor.

Sailor shrugged. "Nowhere, really. Past few days, I've been sort of…you know…bumming around."

"Stick with me and I'll make sure you get the money for your clothes, ID, and shit. In the meantime, you can stay with me."

He studied her face. "Really?"

"Uh-huh," she said nonchalantly.

"Hey, that's real cool. Thanks."

"Welcome. My place is small, but I'll make room for you. Do you have a cell?"

"No, I have to get it turned on."

"Hmm. Good thing you'll be staying with me. Having you close by is more convenient than having to chase you down every time I get you some work."

"Yeah."

"I want to sample the goods anyway," she said in a matter-of-fact tone.

"Sample the goods?" He stared at Misty like he didn't understand.

"Do you think I would send you out to one of my loyal customers without knowing how you holding? Besides, you should feel honored that I'm going to let you smash."

"I am. I'm more than honored. I'm in shock that a hot-looking chick like you wants to go to bed with me."

"Don't get it twisted. It's not that I want to. It makes good business sense for me to find out your strengths and weaknesses in the sex department. I need to find out how long you can last."

"Oh." He nodded, eyes drifting away in thought. "I'm good in bed. At least that's what I've been told." He laughed nervously, his face reddening in embarrassment.

"How good you are remains to be seen. By the way, how are your oral skills?"

"Uh…" He looked mortified. "My oral skills are pretty good."

"I'll be the judge of that."

"Cool," he said with uncertainty in his voice.

"When we get to the crib, we're going to practice. I'll have someone playing the role of voyeur, so you can get used to an audience when you're sexing a chick."

Sailor looked ill, but managed to crack a smile.

Pleased with herself, Misty honked the horn, startling Sailor. Like a faithful puppy, Troy came rushing out of Burger King, wiping his lips with a napkin.

"Who's that?"

"That's Troy. He's on my payroll, too. You're going to be spending a lot of time together."

"You ready, Misty?" Troy asked, cutting a hopeful eye at Sailor, obviously hoping that Misty had sealed the deal.

"Yeah, I want you to meet your partner-in-crime," Misty said with joyful laughter.

Counting money in her mind, she absently muttered introductions. Troy shook Sailor's hand. He was so grateful for some help with the work load, he didn't stop shaking Sailor's hand until he noticed Misty's eyes shooting him daggers.

"My bad," Troy said, and released Sailor's hand.

"You hungry, Sailor?" Misty asked.

"Starving."

"I can't have my new worker skipping meals." Misty dug into her purse and slid Sailor a ten. "Get yourself a platter. Go with him, Troy. I need some privacy while I make an important call."

CHAPTER 7

Though Sailor had an exotic look, his head covered in a fluff of dark curls, he acted like a white boy. Misty had no idea how Eskimos got down, but it was obvious that Sailor's father had never given him any Eskimo tips. Sailor walked, talked, and acted like a white boy. Straight up. Having him around felt foreign and was going to take some getting used to.

What she liked was how quickly he had come to idolize her. During the drive back to the apartment, Troy sat in the back and Sailor sat beside Misty, gazing at her like she was a goddess. That shit turned her on.

"You're so beautiful. Seems like just a few minutes ago, I was feeling down and out. Then you came along. Like an angel."

Though she was more like a sexy devil than an angel, Misty smiled because she loved being called beautiful. There was no doubt that she was one of the most gorgeous people on earth, but she could never hear it enough. Sailor didn't realize it, but he was already starting to get her coochie wet.

In the backseat, Troy was oblivious to the conversation

up front. He pushed buttons on his cell, smiling as he sent and received text messages.

"Yo, Misty. Can you drop me off 'round the way? I need to holla at some of my homies."

"Fuck your homies. You got work to do."

"I thought ya boy up there was takin' care of that job."

"He is. But I gotta try him out when we get back to the crib. I need you to play the part of Horny Hubby. You know...watch us while we fucking. If he's laying pipe the way he's supposed to, then you should be in the background making noises. You know...breathing hard and beating your meat. Sailor gotta get used to all types of freak shit."

"Oh. Aiight. I gotchu." Not wanting to rile Misty, Troy kept the disappointment out of his voice.

Smiling, Sailor shook his head. "I can't believe I'm agreeing to do this. But you make something bizarre and unnatural seem so normal."

"Sex is the most normal thing in the world. You must have lived a sheltered life in that crazy-sounding place in Wisconsin."

"No. My mom was liberal. I wasn't overly sheltered."

"Seems like it to me. I mean...you never been in a threesome before, have you?"

"No."

"You ever had your dick sucked while somebody else was licking your balls?"

He shook his head and then, frowning, he looked over his shoulder, scrutinizing Troy.

"I'm not gay," Sailor said, cutting another look at Troy.

"Me either," Troy defended.

Sailor looked relieved.

"I don't hire gay men." Though Misty had no intention discriminating against gay men or anyone of legal age, for the moment she said whatever she thought Sailor wanted to hear.

She smiled at Sailor. "You and Troy are gonna be like brothers. Your only responsibilities are to keep your customers happy and to make sure that I'm sexually satisfied."

"Gosh. You're hot. And so beautiful. I'll do whatever it takes to keep you satisfied."

Loving to hear about her beauty, Misty gave him a big smile.

❦

Sailor felt self-conscious about Troy being in the bedroom, but he managed to block Troy out of his mind while he burrowed his tongue into Misty's coochie.

Not interested in the least, Troy sat in a chair looking down at his cellular... fingers moving...still texting.

Misty sat up suddenly, but placed her palm on top of Sailor's head, keeping it in place.

"Troy! I know you don't think you gon' sit over there and play with that damn phone while me and Sailor are over here getting busy!"

"I ain't hear you moaning or nothing. I didn't think it was time for me to make no sound effects."

"Sound effects! Is that all you think I want you to do?"

"That's what you said. You told me to act like that married guy."

"Whatchu tryna say, Troy? You don't wanna eat my coochie?"

"Yeah, man. I stay with my face between your legs, but I thought Scooter was handling that."

Sailor lifted his head from Misty's crotch. "My name is Sailor."

"My bad," Troy said.

The sound of Sailor's voice vibrated against Misty's sensitive area. His warm breath sent hot sensations straight to her clit. A moan escaped her lips. She wanted to wrap her thighs around Sailor's neck, but controlled the urge while she got shit straight with Troy.

"What's your problem, Troy?"

"Nothing."

"Well, act like you're interested."

"I am," he said, still fiddling with his phone.

"Put that shit down. Take your clothes off and get in the bed with us. If you could see how good Sailor's lapping up my juices, your ashy dick would be getting as hard as a rock and then you'd be making the moaning sounds he's gotta get used to hearing."

"Oh, aiight," Troy said, annoyed. Reluctantly, he put his cell down and started peeling off clothes.

Sailor's body tensed and Troy's footsteps approached the bed.

Misty stroked the top of Sailor's curly head. "Troy's not going to touch you."

"Man, ain't nobody tryna get with you. I ain't no fruit." Agitated at being forced to join in a boring sex session that didn't pay, Troy flopped down on the side of the bed. Half-heartedly, he caressed Misty's stomach, while his eyes kept roaming over to his cell.

"You too attached to that phone, Troy. Don't make me do an intervention and cut that damn thing off," Misty threatened.

"Stop playing, man."

"Then get focused." She closed her eyes, dismissing Troy, and resumed enjoying Sailor's thrilling tongue.

Reacting to Misty's moans and the wet sounds emanating from the bottom of the bed, Troy finally took interest. Observing the white-looking dude's tongue slipping in and out of Misty's coochie had the effect of watching porn. This live performance he was viewing sent an unexpected wave of heat traveling swiftly through his shaft.

He watched Sailor's tongue swiping between Misty's folds.

"Mmm," Troy grunted.

"Go get the baby oil," Misty told Troy in a voice barely above a whisper.

Expecting Misty to use the baby oil to give him a badly needed hand job, Troy rushed to get it. When he returned to the bed, Misty was wriggling wildly as Sailor filled her with the full length of his tongue.

CHAPTER 8

Without a word, Misty stretched her arm out over the side of the bed, palm open. Troy squirted a generous amount of lubrication into Misty's palm and thrust his lengthened dick inside her hand.

She put a stranglehold on Troy's long pole, preventing him from freely gliding in and out of her oiled palm.

"You want me to jerk you off, Troy?"

"Yeah, Misty," he said hoarsely. "I need that. Watching y'all got me fired up."

"Nah, you gotta earn a hand job."

"What I gotta do?" Troy asked, sounding desperate and no longer distracted by his cell or anything else except his primal urges.

Aroused by the taste of Misty's pussy, Sailor groped his manhood, soothing himself while waiting for Misty to tell him she was ready for penetration.

"You like the way he's eating my box out?"

"Yeah, you know I do," Troy said in a voice barely above a whisper.

"Then show me."

"Whatchu want me to do?"

"After all this time we've been together, how you gon' let Sailor take over your position? You need to man-up, Troy!"

"Getcha face outta her box, man. That shit ain't cool." Troy's face was frowned up, muscles tense. And though he was much leaner than Sailor, he had enough thug in him to sound intimidating to someone from Oconomowoc, Wisconsin.

Alarmed, Sailor lifted his head. "Easy, dude. What's happening here?" He looked at Misty for an explanation.

Though she was clearly the instigator, Misty shrugged. "Troy be buggin' all the time," she said, blaming the turmoil on Troy. "He's acting like a big baby, so let him suck on my clit for a while." She twisted away from Sailor's warm mouth.

Sailor stood up. And Troy immediately took his place, swishing his tongue around swiftly, rushing through the task, trying to quickly earn some sexual relief.

"Slow down, Troy. Don't be tryna punish my coochie because you got some competition."

Troy stopped licking. "That white boy ain't no competition for me!"

"You ain't gotta be calling him names. Act nice, Troy. Y'all gotta keep your tempers in check and try to get along together," she said, now blaming both Troy and Sailor for the chaos she'd caused.

Looking confused, Sailor scratched his head while Troy worked on Misty's clit.

Misty crooked her finger, beckoning Sailor. Led by his stiff dick, Sailor rushed to Misty's side.

"Take your clothes off."

Too worked up to be bashful, he pulled off his skateboard T-shirt.

Wow! His torso was the truth. Broad-ass chest, contoured waist, and a fucking eight-pack! Those two strips of muscles that ran parallel to each other had individual blocks of four muscles on each side. Amazing!

By the time he came out of his jeans, Misty was more than impressed. Sailor's body was cut so nice, he reminded her of a Greek muscle god of the Olympus.

He slipped his average-length, but extremely chunky width of a dick into the palm of her oiled hand.

While Troy ate her pussy, Misty gave Sailor hand relief.

Hearing Sailor's low moans along with the sloshing sound of his flesh slipping in and out of Misty's tiny hand was more than Troy could stand, but he knew better than to stop flicking the tip of his tongue against her firm clit. Misty was trembling. Close to cumming. She'd go ballistic if Troy quit while she was so close to the edge.

But Sailor reached the finish line before Misty. "Ahhh," Sailor gasped as he ejaculated, sending a splatter of sperm onto the sheets.

"Damn. You were really backed up," Misty commented. "Go get a paper towel…a washcloth, or something. Clean this mess up."

His eyes squeezed shut, holding his dick and breathing hard, Sailor didn't move. He was too caught up in the euphoria of busting a nut to make sense of Misty's order.

"Yo! Snap out of it!" Misty hollered.

He opened his eyes. "Huh? What?"

"Handle this shit." She frowned at the milky puddle on the bed.

"Oh, sure." Sailor took off toward the bathroom.

Turning her attention to Troy, she patted the top of his head. "Stop. That's enough. It's time to fuck."

Troy looked at the load Sailor had left behind and wrinkled his nose. "Damn, my man got his seed splattered all over the bed and shit."

Misty moved to the other side of the bed.

"Umph," Troy grunted, his primal urges taking priority over his squeamishness. He lay on top of Misty and started slowly, easing in increments of hardness.

When Sailor returned with a wad of tissue paper, Troy was putting in work, giving up long strokes.

"Your oral skills are on point," she said as Troy pounded into her.

"Thanks," Sailor replied, appreciative of the compliment, but uneasy about talking to a girl while she was being fucked.

"But there is room for improvement," she continued, her voice coming out in gasps as Troy tried his best to knock her back out.

"On the bright side, it's a good thing that you shot off

that load before you got with the clients. Feel me? It would have been a disaster if you came too quick."

"I can usually go much longer than that," Sailor said in his defense. Having a conversation with Misty while she was being sexually penetrated was darn uncomfortable. It seemed perverted as all hell, but Misty acted like it was the most normal thing in the world, so Sailor did his best to hold up his end of the conversation. As long as he kept his eyes latched on Misty's face, his gaze never straying in the direction of Troy's gyrating lower body, he could pretend that he was having an ordinary discussion.

"It's just that…well, it's been a while," he explained. "And you had me so excited. I never met a woman like you before. So in control and so gosh darn beautiful. You're like a heavy dose of E."

Misty giggled, and then patted the side of the bed.

Obediently, he sat down. She slid her finger in his mouth.

Blocking out Troy, Sailor closed his eyes and adoringly sucked Misty's finger.

With her free hand, Misty squeezed Troy's buttock, digging her fingernails into his flesh, demanding deeper penetration.

While one man sucked, the other fucked. It was what Misty had always wanted. Two men. On call to take care of all of her wants, needs, and every freaky desire.

CHAPTER 9

Misty was trying to luxuriate in the bathtub but it was hard to relax when she was surrounded by cracked tiles and had to listen to the sound of a toilet that constantly ran. *I need to move out of this shit hole. No, not yet. I need to upgrade my whip first.*

Sailor's sexual stamina and earning power put Troy to shame. With Sailor bringing home the bacon, she had been hitting up the malls again. Shopping like there was no tomorrow…making up for lost time.

But it was time to get her priorities in order, time to put the shopping sprees on freeze. She needed a luxury apartment and a fly set of wheels. But there wasn't enough money to do both. In addition, her credit was fucked up. Misty let out a sigh of frustration. *Where there's a will, there's a muthafuckin' way. It's time for me to come up.*

If Troy's whining bitch-ass worked half as hard as Sailor, there'd be money to blow. But Troy was immature, always hanging out with his friends, which was what he was doing at that very moment. Dressed in the new clothes and sneakers she'd bought for him, he had hopped on public transportation...going back to his old 'hood to stunt for his homies. Shit, if any of his friends were worth a fuck, they'd be on her payroll, slinging dick instead of hugging a dead-ass block.

Sailor, on the other hand, was a homebody, reminding her of Brick in so many ways. Like Brick, he liked to relax and watch TV or play video games during his down time. And like the old Brick who used to love her, Sailor was also smitten by her beauty. He constantly strived to please her.

"Sailor!" Misty yelled. She counted silently, curious to see how many seconds it took him to respond.

Twelve seconds later, he appeared in the bathroom. "Hey," he said cheerfully.

Misty felt a little let down. The last time she'd timed him, it had only taken ten seconds.

"What's wrong?" Sailor asked, sensing her mood.

"Nothing," she said, pouting. She squeezed soap on her large, pink sponge.

"Want me to wash your back?" His eyes adored her, but that wasn't enough. Misty needed more verification of his affection.

"I guess," she uttered. Her eyes watered.

"S'matter?"

"I don't think you really love me."

"I do." He sat on the side of the tub and wiped the manufactured tears from her eyes. "What can I do to prove it?"

"I'm not used to living like this, Sailor. You gotta get me outta this dump."

"I'm trying. I work hard for you."

"But you're so picky."

"Whaddya mean?"

"You know…the way you only deal with female clients."

"Not true. I take care of that married couple."

"Yeah, but…" She lowered her eyes.

"What?"

"Bitches are so cheap. We could make so much more money if you'd start servicing men."

"I can't do that. It's gross."

"You let Horny Hubby lick your nut sac."

"That's different…I guess. With his wife there, I don't feel like I'm doing anything gay."

"And I'm not asking you to do anything gay. All you have to do is let my male clients give you a blow job. How easy is that? Stand still and get your dick sucked."

Looking troubled, Sailor scratched his head. "I don't know. Seems gay."

"You're not a homosexual. In my opinion, you're all man. Doesn't my opinion matter?"

"It matters a lot."

"Okay, then. Let me line you up with one of my loyal clients. I'll go with you, if you want. I'll even hold your hand. You're the only person I can depend on, Sailor. Troy's not holding up his end like he should. When I get on my feet, I'm kicking Troy out of the crib."

"Really?"

"Uh-huh. I'm getting tired of his triflin' ways."

"It's just gonna be you and me living here?"

"Yes. But you have to do your part. Please, Sailor. You gotta do this for me. Do it for us."

He closed his eyes and lowered his head and nodded. "Okay, I'll do it."

Misty squealed with joy.

Sailor swallowed hard. "This has to stay between us. I realize that Troy does that kind of work, but I'd feel really uncomfortable if Troy or anyone else found out."

"What you do behind closed doors is your business and mine. Troy don't need to know."

"Okay," he repeated, sounding like he was trying to convince himself that he was making the right choice.

"I'm in love, Sailor."

He lit up. "You are?"

"Yeah," Misty responded breathlessly, picturing her hands gripping the steering wheel of the new Lexus RX that was being advertised on TV.

Sailor bent his head and kissed her. "I don't know what's better, kissing your beautiful lips or your sweet cunt."

"Make a choice."

"Uh…"

"If you could only kiss one set of lips, which would you choose—my mouth or my coochie lips?"

Put on the spot, Sailor's cheeks tinted crimson.

Wearing a devilish smile, Misty rose up from the sudsy water. She faced Sailor, who sat on the side of the bathtub. She pressed her coochie against his mouth and whispered, "I'll decide and make the decision on which lips get kissed."

❧

There was tension in the car. Looking battle-weary and shell-shocked, Sailor stared into space during the drive home. Misty turned on Power 99, and then switched to a station that played the kind of white-boy music that Sailor liked.

A song by the band Train was playing. Stuck in some kind of trance, he didn't light up or bob his head to the whack music he usually enjoyed.

"Yo, Sailor." Misty waved her hand in front of his face. "Snap out of it. You're creepin' me out, dude," she said, chuckling as she spoke in Sailor's vernacular.

"I don't wanna talk right now. I'm feeling kinda nauseous."

"Stick your head out the window if you planning on throwing up in the car."

To her amazement, he leaned out the window, and started making gagging sounds.

Misty snorted in disgust. "Dr. Hardy slobbered on your dick a little bit. So what? It's not that serious. You tryna throw up and shit, acting like somebody spread your ass cheeks and took your manhood."

Unsuccessful at retching, he pulled his head back inside the car. "I don't wanna talk about it. Is that okay with you?" he yelled.

Misty hit the brakes, holding up traffic, forcing motorists to have to swerve around her. "Hold up." She waved a finger in Sailor's face. "Mufucka, you don't think I'ma let you talk to me any ol' kind of way. You can get the fuck outta my whip. Go holler at the moon like a goddamn werewolf if you need to be raising your voice, but I'll be goddamaned if you're gonna sit in my ride and scream at me. Get out!"

Sailor was aghast. "Get out? Are you for real?"

"Fuckin' right. I can't stand an ungrateful bastard. Get the fuck out. I'll stick with Troy. Troy don't like to hustle hard, but he's loyal. He don't bite the hand that feeds him. I took your ass off the streets, so go back to whatever hole you crawled out of."

"Misty? I don't get it…what did I do that's so terrible? I was only expressing my feelings. I'm confused and hurt over what happened at that doctor's office."

"You acting like a bitch-ass. Complaining and pouting instead of staying focused on getting money. I don't need this kind of bullshit. I'm not gon' be babying your ass every time a muthafucker gives you some god damn head."

"I'm not upset with you, Misty. I'm confused and mad at myself."

"Whatever, Eskimo-ass nigga. Get over it."

He winced at the name calling, but quickly recovered. "Okay. I'm over it."

Somewhat satisfied, she took her foot off of the brake and accelerated.

"Hungry?" she inquired in a sudden sugary tone.

"Starving," he responded with an appropriate amount of enthusiasm.

"Wanna get some seafood at Joe's?"

"Super!"

Sailor's swift change of disposition filled Misty with warmth. She'd won the power struggle. She would ride him like a stallion later when she got him at home and in bed. There was something about a cooperative man that made her coochie act up. Dripping and drizzling and running like a faucet.

CHAPTER 10

S ailor had been whining about getting his belongings. Misty had no interest in helping him get his corny clothes, but she did want to get her hands on his personal ID. She couldn't say for certain why she wanted Sailor's ID, but it seemed like something she needed to have in her possession. Maybe one day she'd see a shrink about her control issues.

But in the meantime, she had to make it her business to charm this Uncle Marshall character into giving up Sailor's possessions, and she didn't intend to give the greedy, thieving old man one red dime.

After sneakily thumbing through Sailor's pocket-sized composition book, Misty found Uncle Marshall's phone number and address.

Misty dolled herself up, showing lots of skin. The summer sun had turned her skin to a coppery color, enhancing her exotic beauty. Merely gazing at her would probably cause the man to cum in his pants.

According to Sailor, Uncle Marshall was in his fifties. She hoped her drop-dead gorgeousness didn't give the ol' head a heart attack; at least not in her presence. She was not in the mood for the images that were running through her head.

In her mind, she could hear an EMT worker asking her what had happened to Uncle Marshall. She saw herself shrugging and then nonchalantly stating, "Ol' head took one look at me and the nigga dropped. His heart couldn't take all this lusciousness and beauty." Her musings had her laughing out loud.

But she took the dire possibility of ending up with a body seriously. That would be entirely too much drama for her tastes. Needing to rethink her wardrobe selection and come up with something less lethal, Misty waded through fabric in the small closet that was jam-packed with her wardrobe and only a meager few items that belonged to Sailor.

Troy stayed garbed up in fresh gear. For a person whose elbows and kneecaps stayed ashy all the time, Troy had some nerve being so particular. He was like a bitch when it came to his clothes. His jeans and T-shirts were folded in neat piles on the single shelf inside the closet. His sneakers were kept in pristine condition, contained in their original boxes and stored under the bed.

Uncle Marshall lived in Germantown, a couple of blocks from that homeless place where Sailor had been staying. He lived in a big stone house on the corner. Long, interesting windows that were without curtains or shades drew Misty's attention.

From across the street where she parked her car, she could see movement inside the spacious single home. It seemed like Uncle Marshall was openly bragging about having a big house with high ceilings and lots of open space. Obviously, Uncle Marshall had big bank.

She thought about the cramped little apartment she called home and became instantly irritated. Sailor should have prepared her for the way Uncle Marshall was living. She would have enticed Uncle Marshall with some sinfully skimpy clothes had she known the ol' head was stacking paper like this.

Fuck Sailor's ID; she needed to get on Uncle Marshall's good side. She'd flirt with the older man and get him to come up off of a weekly allowance. Nah, she needed more than that. Ol' heads usually had good credit and since Misty knew her mother wouldn't dream of helping her out anymore, she had no choice but to use her good looks to bedazzle Uncle Marshall. She'd hoodwink the old fool into putting some cash down and co-signing on that new Lexus she'd been lusting after.

💋

It was raining men up in Uncle Marshall's crib. Gorgeous men that looked like they belonged on a billboard decked in Calvin Klein underwear. Through a window, Misty could see a bare-chested, black-as-tar, gladiator-looking mufucka doing pushups on the hardwood floor. *Damn!* She licked her lips as her eyes roved to a mocha-colored hottie. His hands were clasped at the back of his head as he lounged on the couch, watching TV.

Another stunning physique passed by a window. This one was tall and medium brown. Resembling an ebony demigod, his lower body was displayed in a pair of boxer briefs. In the front of his underwear, a bunched-up bulge of manliness tantalized her. Misty's mouth watered with lust. *That mufucka is holding down there.*

Someone wearing a white wife beater said something to the dude holding the remote. She was only able to get a quick glimpse of him. From what she'd seen of him... sculpted torso, bulging biceps. Mmm. He could get it.

She moved her gaze back to the black gladiator. He hopped up from the floor. Pellets of sweat trickled down his beautiful frame. Her breath caught in her chest. She watched, awestruck as his Adam's apple bobbed while he chugged water from a gallon container. The innocent act of swallowing was a provocative and alluring sight.

Uncle Marshall's house was filled with male eye candy. Misty had a powerful sex drive and these hard-bodied men looked like they could provide the kind of work-over she'd been craving. Each man looked equipped to satisfy her darkest desires. Men like these were designed to provide maximum pleasure.

She wanted to fuck. Her coochie clenched with need. It didn't appreciate being denied something it wanted.

Misty could feel her pussy folds swelling. She squeezed her thighs tightly together. Her temperamental coochie was trying to throw a fit. Bad. Her body's reaction to all that unexpected testosterone was overwhelming. Her nipples were erect and a fiery liquid passion slid down her slender thighs.

Get yourself together, she told herself as she flipped a long swath of hair over her shoulder. Taking a deep breath, she pressed the doorbell.

She heard movement. Lots of movement. Taking a peek inside, she saw masculine forms retreating into the shadows.

What the fuck?

The door opened. "Yes? May I help you?"

The man standing in the doorway was long and lean. He stood with the erect stance of a dancer. His lips were pursed, his hands clasped together. His complexion was eerily flawless…not a wrinkle in sight. The smooth skin, no doubt pulled tight by a surgeon's hands. Additionally, he had that frozen-in-surprise, Botox look. His jet black hair had tight, processed curls. His eyebrows were arched with dramatic flare, and were dyed black—matching his tinted hair.

It was a hot sunny day, yet he was dressed in a blue jacket, a glittery shirt, and white flared pants. His neck was swathed in a white silk scarf, as though he was so fragile, the air conditioned chill might have an ill effect on his health.

The man obviously thought he was grand, but to Misty he looked a hot mess in his costumy...over-the-top, elegant attire. This man was no trendsetter. The old kook was biting off the fashion style of the silver screen-era.

Misty wrinkled her nose. Seemed like she'd caught a whiff of an unpleasant scent. *Did ole boy pull his gear out of a trunk filled with mothballs and shit?*

"Uncle Marshall?" Misty couldn't help from giggling. The man looked like a complete fool.

Taken aback, he blinked a few times. "Only close friends call me Uncle Marshall. What can I do for you?" he said, sounding very annoyed.

"I'm a friend of Sailor's." She waited a beat, allowing him a few seconds to read between the lines. Her tone of voice accused him of a host of heinous crimes.

Acting guilty, the man Misty presumed to be Uncle Marshall inhaled sharply at the mention of Sailor's name.

"I'm here to pick up his ID and the rest of his things," she said, cutting to the chase. The seduction she'd planned for Uncle Marshall was pointless. Limp-wrist mufucka had more sugar in him than Kool-Aid at a neighborhood block party.

Trying to put two and two together, Misty ventured a peek over Uncle Marshall's shoulder. Not a muscle man in sight. They'd all fled to other parts of the house... to secret places where they wouldn't be detected. *Something's not kosher up in this dip.* Misty turned up the corner of her top lip. She didn't like Uncle Marshall at all. He was full of his faggoty-ass self for some unknown reason. She couldn't imagine why. He was a throwback from ancient times and his wardrobe sucked. He was a fake-ass, black Hugh Hefner. But instead of a having a bunch of bunnies hopping around, he was surrounded by beautiful young men.

Gathering his wits, Uncle Marshall smoothed out his jacket. "Did Sailor send the money he owes me? He ran up a huge tab."

"A tab? You make it sound like you running a casino in ya crib. What kind of tab did Sailor run up?"

He tsked and waved his hand, as if brushing away an annoying insect. "Nothing illicit. Sailor owes me room and board."

"Oh yeah," she said, her voice colored with suspicion. "Are you a landlord or something? I mean…damn, you act like Sailor broke the lease that he signed."

The prissy man smiled indulgently. "Sailor and I were not bound by legalities. We had a gentlemen's agreement, which he reneged on." He released a titter of laughter that had an ugly, malicious sound.

Misty was starting to get the picture. Somehow, Uncle Marshall had lured handsome, young men into his spacious home. How he kept them there was anyone's guess. Misty had a strong suspicion that the hunks she'd seen through the window had all come from that Caring Cottage place where Sailor had been staying.

She glared at the homosexual. *Nasty-ass, deviant bastard.*

He returned her look of loathing with a scornful roving gaze that traveled from her red toenails, past her tight jeans, and up to her dark, shimmering mane. "Our little chat is over. Tell Sailor that I'm willing to discuss his financial responsibility…" He paused and glanced at his manicured nails, and then began twirling his hand around with great flourish. "Sailor and I can sit down and discuss the matter, man-to-man. There's no reason for you to return, my dear. There's nothing here that concerns you."

He started to close the door, and then stopped. He arched a dark, tinted brow as though he'd been struck with a bright idea.

"Don't let Sailor's good ol' boy routine fool you, Miss Thang. He's not as innocent as he appears."

With those words, he stepped back, looked over his shoulder, and cast a smile at someone who was out of Misty's visual range.

Blushing, eyes twinkling like he had something naughty to attend to, he flagged Misty with a motion of his hand. "Be on your way, Miss Thang. There's nothing here for the likes of you."

While Misty was drawing enough breath to fire off a round of obscenities, he gave Misty a wink and then, ever so gently, closed the door in her face.

CHAPTER 11

*N*o, that flaming fag did not wink at me and then close the door in my face! I'm surprised he could even work his paralyzed eye muscle into a wink. I should have ripped that scarf off and exposed that wrinkly neck he's tryna hide. Shoulda put a chokehold on his freak ass. Nah, I should have sucker punched ol' boy...put a crack in that frozen face.

Misty stood fuming for a few seconds before stomping away.

Sailor had some explaining to do.

All total, Misty had counted four buff men, and she was willing to bet that there were other hotties roaming about.

What the hell was going on in Uncle Marshall's house? How had that flaming fag attracted all those young, hot men? Maybe it would make a little more sense if Uncle Marshall was living in a Playboy-type mansion like the real Hef. But ol' boy wasn't stacking like that. His crib looked alright from the outside—it was spacious and everything—but it wasn't a damn mansion.

Every man she glimpsed was unusually good looking. All of them had spectacular bodies. If she had those hunks working for her, her pockets would be fat.

Driving fast, she could hardly think straight. Her thoughts shifted from steamy group sex to stacking money. She imagined lining up those rippling studs and giving each one a test run.

If the man passed inspection, she'd send him out to her high-priority clients, charging them triple their usual fee. Those hot boys were worth a damn fortune.

What the hell were they doing wasting their time hanging with freaky Uncle Marshall?

Sailor had better come correct and start talking. Misty wanted to know how a haggard homosexual had the wherewithal to accessorize his home with hunky, male eye candy.

❧

She burst inside her apartment and slammed the door hard.

On the floor doing crunches, Sailor stopped mid-crunch and stared at Misty in confusion.

Her hot gaze pierced his questioning eyes.

He wiped away perspiration with the towel that lay beside him. "Who pissed you off?" There was nervousness in his voice.

"You'll never guess."

He held out his hands. "I give up," he said with a chuckle, trying to lighten up the tension in the room.

"Uncle Marshall. I paid him a visit…trying to get your things. He refused. He's not a very nice man."

"He's okay. He's a stickler for rules and keeping the guys disciplined."

"About the guys…"

"Yeah?"

"Wanna explain? First of all, you never mentioned that Uncle Marshall was a flaming fag. Second, you didn't tell me that the dude's crib is the hangout for hot boys. What's going on over there?"

"I never questioned Uncle Marshall about his sexuality. It's not my business. To me, he's only a friend. I don't know whether he's gay or not."

"Stop playing dumb, Sailor. You know that mufucka's flaming."

Sailor dropped his head. "I really don't know," he insisted.

"Yeah, aiight. So why were you and all those other hot-to-death boys hanging around that old, mothballs-in-his-clothes-wearing pervert?"

Sailor frowned at Misty's derisive description of Uncle Marshall. "Uncle Marshall's not a pervert. He helps young men get into the modeling field."

"That's a bunch of crap."

"Seriously, Uncle Marshall was a former male model here in the States, but mainly in Europe."

"Uh-huh," Misty said doubtfully. She held up her hand. "Okay, fuck all that. Where did that ol' head find all those good-looking men with fabulous bodies?"

"Most of them are from Caring Cottage."

"You're kidding me? Do you mean to tell me that all I have to do is hang out at that homeless shelter and I can grip me up a gang of fine-ass dick slingers?"

"Not exactly."

"Well, spit it out. How could you keep that kind of information from me? You've been watching me busting my ass, tryna make major moves with only two damn dick slingers. Why ain't you open your mouth and say something?"

"What was I supposed to say?"

"You should have pointed me in the direction of Uncle Marshall's house. My operation could use a few more good men. That faggot done scooped up every pretty nigga that has ever stepped foot in Philly."

"None of us guys understood how to get our bodies in condition until we moved into Uncle Marshall's place. He's like a mentor to young men. All he asks is that you make yourself look your very best."

"Oh, really now. What kind of commitment?"

"A commitment to train our bodies to exhaustion…to fuel it with only healthy food and to shun a mediocre existence as if it were a disease…to strive for a life of excellence."

As Misty absorbed Sailor's explanation, it was clear

that he'd been brainwashed by that lustful queen. Sailor sounded like he was reciting a mission statement or a pledge of allegiance or some shit. Spouting off words that were put in his head by that freak.

She looked at Sailor with a narrowed eye. "Your body's tight. Where did you fall short?"

"Uh…I didn't fall short. I followed all the rules."

"If you followed all the rules, how did you wind up owing that creep six hundred dollars?"

"That's the figure he came up with. I probably owe him much more than that."

Aggravated by what sounded like sheer stupidity, Misty grimaced as she spat, "How do you figure that? And why are you defending that sleaze-bag thief?"

"Uncle Marshall's not a thief. I can't say anything bad about him. He helped me out when I didn't have a friend in the world."

"So what happened to the friendship? Why'd he put you out on your ass?"

"It's a long story."

"I'm all ears," she said, taking a seat. Impatient fingers combed through her hair while she waited for Sailor to pour his heart out. She was willing to endure listening to Sailor's boring story, hoping to glean some information that would put her on the right track to scooping up all the hard-bodied men inside Uncle Marshall's house.

It was an exciting thought. Uncle Marshall had enough in-house manpower to give Misty's business a big boost.

CHAPTER 12

Sailor told Misty that he'd ended up in Philly while working for a traveling sales crew. Trying to raise money for college, he'd left home to work for a company that had advertised in his local newspaper. Within hours of being hired, he was on the road, told that he could make a fortune if he joined the traveling sales team that was staffed with teens and young adults who peddled cleaning products outside of malls, on busy thoroughfares, and some even went door-to-door... desperate to earn their commission.

Knocking on doors in the 'hood made Sailor an easy target. Robbed of his inventory and money, the company fired him, leaving him stranded in Philadelphia.

"Boy, it's obvious that you don't know anything about the 'hood."

"Yeah, having a gun pointed at me was the scariest situation in my entire life."

"You're lucky you came out of that situation with your life," Misty told him, shaking her head at his naiveté. "I know some niggas that woulda pumped some slugs in your dome and left your brains splattered on the sidewalk just for the hell of it."

Sailor shuddered at the visual. "With no money and no place to go, I was lucky to get into the Caring Cottage. They offered housing and job-search training."

"So what happened with that?"

"Uh…I met Uncle Marshall. One day while I was shooting hoops in the park, he approached me. He gave me his card. Told me that he was in the fashion industry and that with my face and physique, I could earn a million a year. He said he could get me in, but I needed to work on my upper body and abs."

"That ol' buzzard got game. He be hanging out in the park leering at young niggas."

"He's a pretty sincere guy. He searches in the park because that's where he can find raw talent."

"I bet." She rolled her eyes. "Is the park near that shelter?"

"Yeah, the park is a couple blocks away. A lot of the guys from Caring Cottage hang out in the park during free time." Her mind started putting together a plan to sell a dream to some of those youth at the Caring Cottage. At least the dream she was selling had some validity.

"Uncle Marshall's a crafty ol' queen. Queenie got good game…telling desperate youth that he can give them modeling careers."

"He's not lying," Sailor defended. "He showed me pictures of him in magazines—"

"Get outta here…ain't nobody hiring that old fool to model anywhere."

"Uh-huh. He has tons of magazines with him on the cover—"

"Oh yeah? What magazine? *Geriatric Times*?" Misty scoffed.

"No, pictures of him were inside the pages of *Ebony* and *Jet*. And *Essence*. Lots of others. He had cover shots on a few foreign magazines. He was an international model. A long time ago. He had a very lucrative modeling career and he said he's still well-connected."

"So he says. I bet those magazines he posed for are older than dirt."

Sailor chuckled. "Yeah, they were pretty old. But he's working behind the scenes now."

Sailor was so gullible, it was a disgraceful shame.

"Uncle Marshall has photography skills as well. He did many photo shoots with guys he believed had bodies that were camera-ready."

Misty raised a brow. "Did he get anyone a modeling job?"

"No. Not yet. None of the guys are ready. Every one is still training…strengthening their bodies. Some have advanced to working on their portfolios."

"Did you start working on your portfolio?" Misty's mind was racing, thinking that any photos the pervert had taken of Sailor would be a good temporary marketing tool for her business. Once she had her money right, she'd spice things up and shoot racy pictures that would be downloaded to her site. *It won't be long now!*

Sailor blushed. "Me? No. I was the newest guy in the house."

"You look camera-ready to me." Misty imagined taking a picture of Sailor while he jacked off in the shower. *Steamy!*

"My time would have come. I would have gotten a photo session." He lowered his head. "But Uncle Marshall asked me to leave."

"Hmm. What kind of beef did you have with ol' Queenie? Why'd he kick you out?"

"It was a sort of punishment. Uncle Marshall wanted me to experience the stresses of the outside world, hoping I would see how easy I had it at his place."

"Yeah, yeah. You told me all that. Now tell me exactly what you did to get Queenie's feathers ruffled."

Unable to meet Misty's eye, Sailor looked away.

"What happened?"

"One day when Uncle Marshall was checking to see if I was camera-ready—"

"What did that involve?"

"Well…he'd look me over. Nude. And sort of…you know…do a muscle check."

"A muscle check?"

"Feeling my muscles, testing the bulk."

"He was getting cheap thrills, huh?"

"It creeped me out at first, but I got used to it. And it was for my benefit that my muscle toning was right."

Misty wore a sneaky grin. "Did he feel up your love muscle?" Her eyes zoomed in on his crotch.

"No!"

"Well, what the fuck happened? Stop beating around the bush."

"After the check, he asked me for a friendship kiss."

"Fucking pervert. What's a damn friendship kiss?"

"A kiss on the lips. But no tongue."

Smiling knowingly, Misty shook her head. "Did you go for it?"

"No, I recoiled. His feelings were hurt. Then he got angry."

"I bet Uncle Freaky threw a hissy fit. That lil' kiss would have led to him wanting to slobber on your dick."

"I don't think so. He just wanted a kiss. Despite all the boys he has in his house, I think he's lonely."

"Greedy is more like it. That ol' pervert has been doing a lot more than friendship kissing up in that dip. Good thing I got my hands on you before Uncle Freaky turned you out."

"Isn't that what you've been trying to do?"

"Trying! You're already turned out. But at least I pay you. What did he do except feel you up and fill your head with pipe dreams?"

"I don't want to do this work forever, Misty. I still plan on going to college."

"I know. But in the meantime…while you're stacking your college fund, I need you to put me on with those other dudes inside Uncle Freaky's house."

"I don't think you can do it. They enjoy all the perks that Uncle Marshall provides."

"Such as?"

"Free food. Everyone has a laptop. Only two to a bedroom. At the Caring Cottage, there were six of us sharing a dorm."

"But he's not giving those guys financial independence. That's where I come in the picture. Now give me the scoop. How many dudes live in that crib? What are their names? When do they go shoot hoops?"

"Never. Not anymore. Uncle Marshall doesn't like the guys associating with thugs or any girls who could use a fake pregnancy to ruin our careers. He doesn't want to risk the chance of any trifling behavior rubbing off on his boys." Sailor smiled embarrassedly. "He refers to all of us guys as his boys."

"Mmm-hmm. I see." *Uncle Freaky has control issues.*

"He's looking out for everyone's well-being."

"He brainwashed you, Sailor. He was using all of you... keeping all that male eye candy for his damn self. If he could really get you some work, he'd be earning money off of at least one of the guys. Now tell me how I can get those houseboys. I can do more for them than Uncle Freaky can. That bullshit he's talking ain't nothing but a pipe dream."

CHAPTER 13

Turned out Uncle Marshall had a vice: the daily lottery. According to Sailor, Uncle Marshall selected two of his houseguests to go play his lottery numbers. Sailor said the two guys would show up at Best Check Cashing at approximately four-fifteen.

There was no available parking near the check-cashing place, and Misty had parked a block away. Refusing to stand around in the sun waiting, Misty cooled off inside a cheap shoe store, while Sailor was keeping watch outside on busy Chelten Avenue.

Sailor popped inside the shoe store. "Lennox and Izell are coming down the street!"

Misty yanked off the sandal she was trying on. Tossing it inside the box, she jumped up and pushed her feet back into her Coach sneakers.

"Do you want the sandals you tried on?" the sales girl asked.

"I don't wear cheap shit," Misty snarled as she ran out of the shoe store.

Outside, Sailor pointed out two hunks who were heading in their direction. Misty recognized one of them; the dark chocolate brother that she'd seen him through the window doing pushups. The other one was a lighter shade of brown with short, russet-colored locs. Both men were hot to death, showing off their triceps with sleeveless shirts.

Misty's twitching coochie was frothing at the mouth and going into convulsions.

"Sailor! Whassup, dude?" the dark chocolate hottie said as they approached.

"We been worried about you, man," the other hunk added, brows furrowed.

"I'm doing alright." Grinning, Sailor was obviously glad to see his old housemates.

Misty elbowed Sailor. "Introduce us."

"Oh, yeah. I want you guys to meet Misty. I'm staying at her place." Pointing at his two friends, Sailor turned to Misty and said, "That's Izell and Lennox."

"Hi," Lennox said.

Remembering how he looked shirtless, Misty had her eyes glued to Izell's broad shirt.

"'Sup, Misty?" Izell said, darting an eye at Sailor that suggested approval of Sailor's taste in women.

Misty was feeling Izell. She could tell that he had a little bit of thug in him. Envisioning all the money she could make off of the brawny pair, Misty graced them with a beautiful smile. "I'm good."

"Good seeing you, Sailor," Izell said. "Glad you aiight."

"Yeah, we have to do the lottery thing and then get back for our evening training," Lennox added.

"Are you going to give up on modeling, man?" Lennox inquired.

Sailor nodded. "I'm not cut out for that. I'm working hard, trying to get my money together so I can get in school in the fall."

"Where are you working?" There was pity in Lennox's eyes, like he expected to hear that he was cleaning toilets in a public restroom.

"He works for me," Misty cut in. "Easy work with good pay."

"Good for you, Sailor. Glad to hear it. We have to play Uncle Marshall's numbers. Take care of yourself, man," Lennox said, unwilling to take the bait.

Sailor's friends are as corny as he is. Nothing 'hood about either of them.

"Aren't you two curious? Wouldn't you like to get paid some serious dough?" It was difficult for Misty to maintain her smile. With two potential meal tickets trying to slip out of her grip, she was beyond irritated.

"Not interested. We're in training, getting ready—"

"To make it big in the fashion industry," Misty interrupted.

"That's right," Lennox said. "A couple more shoots and my portfolio will be ready."

Sailor slapped Lennox's hand. "That's great. Congrats, man."

They were there to pull Lennox and Izell, so why was Sailor slapping his hand? She glowered at Sailor.

There was a smug look on her face as she asked, "So how are you getting money in the meantime?"

"Our needs are met," Izell piped in.

Damn! Uncle Freaky must be giving up a lot more than some friendly kisses to have these dudes hanging around his homo ass for free.

"Wouldn't you like to do better than having your needs met?" She unsnapped her clutch bag, revealing a pile of one hundred dollar bills. It was money she'd acquired from Troy's and Sailor's sex labor. "I can make sure you keep cash in your pocket while you're waiting for your next close-up."

Instead of breaking his neck to play Uncle Freaky's number, Izell lingered. Apparently, the sight of Misty's thick stack had Izell's wheels spinning. "What's the job and how much does it pay?"

"I'm gonna keep it real with you. I sell sex."

Izell and Lennox both raised a brow.

"You wouldn't be doing much more than you're doing now."

"All I do is pose for the camera," Lennox said smugly.

"You'll be posing, but my clients like to touch the merchandise. Just like Uncle Marshall does," she said with a knowing wink.

Lennox and Izell exchanged a meaningful glance.

"The only difference," she continued, "is that my clients pay to handle the goods. And they pay well."

"Your clients are females, right?" Lennox's interest was piqued.

"A few. Most are males. You won't have to do much of anything. Just look luscious while my clients admire those muscles you've both worked so hard to build."

Izell stared at Misty, as though searching for the truth in her eyes. "It's got to be more to it than letting somebody cop a feel."

She shrugged. "Not really."

"How much do we get paid?" Lennox asked.

"Depends on what gets touched." Misty sighed. "Let's keep it real, okay? That old freak you live with sneaks a feel when he's examining your muscles. He probably does more than that." Misty looked at Izell and Lennox with suspicion.

"Whatever," Izell said snidely. His tone suggested that Misty had a vivid imagination.

Trying to hide the embarrassment coloring his face, Lennox looked down, suddenly engrossed in his sneakers.

"I realize what's going on up in that crib. I heard Uncle Freaky likes to kiss the boys," Misty said tauntingly.

Izell's gaze jerked to Sailor's face. His dark eyes glistened with accusation.

Guilty of telling secrets, Sailor looked away.

"I don't fuck with other men," Izell asserted.

Misty softened her tone. "I believe you. But you'd be a fool to turn down this good money I'm offering."

Izell relaxed. His body language became less confrontational. "How much did you say you're paying?"

"I can start you off at three hundred per client. As you build up your clientele, I'll gradually raise you up to five hundred a pop."

"When can we start?" Izell's voice was steady and controlled, but Misty could sense his enthusiasm.

"I could get you some work tonight," she said confidently, though she wasn't really sure if she could wrangle up a client. Dr. Hardy, one of her most loyal clients, could usually be counted on for an impromptu sex session. Though he kept complaining that no one compared to Brick, the good doctor would not turn down an opportunity to get with new talent.

"I don't know about tonight. How about tomorrow?" Izell said.

That sounded good to Misty. She needed the extra time to line something up. "Cool. But there's a condition."

"What's the condition?" Izell folded his arms. His biceps bulged like crazy.

Looking at his bulging biceps, Misty was transfixed for a few seconds.

"I need more manpower."

"Uh-huh…"

"For every stack you make, you need to provide me with a new recruit."

"I can do that," Izell said confidently.

Lennox nodded. "We know a lot of dudes who could use some fast money."

Images of a stable filled with bulky, fine-ass men put

a grin on her face. She'd keep Troy's skinny, ashy ass around as a novelty act for extreme perverts, but it was now mandatory that everyone on payroll be beefed-up and beautiful.

Thank you, Uncle Freaky!

CHAPTER 14

Misty sat on the side of the bed. "Take your shirt off."

Standing in front of her, Izell didn't hesitate to pull his shirt over his head, and then tossed it on the floor.

Her eyes glossed over his abs, which were laced tight with muscles. His body was so hot, it took all of her willpower not to drool. "You're such an exhibitionist," Misty teased, showing no sign that she was impressed.

"Is that a crime?" Izell was full of himself, but Misty didn't care. As long as he could put it down in the bedroom, she didn't care how much he loved his body.

"Not in my world." She flung her hair out of her face, trying to shake away some of the lust that was over-powering her senses.

She would have loved to take her time and fondle every muscle on his chiseled torso…to lick his body up and down. But she was in a time crunch. Sailor had to be picked up from his appointment in an hour.

"Wanna see more?" he taunted, pulling at his belt.

"Not yet. Your clients are going to adore you. Are you going to be able to deal with having a bunch of body worshippers?"

"I won't mind. I worked hard on my body so it can be admired."

"My clients will be doing a lot more than admiring."

"Oh, yeah?"

"Uh-huh. They'll be willing to spend a lot of paper to touch your dick."

"Mmm," he moaned. "You got my joint hard."

Misty noticed the bulge in the front of his pants. Unable to resist, she rubbed the hardened lump. "If you let them kiss it, you can make a whole lot more."

He gripped his erection through his pants. "Stop, girl. Don't get me all worked up if you're not prepared for this."

"Are you holding?"

"Find out for yourself." His tobacco-brown eyes were bright with confidence.

Eager to find out what he was working with, Misty pulled his belt loose and unzipped his pants.

When his khakis dropped, Misty's mouth watered. Izell's body was tight, but his dick was a masterpiece. It was big, black, and heavily veined; a savagely beautiful dick. So stunning, Misty would have loved to claim it, frame it, and hang it on a wall.

She didn't know whether to suck or fuck the tantalizing dark spear that was pointed at her.

When it came to oral sex, Misty preferred being on the receiving end, but with a dick as well-formed and delicious looking as Izell's, how could she resist?

Unable to restrain herself, she gripped his hips, and took in a mouthful of raw meat.

Izell's body vibrated with arousal. His fingers spiked through Misty's hair, his breathing became raspy as he inserted more of his iron-hard dick between her suckling lips.

Sexual agony knifed through her. One hand clenched his ass; the other was wrapped around his hard, heated flesh, as she pulled in as much of his dick as she could fit inside her hungry mouth.

Clasping her head, Izell pulled out suddenly.

Misty was shocked. Her eyes were wide and ablaze with anger. "What are you doing?" Izell was hot and everything, with a body that looked like a work of art, but Misty still called the shots.

She wiped her mouth with the back of her hand. "I didn't say I was ready to fuck," she snapped, though her restless coochie had a different opinion.

"I had to stop. Felt like I was about to cum."

"Already?"

"I'm pretty quick the first go-'round."

That admission took him down a notch in her opinion. "How quickly can you recharge?"

"Immediately."

"That'll work." She made a fist around his slippery pole, sliding it up and down, putting friction on his manhood.

Grimacing, he thrust inside her cupped hand, fucking her palm like he was deep inside a tight pussy. A growling sound in his throat and the dip in his knees were telltale signs that although Izell was fighting to hold back; he was about to shoot off his first load.

Witnessing a brawny man at his weakest moment gave Misty a feeling of power. But her coochie, yearning for attention, clenched unmercifully, making her weak. She pressed her thighs together, attempting to ease the demanding throb.

She tried to pacify her pussy by rocking back and forth on the edge of the bed. It didn't work. Finally, she pushed four fingers past the swollen lips of her sex. One hand stroked Izell while the fingers of the other hand dove in and out of her snatch, the slurping sounds inciting Izell to explode with a loud groan.

Misty extracted glazed fingers and began stripping off her clothes. Naked, she lay on her back; her pussy was creamy with need. Erect nipples broadcasted her desire.

True to his word, Izell was rigid within seconds. She could feel the heat of his passion as he began mounting her. Desperate to feel his naked flesh against hers, Misty's hands went around Izell's waist and pulled him on top of her.

He lowered his head and covered her lips with his. His emboldened tongue explored her mouth while his hand sought the hot lust between her legs. He slid a thick finger inside her wet pussy, pushing in deeply. His lips traveled from her mouth and down to her neck, where he nipped at her delicate flesh while twisting his finger, making her gasp for breath and utter his name.

Her senses overstimulated, Misty moved her hips and humped on his finger. The intensity of the sensation he was giving her was similar to getting a good fuck.

When he withdrew it, she grabbed his ass and tried to force his dick inside to fill the emptiness. Her yearning had her whimpering as the head of his dick touched her hot flesh.

She ran the tips of her fingers in a steady rhythm along his spine. Then her movement became erratic as she raked her fingernails against his back. Needing to feel his heat, she dug into his ebony skin, forcing him to press closer.

The cries of pleasure that spilled from her lips rose in volume as the head of his dick opened up her slick folds. Inch by inch, he tunneled inside, filling her up with his shaft. In-and-out motions delivered sensations to her engorged clit.

Sensing that her clit needed attention, Izell caressed it with his thumb; each stroke felt like a burning lash of unbearable pleasure.

"Stop." Misty writhed beneath his powerful frame.

His hips circled at a slower pace. He looked down at her. "You're talking shit. You don't want me to stop." he said, his voice rough.

"I can't take it. You're driving me crazy," she said hoarsely.

Izell stilled his circling hips and began teasingly with-drawing small increments of his length.

Possessively, Misty's coochie tightened around his thickness. Mindless with lust, she had a sudden change of heart, and screamed, "Don't stop! Fuck me! Hard!"

Giving her what she wanted, Izell lifted her legs and held them open, plunging into her quivering sex with ferocious thrusts.

She matched his tempo, stroke for stroke, until an orgasm jolted through her core, jerking her head from side to side, bucking her body uncontrollably.

Her orgasm excited him. The speed of his thrusts increased. His breathing became harsh. The sounds he uttered were throaty and primal. He pulled out. Releasing her legs from his grasp, Izell clutched his dick and shot out streams of milk-white fluid over her small breasts.

Misty looked down at the cum shots that slid down to her tummy. Her mouth fell open in shock. "Nigga, is you crazy? I'm not into this freak bullshit. I didn't give you permission to be skeeting your seed all over me."

"My bad."

She looked down at the creamy glob that was pooling in the curls of hair that covered her mons. "Ew. This is so nasty."

"That's protein," Izell said nonchalantly. "A little bit of cum is good for your skin."

Furious, Misty glared at Izell. Her thoughts turned to her former lover, Dane. Seething, she remembered how dick-whipped she'd been. Dane stole her business, her luxury vehicle, and one of her good workers. The untimely death he met was too good for him. She hoped the bastard rotted in hell.

She wasn't about to let another good-fucking nigga take her under.

Waving a finger through the air, she said, "Let me tell you something; your sex game is on point, but I'm not a sucka for a dick. Once I bust a nut, I'm back to business as usual."

Izell glanced at the white spatters on her breasts. The smirk on his face revealed pride in his handiwork.

"Fun and games are over, mufucka."

Izell's lips twisted bitterly. "Watch your mouth."

"I don't have to watch a goddamn thing. If you want to work for me, you better treat me with some respect. Apologize!"

"Apologize for what? It's not that serious."

"Don't tell me what's serious. You don't run shit. I do!"

"You a trip."

"I want an apology," she insisted. "Or you can forget about our business arrangement."

She waited, allowing her words to sink in. She watched his face tense as he ruminated on her threat.

His features contorted as he engaged in a mental battle with himself. Coming to a decision, Izell's expression became relaxed. "I didn't mean no disrespect."

"Is that an apology?"

He coughed and looked embarrassed as he said, "Yeah, my bad. It won't happen again."

"Alright." She sneered down at her pubis. "Go get a washcloth to wipe this nasty crap off of me."

Izell gave her a look of disbelief and turned around

slowly. He stood for a few seconds, as if debating whether to follow her order.

The back of Izell's body—the defined slabs of muscle on his back, his firm ass, and his well-developed hamstrings—was a stunning piece of sculpture.

He began moving toward the bedroom door. His naked body, a smooth flow of sepia-toned muscle, was poetry in motion.

Misty's anger was diminished by a twinge of arousal.

She'd gladly put their little misunderstanding behind them if Izell proved to be the sexual beast that she needed him to be.

With a smile on her face, Misty reclined. She decided that after Izell cleaned his gook off of her, she'd put him through the test...see if he could get it up one more time.

Tomorrow, she'd find out if Lennox was on top of his sex game.

CHAPTER 15

With Izell and Lennox added to the roster, money was coming in more regularly. Misty bought a refurbished laptop, and once her website was up, she was expecting to really get her money right.

Sailor was a computer guru. He was a former member of the Geek Squad at one of the big computer chain stores. Why he'd left that job to go peddling cleaning products was anyone's guess. Misty really didn't give a damn. She was glad he was using his computer skills to launch her new web site.

Though she had basic computer knowledge, Misty was glad to allow Sailor to take over that task. Unlike that slimy Dane...may he never rest in peace...Sailor was trustworthy. Honest to a fault. Misty didn't have a problem letting Sailor have access to such sensitive information.

Standing behind him, she looked over Sailor's shoulder as he swiftly set up a page that featured Izell and Troy.

As she'd done in the past, Misty intended to post illicit

photos on the site. Now that she had Sailor's assistance, she was upgrading and adding options.

It was Sailor's idea to add the option of a still photo or a sex clip. It was a brilliant suggestion that would bring in some major paper.

Convincing Izell to participate in a cum-shooting video had been easy. Misty realized firsthand that Izell had a thing about squirting out his load on human flesh.

The difficult part of getting the video filmed was getting Troy to agree to participate.

After cajoling, bargaining, and then finally threatening him, Misty persuaded Troy to play his part. Troy was furious and embarrassed when Misty instructed him to bend over and let Izell use his ashy ass as the bull's eye for his far-reaching cum.

She named the video *Lotioning Up An Ashy Ass.*

"How much longer is this going to take?" she asked impatiently.

"A few more minutes." Sailor kept his eyes glued to the screen, his fingers rapidly clicking away on the keyboard.

"Can't you hurry up?"

"I'm going as fast as I can, but it would be helpful if you stopped hovering."

Misty scowled. "I know you're not talking to me. You don't run shit!" she spat, her lips twisted in indignation. "I can go to Best Buy and hire any geek I want."

Sailor sighed. "I'm not deliberately being a dick," he said, sounding like a white boy. "But it's hard to concentrate when you're standing over me. I'm starting to feel rushed."

"Good. That's how I want you to feel."

"Didn't you tell me that I'm your right-hand man?"

"Yeah, but that doesn't mean you can sit around bull-shitting. I gotta get my money right."

"I want you to make money, Misty. I have a personal interest in your business."

She gave him the crooked eye. "Whatchu talkin' 'bout, Willis?"

There was a blank look on Sailor's face. Apparently, they didn't watch reruns of *Different Strokes* in his weird-ass hometown.

"I'm still trying to raise the money for my tuition," he explained.

She turned up a corner of her top lip. "Tuition? Ew. That's a waste of money."

"You can't get anywhere in life without a proper edu-cation."

"Says who? Haven't you heard that most filthy rich people are self-made entrepreneurs?" She waited while Sailor marinated on her words.

He shook his head. "Never heard that."

"Well, it's true. And the right-hand man usually gets a good come-up by holding on to the business man's coattails."

Sailor chuckled.

"Do you mean to tell me that you'd rather go to college

than ride my coattails?" Her suggestive body language and the sassy lilt in her voice made her question sound naughty.

"Uh…I'll take the ride," Sailor said, blushing.

"Smart choice. Look, I'm going out for a few hours. I need some retail therapy. Do you think you'll be finished by the time I get back?"

"Of course. I'll have everything in place by then."

"To be a computer geek, you sure are taking a long time," she complained.

Sailor gave her a patient smile. His warm feelings for her were apparent in his gaze.

"Don't be staring at me like I'm a muthafuckin' computer screen," she hissed and rolled her eyes.

Sailor shook his head, as if Misty were an adorable brat. He returned his gaze to the monitor and then suddenly looked up. "Oh, did I tell you that Lennox called this morning?"

"What now? Lennox is starting to get on my nerves. He's so fuckin' greedy. I gave him back-to-back work and he still wants more."

"That's not why he called."

"Oh. What did he want?"

"He said he convinced another dude from Uncle Marshall's house to come work for you. When he gets here, I'll take some shots of him."

"Hold up. Slow your roll. I need to look the dude over so I can figure out what kind of shots I want to take."

Sailor gave her a look. "I know what kind of shots to take. You said that I'm your right-hand man, so let me handle this for you. I guarantee that you're going to love the pictures that I post."

In a split-second, Misty's sour mood changed to joyous. "You're gonna hook everything up and have the new recruit added to the roster? Yo, I'ma be making money off that mufucka before I even meet him?"

"That's the plan," Sailor added with pride.

"Wow! That's whassup." Misty dipped down and kissed him on the cheek.

"You're the man, Sailor. I'll see you when I get back from my shopping spree."

Wearing a big smile, Misty sailed out of the apartment. Knowing that she was about to get her paper straight, she couldn't decide whether she should go to the mall, look for a bigger apartment, or go buy herself a classier whip.

With the jacked-up credit she had, she wouldn't be able to get anything that required a payment plan. Hopefully, she'd find a fly whip that she could afford to purchase with cash.

A new apartment would have to wait. Her public image was more important at this juncture.

At a car dealership on Baltimore Pike in Springfield, she traded in her hooptie and bought herself another BMW X5. It cost her fourteen stacks, which she paid in cash. It was the same color as her previous X5, but this one was much newer than the one that no-good, dead-ass Dane had ruthlessly stolen from her.

But no one could tell that this X5 wasn't spanking brand-new. The body of this model didn't change from year to year. The interior was in pristine condition and the exterior didn't have a nick, dent, scratch, or any type of mark.

Behind the wheel, she fiddled with buttons and knobs, quickly orienting herself to her new ride. When the radio came on, a Nicki Minaj song pumped through the speakers. As usual, Nicki was bragging through the song… talking mad shit. But Misty wasn't even mad at that fake-ass Barbie bitch. Nothing and nobody could darken this sunshiny day.

So what if she'd spent most of her cash on hand? The way she was slowly ripping off Uncle Freaky, it was merely a matter of time before the big bucks started pouring in. She continued fiddling with buttons and knobs until the sunroof slid back. A gentle breeze wafted through her hair.

This was the beginning of a fabulous new life. She could feel it in the air.

Feeling more relaxed and happier than she'd been in a long time, Misty steered the vehicle in the direction of Springfield Mall. The money she had left over was burning a hole in her pocketbook.

With a plan in mind, she parked. Then she hit the alarm button on the X5 and whisked inside Macy's for some serious shopping.

CHAPTER 16

Misty had been waiting for fifteen minutes when the 52 pulled up. The beat of her heart drummed erratically, and then picked up enormous speed. Despite the chill of the air conditioner, her face felt hot and flushed, and her skin had became moist and prickly when she'd seen him intermingled with the other passengers who were getting off the bus.

Excited, she gazed at her reflection and fished inside her purse, searching for lipstick. Retrieving the sleek, expensive case, she applied a glossy cherry color to her lips. It was time for a showdown with this nigga. Talk some sense into his head.

Guzzling a bottle of VitaminWater, hard hat on his head, tool belt hanging, Brick headed toward his home.

Her mouth parted; a soft moan escaped. Hot-boiling yearning pooled between her legs. Misty squirmed in her seat.

Brick was walking with that same confident swagger he'd had at the hospital. Brick had become a very self-assured man. A knot of resentment tightened in her chest.

With her new whip pointed in his direction, Misty

watched him. Despite the fact that Brick was frontin', she didn't think she'd ever seen a more desirable sight. As he grew closer, she could see beads of perspiration trickling down his arms and over his massive biceps. *Oh, Brick!*

Her tongue darted out and moistened her lips. Butterflies flitted in her stomach. Then she rolled her eyes at him, feeling both excited and vexed at the same time. *Look at this mufucka…strutting down the damn block like he running shit.*

He passed by without even noticing her. She beeped the horn. He turned around. Spotting Misty, Brick gave a look of recognition. He didn't appear to be impressed by her new ride, but there was something in his eyes… something hard to distinguish. If she didn't know better, she would have sworn that she saw pity in his eyes.

"What's good, Misty?" Brick said without emotion or any mention of the X5.

This bus-riding, jealous-ass nigga getting on my nerves already, tryna act new.

"Is my mom home? I picked up some gifts for my little brother." She motioned toward the back seat, which was crowded with bags from Macy's, The Children's Place, and Toys R Us.

"Looks like you went a little overboard for my son," he said with a chuckle that held a trace of pride.

The sound of Brick's laughter gave Misty hope. "Your son is a part of me, too, Brick." She gave him a long look.

Making a baby with her mother was the ultimate betrayal. The two people she'd trusted most in the world had stabbed her in the back and turned the knife.

Her eyes clouded. "Nothing's too good for my blood," she said softly, trying not to choke up.

Brick eyed her closely, as if checking for deception in her eyes, but Misty hid her ulterior motives behind a pool of tears.

"Your mom's not home right now. She took the baby to his doctor's appointment. But I can take the bags," he said in a firm, cool voice. He reached for the handle of the back door.

This wasn't in the script. Misty had planned on visiting for a while. She wanted to get inside the house and secretly observe Brick. While her dumb mother gushed over the expensive gifts, Misty intended to search for signs of Brick's boredom. Brick was a freak. She knew how he liked to get down. He had to be bored with her mother by now. That bitch was home on disability. She allegedly had complications after giving birth. Lazy hoe. Brick knew good and well that he missed her tight coochie. Nigga couldn't be feeling shit when he pushed his dick inside her mother's baby-birthing, loose-ass pussy walls.

Thomasina could not compete with Misty's bedroom skills. Misty had always kept Brick sexually stimulated with the dirty words and the raunchy scenarios she whispered in his ear while they were fucking. And she didn't just talk good game, either. She did everything within her power to allow Brick to live out the sexual fantasies that she put in his head.

"Hey, Brick," she said, smiling. "I had a dream about Shane the other night. About the three of us. You know... the way we used to be. I still miss him." She gazed at Brick. Speaking softly, she said, "Nobody understood Shane except me and you."

Brick grunted in displeasure and contorted his face.

"What's wrong?"

"Why you always bringing up Shane? I wish you'd let that man rest in peace. The life that nigga was living wasn't no good for him or nobody else. He was hurting inside. And for that reason, he couldn't help from hurting everybody who loved him—including you and me."

"I know, but I was thinking about the good times."

"Wasn't no good times, Misty. We were three weed heads, staying high and always looking for a quick come-up."

"We were young, Brick. Three kids doing what we could to make our hustle official. I don't see anything wrong with that."

"Whatever," Brick said disgustedly. "Shane was in a dark place back then. Now my man is standing in the light. I believe in letting the past stay where it belongs. Y'ah mean? It would be wise for you to do the same."

Who dis nigga think he is? Half-retarded mufucka knows he's outta pocket. He needs to check himself. Tryna sound all wise all of a sudden. He's kicking it like he got some book smarts.

I don't know who he been listening to, but he can kiss my ass. Since when does Brick give me any goddamn advice?

She felt rage building inside her. She wanted to scream profanities and slap the shit out of Brick. But she clenched her teeth, suppressing boiling anger by taking a deep breath.

"Yeah, I guess you're right," Misty agreed. Though it was killing her to have to suck up to Brick, she had no choice. That saying, "there's a thin line between love and hate," was proving true. She hated the smug expression on Brick's face. But wanted to fuck his brains out for turning out to be all hot and sexy. Damn, this shit was confusing. Absolutely ridiculous.

She wasn't used to caving in for anybody...and certainly not for Brick. Fuck! She was the mastermind in their relationship. She'd started schooling him back when they were kids. Now he had his head up her mother's ass, trying to act like he had grown his own set of big balls. Ungrateful bastard.

To be a pervert mufucka, he sure had some nerve... acting all opinionated and arrogant. Brick used to be so whipped he would bow down and sniff Misty's coochie if he thought she'd been out cheating. Freaky mufucka used to get off by trying to catch a whiff of another man's scent.

His cocky attitude was her mother's fault. That bitch was blowing up his dome. Making him think he was somebody special. Never in his entire life had anyone cooked, cleaned, or catered to Brick.

Somebody needed to whip her mother's ass for doting

on him. Brick was a good damn man gone bad. *Fuck!*

Misty used a different ploy. "Remember that Betty Boop apron you used to like to wear?" she asked, hoping to arouse him with a kinky memory of his submissive tendencies.

Brick snorted. "Yeah, I was a sick mufucka back then. Yo, it's obvious that this is not a goodwill visit. So do me a favor…take all that shit you bought back to the store. I takes care of mine. My baby boy don't want for nothing."

"I'm sorry, Brick. I was only tryna make you laugh. I didn't mean—"

Brick turned his back on her.

With great regret, she watched him walk away from her, his broad shoulders dipping in defiance as he sauntered up the narrow walkway that led to his front door.

She turned on the engine and gave Brick a long last look.

It's not over, Brick. We belong together. You need to be rolling hard with me, instead of fighting destiny.

CHAPTER 17

Brick heard the clatter of the stroller and rushed to the front door. He raced down to the pavement and unlocked the safety belt, and gripped up his son.

"Baby boy. Baby boy! Daddy sure missed you!" Brick held the giggling child high in the air and gazed up at him lovingly.

"Oh, ignore me like I'm not even standing here." Pretending to be insulted, Thomasina let go of the handle of the empty stroller.

"How's my big girl doin'?" Brick moved next to his wife and kissed her on the cheek. He could see her eyes darting toward the nosey neighbors who were sitting on lawn chairs with their eyes fixated on the May-December couple.

"I know you're not worried about what they think," Brick fussed.

"Not at all," Thomasina responded and then placed a kiss on her husband's lips.

Murmurs of discontent floated over to Thomasina and

Brick. Obviously, the spectators would have found it more exciting to see Thomasina and Brick throwing punches at each other than to watch their public display of affection.

Thomasina folded the stroller and began to tug it. Brick relieved her of the burden. Effortlessly, the big man picked up the stroller, looping the handle inside the crook of one arm, while hoisting the baby in the other.

Inside their small living room, Thomasina sniffed the air. "Something smells good." She looked at Brick curiously.

"Dinner's cooking outside on the grill."

"Baron, you didn't have to do that. You work outside all day…toiling under the burning sun. When you get home, you're supposed to rest."

"Ain't nothing wrong with a man cooking for his family every now and then."

"On the weekend, when you've had some rest," she fussed.

"Stop fussing. You love it when your man cooks for you."

Thomasina blushed. "Of course I do. But I don't want you burning yourself out. I'm home all day; I'm supposed to take care of you."

"We're supposed to take care of each other. Yo, I'm only twenty-five years old and I'm as healthy as a horse. Putting in a lil' extra work ain't gon' burn me out. I like the fact that you can be home taking care of our son. I don't want to turn him over to strangers. When your disability runs out, I'ma pick up some extra work."

"Baron," Thomasina said, exasperated.

"Real rap. You've been working all your life. It's time for you to sit back and let your man take care of you."

Thomasina beamed.

Brick set little Baron on the floor, but the child's legs buckled in rebellion. He preferred being in his father's arms, and refused to stand up.

"You spoiled rotten, man," Brick teased. "Come on." He picked him up and kissed him. "If you gon' hang with me, you gon' have to learn how to cook. You feel me, man?"

Tears still flowing, the baby nodded. "High-five!" Brick instructed. Giggling, the baby smacked his tiny palm against his father's enormous hand.

Thomasina looked at the two men in her life with love in her eyes. "I must have done something right," Thomasina said.

"Whatchu mean? Everything you do is right."

"No. I made a lot of mistakes in my life. But I must have done something right or I wouldn't have ended up with a good man like you."

"It's all you. Being with you is making me a better man."

Brick meant it. Thomasina was on extended disability and he didn't want her to ever go back to work. Taking care of their son was all she needed to worry about.

"Gotta check on my food," he said and set little Baron on his feet. The baby cried and took steps toward Brick with his hands outstretched.

In the enclosed and miniscule backyard, Brick let his son toddle around and play with the toys that were scattered about. Brick tended to the array of meats... chicken, salmon, burgers, hot dogs, and ribs.

Watching her weight and blood pressure, Thomasina only ate chicken and fish, but Brick still got down with beef and pork.

As he slathered barbecue sauce on the ribs, his strokes changed from gentle to heavy-handed and angry. What was his problem? Cooking on the grill was something he loved. It was soothing...a pleasurable experience that took away the tensions of the day. But his tension refused to budge and he noticed that he was taking out his frustration on the meat that he was smacking with the barbecue brush.

Misty.

Her unexpected visit had him on edge.

He banged down the lid. The loud sound jolted the baby. Little Baron yelled.

"My bad. Daddy didn't mean to scare you. You aiight, man?"

The young child was resilient and had quickly recovered from the loud noise. "Bird, Daddy." Brick's son pointed upward to a bird that was flying and then settled on the branch of a tree.

"Where'd that bird go?" Brick asked his son.

"In tree!" Little Baron screamed.

"That's right. Boy, you're a genius," Brick said with pride. Then his thoughts returned to Misty.

Cooking usually took his mind off of his troubles, but today it wasn't working.

Brick didn't like keeping secrets from his wife, but some things were best left unsaid. Misty did not have good intentions when she came to visit. No point in giving Thomasina false hope.

Thomasina would have happily invited Misty to join them for dinner with the expectation that they could all coexist as a happy family.

But Brick knew better. Misty wouldn't be satisfied until she'd sabotaged their marriage. Destroyed their peaceful life.

He sucked his teeth, recalling how he'd warned her to stay away from his family…in the hospital…right after his son was born.

Her showing up today was a bold move. She had some kind of trick up her sleeve, and when Misty's wheels started turning, it couldn't mean anything but trouble. She'd relentlessly pursue whatever she wanted.

Misty couldn't dupe Brick. Not anymore. But that didn't mean she wouldn't try to worm her way into their lives…getting to her mother when Brick wasn't around.

For most of his life, he'd loved Misty with all his heart. But now…

Brick yanked up the lid of the grill. A cloud of smoke concealed the glowering mask of hatred that twisted his face as he imagined himself yanking Misty out of her whip and throwing her up against a brick wall the next time he caught her staked out anywhere near his house.

CHAPTER 18

Brick was stretched out on the bed, watching *Any Given Sunday*, an old flick with Pacino playing a tough coach. Jamie Foxx was featured as the quarterback for the team that Pacino was trying to lead to victory. Though nothing compared to his performance in *Scarface*, Brick enjoyed anything Pacino starred in. No, scratch that…he didn't like the movie where Pacino played a blind dude who went around sniffing out pussy all the time. Pacino got props from Hollywood, but in Brick's mind, he should have turned that role down. Playing a horny, blind dude wasn't a cool move.

Pacino and Jamie Foxx were going at it toe-to-toe when Thomasina came out of the shower and entered the bedroom. He caught a whiff of lavender bath gel.

"You smell good," Brick acknowledged, though engrossed in the film.

"Thank you," she replied with a smile in her voice.

She searched among the overflow of lotions, potions, and creams that covered the dresser top. The rattling and clanging drew Brick's attention.

She was naked beneath a large towel that was wrapped around her. Water beads dotted her shoulders, and slid down her arms. Brick checked out the mound of her ass. *Umph!* His pulse kicked up a notch; his manhood grew hard.

"Have you seen my cream?" Thomasina inquired as she continued searching, moving objects and containers around.

"What cream...your lotion?"

"No. My special cream. I usually keep it in the bathroom, but I can't find it."

"Is this what you're looking for?" With a mischievous smile, Brick pulled out a white tube that he'd hidden under his pillow.

"Baron! Why you hiding my cream, boy?"

"Why you always sneaking and rubbing it on while you're in the bathroom?"

"The bathroom is a private place. Some things should be personal."

"Ain't nothing personal between you and me. Come here, baby," he said softly, reaching out to her.

"Hand me my cream. I'll be in bed in a few minutes."

"Nope. Come over here and explain to me what this stuff inside the tube is supposed to do for you."

Unconsciously, Thomasina wrapped the towel even tighter around her body.

"Whatchu tryna hide from me?"

"I'm embarrassed about my stretch marks."

"Yeah, well, it's time to change all that. Right now. Now get yourself over here."

Taking reluctant steps, Thomasina approached the bed.

Brick stood up. He aimed the remote at Pacino, whose gruff voice was interfering with the mood. He clicked to old school slow jams, the kind of music his baby loved to listen to.

He hugged her moist body, and whispered in her ear, "Ever since you gave me a son, you've been uncomfortable being naked around me."

"That's not true."

"Yes, it is. I only get to feel your naked body…under the covers…in the dark. You sexy, baby. Why don't you let me enjoy your body with the lights on?"

"Baron, my stomach—"

"Is beautiful."

"My stretch marks…" her voice trailed off with a sigh.

"You ashamed of you and me?"

"No!"

"You love me?"

"You know I do."

"So why are you embarrassed by the results of our love?" He began undoing the towel. Slowly pulled it away and began drying the droplets of water on her shoulder. He smoothed the towel across her breasts… brushing terrycloth across her stiffened nipples.

A soft moan slipped past Thomasina's lips.

Holding the towel, Brick took a few steps back and sat

on the edge of the bed. He pulled Thomasina forward.

Beneath the bright overhead light that beamed from the ceiling, she stood in front of him. Naked. Exposed. Vulnerable.

He took in her total body. "I like what I see." Male appreciation shone clearly in his eyes as he gingerly dried her tummy, running the edge of the towel up and down each white-streak that she hoped the tube of stretch mark cream would miraculously eradicate.

"Ain't nothing wrong with your body. You're my mate. My other half. And I feel nothing but love and pride every time I look at you."

"I know, Baron, but—"

"Ain't no buts." He stared into her eyes. "There's no reason for you to feel insecure about anything. In my eyes, you are the most beautiful woman in the world."

Thomasina laughed, self-consciously, shaking her head, denying her beauty.

"Believe that," Brick said sternly. "Because it's true." He lowered his head, kissed her soft stomach. Ran his tongue up and down the streaked flesh. "I love you, Thomasina."

Thomasina shuddered and closed her eyes blissfully.

"Now what did you say these marks are called?" Brick asked, bringing her back to reality.

"Stretch marks."

"Nah, them ain't no stretch marks. They look like lines."

"What?"

"Love lines. No, never mind. That's corny. I'ma call these jawns love strokes."

"You crazy, Baron." Thomasina giggled.

"I'm not crazy. Those marks came from a whole lot of stroking." He pulled her on the bed, eased off his boxer shorts, and covered her body with his.

"You never heard of love strokes?"

Laughing, Thomasina shook her head.

The feeling of her dewy skin sent a surge of heat through him. He gripped the base of his erection. "Oh, aiight. I'ma show you what I'm talking about," he said in a lustful groan.

No time for foreplay. His dick was engorged. He'd take care of her later. Right now he had to get his thickness inside her familiar warmth.

"Ah," he sighed with relief. "I love this wet pussy. You believe that, don'tchu?"

"Yes," she panted, circling her hips.

"Open up for me, baby. We 'bout to heat it up."

She wrapped her legs around his back, giving him complete access.

"This is how it all started," Brick whispered. "Remember that night when I was stroking you and begging you to let me plant my seed?"

"I remember."

"You said you were scared."

"I was."

"You didn't want to do it, but you did it for me. You took a big risk for me."

"I don't regret it," she purred.

He thrust inside the hot cavern between her legs. "Do you like these strokes I'm giving you, baby?"

"God, yes!" Her voice was broken with lust.

"Stop tryna hide the evidence—" His words were cut off by a strangled groan as he tried to control himself… tried to fight off the heat of pleasure that burned swiftly through his system.

Tension mounting, his sweat-dampened skin smacked against hers as he pumped his raging hard shaft in and out of her hot syrupy pussy. The feel of her pussy muscles clamping down on his engorged dick was almost too much to bear. Brick growled like an animal, trying to hold on…as her vagina pulsed and clenched, milking him of every drop of semen.

CHAPTER 19

Sailor was serious about getting his belongings. As soon as he made the money to pay Uncle Freaky, he was out of the apartment ready to hand over six hundred dollars for a suitcase filled with bullshit. He was a weirdo. Sweet. But still a weirdo.

Troy was happy to have him out of the apartment until Misty told him about the job she had lined up for him.

"Suppose I catch something?" Troy poked out his lips.

"How you gon' catch something by letting a mufucka jack off on your ass?" Misty rolled her eyes at Troy as hard as she could. The video he'd shot with Izell was getting a lot of hits and bringing in the bucks, but a lot of the tricks wanted to imitate the scene.

There was always a reason for her madness. She took perverted and freaky pictures to put kinky ideas in non-creative mufuckas' heads. Now Troy was frontin'…trying to fuck with her cash flow.

"You gon' have to send somebody else for that job, cuz I ain't doing it," Troy insisted.

Misty glowered at him. "Who am I going to send?

Stop frontin'. You the only person in the world walking around with an ashy-ass behind and you know it."

"Man, my skin only stays dry like that in the wintertime."

"You're in denial. Your ass gets ashy five minutes after you step out of the shower. You go to bed ashy…and you wake up ashy every morning."

"That's a lie."

"You ashy…Cashy! Accept it and get paid."

"No! I ain't like the way it felt when Izell gushed his load on me. No, that shit felt slimy, yo."

"So what, Troy? Cum can't hurt you."

"I ain't with that. I did it for the video—that's it."

Announcing her displeasure, Misty inhaled and exhaled loudly.

"Get mad. I don't care," Troy said boldly. "Anyway, you lied."

"What did I lie about?"

"You said I was gonna get some of the profits from the video. Ain't nothing came my way yet."

Misty's wheels started turning as she mentally browsed through the lie she would tell. "The video is doing well, but I didn't make no money off of it yet."

"Man, you must think I'm slow."

"Seriously. I didn't get shit for that video. Mufuckas have to pay with credit cards. It takes thirty days for that money to clear. I'ma break you off when I get it."

"So how you get the money to drive that new whip?"

"It didn't cost that much. It's used, Troy. Did you check out the miles on this bitch?"

"Nah, I didn't even pay no attention to that." Ashamed, he lowered his gaze.

"See. You always bitching about something and you don't even know what you're talking about. Use your head. Why would I cheat you? You're my best worker. You've been with me the longest. You and me are in a relationship."

"You be talking that same relationship bullshit to Sailor. That half-cracker mufucka be going around telling people that you're his girl."

"Let him think whatever he wants. We needed extra help. I had to pretend to be his girl to pull him. But you know the truth. You know how I feel about you. What you and me have is forever. Sailor is going to leave eventually. He wants to go back to that whack town he's from and go to college and shit. Don't worry about me and him. That's only temporary."

"You be messing with my head, Misty."

"How long have I been fucking with you?"

"A long time. Like a coupla years."

"Don't that count for something? What me and you have is real. And you know it, Troy. But I need you, baby. I need you to do this for me. Please. I'm trying to stack so we can get up out of this dump we're living in. I want us both to be wheeling something fly. Personally, I want a red Lamborghini. Don't you want one?"

"Hell yeah."

"What color?"

"Black on black."

"Let's make it happen. Work with me, baby. You my biggest star. Them muscle-bound niggas ain't got nothing on you."

Troy cracked a smile.

Misty was getting close, but she hadn't sealed the deal. "I'm doing the hardest part. Letting a trick jack-off on your ass is easy. But the good part is when you get finished, you get paid and you get to come home to this." She patted the crotch of her jeans. "That anaconda between your legs be needing to stretch out inside my walls." Troy was weakening. She could tell by the expression on his face. "Fuck Philly. As soon as we get some real paper, we outta here. We gon' get it poppin' with the rich and fabulous in New York. Miami. Los Angeles or somewhere. Feel me?"

"Yeah, I feel you," Troy said, smiling broadly. Nodding his head as he imagined himself poppin' champagne and living it up with the stars.

"Play your part, baby. Work with me. Don't even think about it too hard. Pretend like it's somebody else's ass getting nutted on. But you gotta do this for us. After your work is done, then you can bring your lanky ass home to me."

"I gotchu. I can do that."

Misty smiled with satisfaction.

"When we gon' go test drive the Lambo?" Troy asked excitedly.

"Damn, Troy. One thing at a time. We gotta get a bigger crib, first. Aiight?"

"Yeah, aiight," he mumbled.

💋

After she dropped Troy off at his client, Misty sent Sailor a text. He'd left in the morning and it was eight o'clock at night. All he was supposed to do was pick up his shit from Uncle Freaky's house and then bounce. What the hell was taking so long?

Indignant, she called his cell...the cell she'd paid for so that they could stay in touch. Her call went to voice mail. *What the fuck?*

When her cell suddenly rang, she answered without checking the caller ID. "Sailor! Where the hell have you been?"

"This is Marshall."

Misty let out a shocked gasp. She had never expected to hear that voice again.

"How'd you get my number and what the hell do you want?"

"I want you to leave Sailor and the rest of my boys alone."

"You better kiss my ass. Did Sailor pay that money he owed you?"

"I declined to accept."

"Is he still there?"

"Yes, this is his home."

"The hell if it is! Mufucka, put Sailor on the phone!" she screamed.

"I prefer to keep you two apart. Far apart," he added.

"Do you know who you fucking with? Nigga, I will fuck your faggot ass up. I'ma send rocks through all your windows. Climb through and whip your ass." Blinded by anger, Misty almost lost control of the X5.

"That sounds like a terroristic threat. For the safety of me and my boys, I'm going to have to file an order of protection against your abuse."

"I'ma show you some abuse when I put my foot all the way up your faggoty ass."

The phone went dead. Uncle Freaky had apparently heard enough.

Uncle Freaky was out-of-pocket. Who did that faggot think he was dealing with? He needed an ass whooping, for real. She couldn't depend on Troy for muscle. His skinny self couldn't beat nobody.

It was times like this when she needed Brick to go upside a mufucka's head. *Brick! Damn, nigga. I need you*, she screamed in her head. Misty didn't think she'd ever be able to accept that Brick no longer had her back.

And what was Sailor's problem? He said he was in love with her. Making her have to deal with Uncle Freaky was a fucked-up way of showing his love. *Half-cracka, half-Eskimo mufucka!*

It wasn't fair. Every time she started getting her shit together, somebody came along and fucked it up. Sailor was the link between her and the other so-called models. *How can Sailor do me like this?*

CHAPTER 20

Looking as if he didn't have a care in the world, Troy came bouncing toward the car. Grinning, he opened the passenger door.

Misty held out an open palmed hand and didn't say a word.

"Damn, it's like that?" His hurt feelings could be heard in his voice. He placed the money he'd earned in her hand. "What's wrong now? I did what you wanted and you still ain't happy."

She started the car and moved into traffic. "We got a problem."

"What kind of problem?"

"Sailor jumped ship."

"So! Good riddance to that mufucka." Troy reclined his seat and slouched his long body as if he were preparing for a quick snooze.

"We need him!" Misty said sharply.

"For what? He don't do nothing but fuck around on the computer. Me, Izell, and them other dudes be doing all the hard labor. All the dirty work. What does Sailor really do? Nothing!"

She glared at Troy. "You a stupid ass."

He readjusted his seat to an upright position. "Yo, why you coming at me? What I do to you?"

She gripped Troy's shoulder with her free hand, using her fingernails to hurt him. "You always saying dumb shit. You don't think before you open your mouth."

Frowning, Troy jerked his shoulder away. "Man, fuck this. Take me to my mom's house. I done been through hell and now you expect me to listen to you while you bitch about that cracka bull."

"Oh, so now you gon' leave me, too?"

He sucked in a harsh breath. "Man, I just did the dirtiest shit I ever did in my life. And I did it because you begged me to. Now you want to whine about that half-cracka nigga. If Sailor don't want no come-up, that's his business. Leave his bitch ass alone."

"You're letting your emotions get in the way. It's obvious that you feel threatened by Sailor."

"How you figure that?"

"You're glad he's gone because you're jealous of him. If you were thinking about stacking, you'd be looking at the big picture the way I am."

"Uh-huh. Whatever," Troy muttered.

"Don't you get it? Because of Sailor, I had access to the services of a shitload of muscular, fine-ass niggas. Mufuckas with eight-packs and shit. They looked good enough to be smiling down from a billboard and some shit."

"They wasn't all that."

"Shut up, Troy. If I lose all that money, I'll never forgive myself. I won't forgive you."

"What I got to do with it?" Troy frowned excessively. "I ain't tell that cracka bull to roll out."

"But it's still your fault."

"How?"

"Because." Misty gathered her thoughts. "If you weren't in my ear bugging me about having some alone time, I would have been on top of my game. I wouldn't have let Sailor go back to Uncle Freaky's house."

"Man, I'm sick of hearing about this Uncle Freaky bullshit. Take me to my mom's house. For real, man. You don't nevah appreciate nothing I do for you."

"Aiight, then. I'll take you where you want to go. But when you get out of my ride, I hope you realize there ain't no coming back."

"Whatever."

"Seriously. I'm getting me some real niggas that know how to act." She thought about that Caring Cottage place that Sailor had told her about. She envisioned herself gripping up some of the homeless mufuckas. Some niggas who appreciated a hand-out.

She could buy some weights and a treadmill and a whole bunch of exercising shit. She'd beef up her own men. Train them to look and act the way she wanted them to.

"Real rap, Troy. I'm sick of niggas walking out on me.

How mufuckas gon' keep on leaving me anytime they get good and ready." Fuming, Misty was on a roll. She picked up speed as her anger intensified.

Cautiously, Troy buckled up.

"First, my mother takes my man. My childhood sweetheart. The only nigga I ever really cared about. And then the bitch had the nerve to get knocked up. I told you how she tricked Brick into marrying her. He felt sorry for her. That's the only reason he married her old ass."

Troy didn't say a word.

Misty seethed silently for a little while, and then resumed her tirade. "How many women do you know who could survive having their own mother marrying their man? Make it so bad…Brick is still in love with me. He don't want her. He'll always love me. But he's the type of man who'll try to stick it out for the sake of his child."

"Yo, Misty. Did you forget that Dane was a friend of mine? You dropped that nigga, Brick, after you met Dane. At first, you was fucking with Monroe. Then you acted like he was only a friend after you met Dane. You said Dane reminded you of some nigga who killed hisself."

"Don't you mention Shane's name. I swear to God, Troy. If you say something bad about Shane, I'm gon' spazz out on your ass."

"I can't say nothing about that suicide dude. I never met that man. "

"So what, Troy? Leave him out of this."

"I'm just saying…you kicking it like Brick and your mom played you, when the way I remember, you moved Dane into your crib while Brick was still living there. What did you expect him to do? I know how Brick felt because ever since you brought Sailor home, you got me in that same kind of fucked-up position." Troy raised an eyebrow. "You some kind of black widow?"

"Shut the fuck up."

"That suicide dude, Dane, and Monroe. All dead. Maybe I should really think twice about fucking with you."

"I'ma pretend you ain't hitting me with those low blows. I ain't have shit to do with Dane and Monroe's death. Bastards took my money and stole my whip. That was karma."

Troy looked at her without commenting.

"Dane and Monroe got what they had coming. My own mother betrayed me. And believe me, she gon' get hers someday. But now a goddamn faggot is fucking with me…ripping my entire operation apart. I swear to God…I can't take no more."

She shot Troy a dirty look. "And your ashy ass ain't nothing but a momma's boy, so fuck it…I don't need you. Go 'head. Be with your mother. I don't give two shits."

Misty meant every word. She was never going to let anyone else have the power to fuck up her money. Not ever again.

Sensing that she meant business, Troy spoke softly, "Can we talk about this?"

"Fuck no. You called me a black widow."

"I didn't mean nothing."

"Fuck you, Troy."

"Come on, Misty. I was only talkin' shit."

"Go talk shit to your mother."

"For real, man. I'm sorry about everything that I said."

"Too late. I don't want you and I damn sure don't need you to get a Lamborghini. I can get it myself. You don't believe me...watch me."

"Misty, I'm sorry. Forgive me. I want a Lambo, too. Whatchu want me to do? I'll get down on my knees if you want me to."

She felt her mouth trying to form into a smile, but she prevented that by keeping her lips pressed tightly together.

Troy's begging was not only putting a grin on her face, it was also making her hot. The lips puffed up, and became moist and bubbly, spreading into a big, juicy smile.

CHAPTER 21

Back in the apartment, she flipped open her laptop, intending to immediately change the password on all her accounts. There was no way was she going to sit back and let Sailor wipe her out the way Dane had done.

The video was pulling in bucks. Before pulling up the exact amount, she checked to make sure Troy wasn't peeking over her shoulder. She could hear the water running in the shower.

Troy had better wash his cum-stained ass if wants to get some of this coochie.

Her eyes bulged as she stared at the computer screen. It was unbelievable. She'd racked up five thousand dollars since the last time she'd checked. That totaled seven thousand in one day.

She had to get her imagination going. Think up some more kinky shit. Making sex flicks was bringing in a fortune. This was her passport to success.

Hmm. What else is Troy good for…besides being ashy? Deep in thought, Misty rested her chin on her hand.

By the time Troy came out of the shower, Misty was in a fabulous mood. When she stood up, the closest thing to her lips was his forearm, which she kissed, leaving the imprint of lipstick-colored red lips.

"Yo, that looks like a tattoo," Misty said, admiring the sight of her lips on Troy's arms.

He held his arm up. "Damn sure does."

Her eyes widened with excitement. "Oh, my God. I got a great idea."

"What?" He looked terrified. Misty was famous for coming up with some pretty hellish thoughts. Her ideas always put a smile on her face, while Troy cringed in horror.

"You said you'd do whatever I want, right?"

"Yeah," he responded apprehensively.

"Tomorrow, we're going to a tattoo joint. I want you to have my lips branded on your arm."

"Oh, aiight. Bet." Troy looked relieved. "I never had a tat before, but I heard that only the real big ones hurt."

"You frontin', Troy. You know you're scared of any kind of pain."

"I can deal with a lil'-ass tattoo. I thought your mind might be on some scandalous shit."

"Not yet." She giggled. "All in due time."

Misty had already visualized what she wanted to film next.

Two dicks engaged in a swordfight.

Troy's long dick smacking against a formidable opponent.

Yeah, that's hot. That freaky shit is gon' bring in a lot of paper.

Now all she had to do was find another dick.

❦

Bright and early the next day, Misty and Troy were en route to a tattoo studio.

She kissed a piece of paper, walked inside the place and handed it to the tattoo artist.

"Can you duplicate this?" she asked the tattoo artist, a bald white guy.

"Sure can, but it's gonna cost you a lot more than you need to spend."

Ew! The dude had a big-ass tattoo on his tongue, and some piercings. Nasty-looking shit. Making her flesh crawl. She wanted to grab Troy by the arm and get the hell out of there. "Anyone else work here?" Misty asked, her lips scrunched in disgust.

"Yeah, Lena. She comes in around noon. Why?"

"Just wondering." Misty didn't bother to wipe the frown off of her face. The man's tongue darted in and out of his mouth excessively, like he was being a deliberate creep.

Unfortunately, she didn't feel like waiting until noon and she didn't want to piss away more time driving to another tattoo place. She'd have to put up with the sight of his disgusting tongue. Maybe if she didn't say much, he would take a hint and stop talking.

"Why spend that extra dough on a custom tat when I have dozens of lip designs?"

She tried to avert her gaze. Tried to focus on his neck... his chest...anywhere except his mouth, but her eyes were inexplicably drawn to his monstrous, multicolored tongue.

"Nah, I want my own lips on his right upper arm. Money is no object."

Troy scowled at her. "If money is no object, how come I can't get my own set of wheels?"

"Troy, this is an investment. You're always thinking small. Why don't you look at the big picture?"

"My name's Zelgore," the creepy tattoo artist said as he pulled on a pair of rubber gloves. "You want it placed right here?" Zelgore pointed to the area below Troy's right shoulder.

"Nah. A little bit lower. Troy doesn't always wear a wife beater. I want my lips to be visible when he's wearing a T-shirt."

"Got it." Zelgore cleaned the area that Misty indicated.

Troy fidgeted nervously. "Damn, man. Hold up. Whatchu 'bout to get in to? You acting like you tryna perform some surgery or something,"

"Never been inked before?" he asked Troy with a chuckle.

"Nah, man. Never been interested."

"Be careful. Getting inked and pierced can be addictive."

Troy laughed. "I ain't worried about no addiction. I'm not even doing this for myself. I'm doing this for her...proving how strong my feelings are." Troy looked at Misty. He puckered his lips, pantomiming a kiss.

She smiled at him.

"A better way to prove your feelings is to make sure she's feeling good," Zelgore offered, trying to get on Misty's good side. Then the creep winked at her.

Ew! She sighed audibly, and then switched her gaze to Troy's arm. She eyed the creep's work, prepared to find something to complain about.

Seeing the outline of her lips took away some of her bad attitude. Zelgore was a nutjob but so far she liked what she saw.

"Tats are cool, man. But piercing your tongue or... down below..." He paused. "A piercing in the right place will give her something she can really feel."

The tattooist grinned, revealing his terrible tongue again. Misty released a groan.

Being in a seated position, Troy wasn't forced to view Zelgore's gaudily decorated tongue.

Misty wanted to get out of there. She was itching to go shopping. She needed to do something to take the edge off. But she couldn't leave. She had to make sure the tattoo was done to her exact specification.

As Zelgore became engrossed in his work, his tongue lolled, reminding Misty of the way that Michael Jordan's tongue used to hang out when he was making a shot.

Nasty. Misty looked at the floor, the walls, her cell… the front door. The clock on the wall.

Curiosity got the best of her. "What's that tattoo on your tongue?"

Glad she asked, the nutjob happily projected his wide-ass tongue. Stuck it out as far as he could. *Slimy bastard!*

She gawked at the image inside his mouth and instantly regretted having asked to see it. He was sporting a damn mermaid on his tongue. Two silver balls that pierced his tongue represented her titties. And the bottom part…the fins and the tail and shit…were made up of all kinds of colors. Really fuckin' bizarre. *Goddamn! Why is the world filled with so many fucked-up people?* Misty wondered, shaking her head. She definitely did not consider herself to be one of the multitudes of fucked-up people.

CHAPTER 22

Riding shotgun, Troy carefully reviewed the sheet of paper with care instructions for his tattoo.

"My arm hurts. I need a painkiller," Troy complained, looking down at the bandage that protected the new tattoo on his arm.

"I think we have some Tylenol back at the crib."

"You think? Man, I'm in pain."

"You need to stop whining, Troy. I'm tryna think how I'm gon' pull this shit off. We're back to square one. Just you and me. We gotta start the business all over again."

Troy groaned in displeasure. "Yo, I'm out of commission. I can't work for about a week. My arm really hurts, Misty. I'm dead up."

"Shut up, Troy. You don't use your arm on the job." She gave him a sly look. "That is…I don't think you're using it. You might be playing with mufuckas' dicks and balls for extra tips. You could be on some down-low shit for all I know."

He sucked his teeth. Blew her off with a wave of his hand. "You crazy."

"Then what you worrying about your arm for?"

He shrugged. "I'm just saying…"

Steering the car and keeping her eyes on the road, she spoke without looking at Troy. "You starting to seem suspect. Lemme find out." She laughed; the tone held a malicious, taunting sound.

As she wheeled into a parking spot in front of her apartment building, Troy muttered, "Goddamn. This nigga done brought his ass back."

Misty followed Troy's gaze and was shocked to see Sailor standing on the steps, looking contrite. There were a couple of pieces of battered-looking luggage stacked near the front door.

"I hope you gon' tell him to go back to wherever he came from."

"I know how to handle my business. You said you're in pain, so go inside the crib and lie down."

"Here we go with this bullshit."

"Go take some Tylenol and lay the fuck down!"

Troy seemed to take forever to get out of the car. His body movements were unnecessarily languid and slow.

By the time he made it to the front steps, he found some reserved strength and bumped Sailor with the shoulder of his good arm.

"Watch it, dude!" Sailor barked.

"Fuck outta here," Troy barked. He pulled out his key ring. As he began unlocking the main entry door, he sent Sailor dirty looks, trying his best to dissuade his nemesis from moving back in.

After Troy disappeared inside, Misty beckoned Sailor.

With the engine idling, she waited for him. She already knew she was going to take him back, but she refused to make it easy for him. His bitch-ass needed to sweat.

Sailor took Troy's seat. He covered his face as if coming up with an excuse for his actions was causing him anguish. He finally pulled his hands from his face. His light skin was flushed. "I'm really sorry, Misty. I didn't plan on staying at Uncle Marshall's. Things got a little out of control."

"In what way? Did your gay uncle throw a pajama party for you and the boys?"

"Don't be ridiculous."

"I'm keeping it real! I don't put anything past a mufucka who threatened to get me locked up because I called you! I didn't even call you on his goddamn phone!" she bellowed.

"Calm down. I'm sitting right next to you. I can hear you. I get your point. Geeze, you don't have to yell at me."

"If you don't wanna hear my mouth, then get the fuck out of my ride!" Livid, Misty yelled so loud, she could feel the strain on her vocal chords.

"Can't we have a discussion? Instead of screaming and yelling, let's have some dialogue…like civilized human beings."

"Uncle Freaky didn't talk to me like he was civilized! That pussy threatened me and you ain't stick up for me or nothing!"

"That's not true. I didn't know that you two had spoken until after the fact."

"And?"

"I got a different story from him. He accused you of making terroristic threats. He asked me for your full name and address. He was very determined to file a PDA against you. I refused to cooperate."

"Wow, you're such a gentleman," she said sarcastically. "Why didn't you come back as soon as you paid him for your shit?"

"I'm not a cruel person, Misty. At first Uncle Marshall was angry, and then he broke down...the man was genuinely moved to tears."

"I bet."

"Seriously. That man helped me when I didn't have anywhere else to go. I couldn't callously leave him in such a stressful, emotional state."

"What about me? I was stressed the fuck out, too. I was worried sick. I thought something had happened to you."

"I'm sorry. Can I move back in?"

"I don't know, Sailor. You might be kind of shady."

"That's not true. I was in a sort of moral dilemma."

"How so?"

"Uncle Marshall was hinting at committing suicide."

Normally, Misty would have made a sarcastic comment, but thinking about Shane made her heart sink.

She changed the subject. "Okay, I'm going to give some thought to you moving back in. What about Izell and Lennox? And the new dude? Do they want to continue working for me?"

"Yeah. I got the impression that all the fellas are beginning to feel like Uncle Marshall may not be totally together. You know what I mean?"

"Shit, yeah. One look at that nutty fruitcake and I realized he was thrown the fuck off."

"The fellas are also starting to doubt if he really has any connections in the fashion industry."

"I told you he had game. You didn't want to believe me. All of y'all are young and naïve. He took advantage of you. At least I'm putting money in everyone's pocket."

"You're right. I was naïve. But not anymore."

"I want to believe you, but I don't feel like I can trust you anymore, Sailor."

"I'm giving you my word. Scout's honor." Looking corny, he held up his fingers in some manner that was supposed to instill trust.

"Fuck a scout's honor. I have a better idea."

"Anything."

"Anything?" she repeated.

"Within reason," he said cautiously.

"I want you to get a tattoo. Is that reasonable?"

"Oh, yeah. I can do that." He pulled up his pants leg, showing off his stupid dolphin tattoo.

"I hate that tattoo. What's the deal with you and dolphins?"

"I like them. They're sweet creatures."

"Umph. Whatever. We need to take care of the tattoo. Are you ready?"

"Can I take my luggage inside first?"

She glanced at his funky-looking suitcase and beat-up

duffel bag. Shit looked like it needed to be tossed into a trash bin. "I guess," she said with a reluctant sigh. "Ring the bell. Troy will buzz you in."

"Hey, what's Troy's freaking problem? He deliberately bumped into me…like he's looking for a fight."

"He was taking up for me. Troy doesn't like it if he thinks someone is trying to take advantage of me," she explained, though it was a lie.

"Oh, I'll talk to him," Sailor said good-naturedly.

"Don't even bother. Let him work through his anger issues. He'll be aiight."

Sailor took his baggage inside the apartment building.

She was really glad to have Sailor back on board. And the possibility of getting all Uncle Freaky's boys seemed within her reach.

Misty pressed her palm against her forehead. Damn, she didn't feel like putting herself through another torturous visit with that tattoo artist. Zelgore had to be the creepiest-looking dude she'd ever set eyes on. But she had no choice. She had to seal the deal with Sailor and get him inked. Today.

Zelgore was a wacko for sure, but he did phenomenal work.

However…the next mofo that got tatted with Misty's lips was going to have to take his own ass over to Zelgore's South Street studio.

CHAPTER 23

Having two men bearing the image of her lips was definitely an ego boost.

But there was a downside to being worshipped and adored.

Twice in the same day, Misty had to physically put herself between Troy and Sailor. Under normal circumstances, she'd never put her precious body in harm's way, but she needed these two Neanderthals to remain in one piece so they could go out on jobs and keep the money coming.

It all started while Misty was trying to film them swordfighting. Neither Troy nor Sailor could keep an erection. Instead of battling with criss-crossed dicks, they were throwing punches. She had to put the camera down and stop them from killing each other. *Assholes.*

"Fuck y'all,' Misty snarled. "I'ma get Izell and Lennox to make the video for me."

"Aw, damn. I forgot to tell you," Troy blurted out.

"Tell me what?"

"Um…he…um…" Troy became sidetracked when he

noticed that the bandage on his arm had loosened during the altercation with Sailor. Distracted, he began fiddling with adhesive tape.

"What did you forget to tell me?"

"Oh, yeah. Izell wanted to talk to you about a party."

"What kind of party? Does he know someone who wants to book a party?" Excited, Misty started mentally adding up figures. A party for freaks could bring in a whole lot of stacks.

Troy shrugged. "He didn't mention what type of party."

Misty sucked her teeth. Troy was so dumb. Never could pass on accurate information.

"Get Izell on the phone," she ordered Sailor. "Even though my money bought his fucking cell, I'm not trying get Uncle Freaky riled up. He don't need any excuses to send the law over here."

Sailor began pressing his touch-screen cell phone. "Hey, Izell. Misty wants to talk to you." Sailor handed Misty his cell.

Smiling, she pulled off an earring and pressed the phone against her ear. "What's good, Izell? Troy told me you wanted to speak to me about a party."

"My cousin works with D.B. Spydah."

"Never heard of him."

"Rapper. Underground, mostly. But he gets a lot of play in Miami. Anyway, Spydah's on the show with Smash Hitz—"

"Smash Hitz!" Misty's voice was high-pitched with

excitement. Smash Hitz was one of the most famous and wealthiest rappers in the game. He owned his own record label, a clothing line, restaurants. There was gossip that he was about to buy a damn football team.

Misty's mental wheels began spinning fast. Her chest fell and rose rapidly. *Calm down, heart.* She rubbed the middle of her chest.

Composing herself, she exhaled. "How do I fit into this equation?"

"The show is scheduled for tomorrow, but Spydah and his associates hit town today. They got three suites at the hotel and asked me to bring some honeys through." Izell laughed uncomfortably. "I don't really know that many girls in Philly, but I figured you and some of your friends might want to—"

"Hold up. Is this a paid gig?"

"No, they just want some girls to party with."

Misty couldn't believe what Izell was saying. Seething, she began pacing the length of the studio apartment. "I don't take charity cases. I'm running a business… building a damn dynasty. What makes you think I have time to go round up a bunch of bitches to party with some unknown artist and his homeboys?"

"Spydah's big in Florida."

"Look, I never heard of no goddamn D.B. Spydah. I can't believe you came at me with some bullshit like this. My time is precious. I'm about getting money, not fucking around with some broke-ass, opening-act mufucka."

"Can't you please do it for me? You know…on the strength—?"

"On the strength of what? Kiss my ass, Izell."

"Misty, come on, man. Help me out with this."

"Hell no. First of all, I don't fuck with bitches. Fucking with niggas is bad enough, but bitches are entirely too much trouble." Misty thought of that hooker, Felice, with the big juicy pussy lips. That was one worthless hoe. A big-ass, unnecessary headache.

"I'm just saying…" There was desperation in Izell's tone.

"I don't care what you're saying. Don't sound like there's nothing in this situation that would benefit me."

"Smash Hitz put a lot of money behind Spydah's CD. It's about to drop in a few days…it's gon' be big. My cousin said if I come through with some girls, he might be able to hook me up with a job on Spydah's security team."

"You work for me, nigga! You gotta lot of nerve, asking me to help you get another gig."

"Misty, I'm working for you for extra money. Tricking is not a lifetime career." Izell sounded weary. "You know that I want to get into modeling. I might be able to get my foot in the door if I'm working for a celebrity."

"I never heard of anybody going from a security position to landing on a magazine cover," she said sarcastically.

"Maybe not. But being close with one of Smash Hitz'

artists could lead to modeling some of the fashion in his clothing line."

Izell had a point. Misty mulled over his last comment. Somewhere in this situation, there might be an opportunity for her.

"Hold on for a minute. I need to check out this Spydah nigga and see whassup with him."

Setting the cell down, she opened her laptop, and googled D.B. Spydah.

To Misty's surprise, there was tons of information on the young rapper. She clicked on a link that led to a gossip page and peered at a photo of Smash Hitz with his arm around a younger dude. The caption read: *Smash Hitz and his new recording artist, D.B. Spydah.*

This D.B. Spydah mufucka is starting to look kinda good.

She checked out a few more links and scanned the words swiftly. From what she gathered, D.B. Spydah was a fairly successful, mixtape artist with a name that was recognized on the streets of Miami. After a few years on the underground rap scene, he'd done over one hundred recordings…many with high-profile artists. Now that he'd landed a deal with Smash Hitz' label, his hard work was finally going to pay off. Spydah's debut album was scheduled to drop during his tour.

Misty's mind wandered as she picked up the cell. "How many girls does your cousin want you to bring?"

"Uh…as many possible. You know…the more the merrier."

"How many damn niggas are in Spydah's entourage?"

"Uh…I'm not sure."

"So why am I wasting my time talking with you?" she snarled. "What's your cousin's name?"

"Larry."

"Tell Larry to get at me. I need to speak with him directly."

"For real? You gon' talk to him?"

"You don't know shit, so why should I keep talking with you?"

"You're right," Izell said, laughing. "Okay, I'll tell him. Thanks, Misty. I owe you."

"Whatever." She disconnected the call. *Izell's punk ass better be thankful that I'm a visionary. My eyes can see beyond the here and now. I can see the whole, big-ass picture.*

CHAPTER 24

Even though Spydah was rolling with only a four-man crew, his boy, Larry, wanted Misty to bring at least ten girls to the hotel.

"I'm on it," Misty said agreeably. But she was really thinking, *'Ten girls! Nigga, you trippin'.'* She got the pertinent information from him—the name of the hotel and the room numbers, and the time the party was getting started.

Now she had to locate Felice. Felice, AKA Juicy, was the last bitch Misty wanted to see. She suspected Juicy had been fucking around with her ex, Dane. She couldn't prove it, but her woman's intuition told her that Felice and Dane had been up to no good.

Anyway, that big pussy hooker would be perfect. For the right price, Felice would fuck all seven of those entourage mufuckas. The only problem was that this Larry bull and the other seven dickhead, hangers-on didn't think they were supposed to pay for pussy.

I'm gon' have to pay Felice out of my own damn pocket. Oh well, paying for Felice to fuck an entourage was a cheap price to get a pass into Smash Hitz' fabulously rich world.

I'm going to consider any money I part with as a wise investment.

She wondered if Felice still lived at that same spot in North Philly. Misty drummed her finger on the folding table she used as a work station.

How could she get in touch with Felice? When she met her, she was working as a waitress at Hades, a club down on Delaware Avenue. Misty thought of Big Boy, one of the bouncers at the club. Big Boy knew Felice and probably could put Misty in touch with her.

Luckily, she'd kept a lot of her old numbers. She scrolled through her contact list and found Big Boy's name and number. She called him immediately, praying that the number was still good.

"Yo, who dis?" Big Boy answered.

"It's Misty."

"Misty? Hey! What's good, mami? I ain't seen you in a minute. Thought you fell off the earth."

"Nah, I've been in Miami working with this up-and-coming rapper named D.B. Spydah."

"Oh, yeah? I think I heard of him."

"He 'bout to blow up. Just signed with Smash Hitz. Yo, Big Boy... I might be able to put you on with some security detail. We flew in this morning to do the show at the Wachovia Center."

"Yeah, I heard Smash was coming to town. I gotta work tomorrow night, though."

"Don't even worry about it. You can still meet him."

"Oh, yeah?"

"I've been searching for a club to throw a fly after-party. I might as well rent out the VIP area at Hades and bring Smash and all his associates through."

"Yo…Misty. You dat bitch."

"Who you telling?" she said, laughing. "I'ma set you and him up with a quick conversation. If Smash is feeling you, get ready to travel, nigga."

"Yo. My bag's already packed." Big Boy gave a loud, belly laugh.

As Big Boy envisioned his life changing from ordinary to super fabulous, Misty switched up the conversation, moving forward to the real point of her call. "By the way…have you seen Felice?"

"Uh…nah. Last I heard, she was working at a strip club."

Misty wasn't a bit surprised. *Fucking hoe.* "Where she working at?"

"Downtown. At that joint on Twelfth Street…Silky and Sweet."

"Okay, I know the spot you're talking about." But Misty didn't have time to run around looking for Felice's dumb ass. "Do you know any of the bouncers who work there?"

"Yeah, my bull, Myron, works there."

"Okay, do me a favor because I don't have a lot of time. I have to holla at my peoples and let them know that we need to get with the management at Hades and set up the after-party for tomorrow night."

"Right. Okay, so whatchu need me to do?"

"Get with ya bull, Myron. Tell him to put you in touch with Felice. ASAP! Lock my number in."

"I gotchu."

"Let Felice know that this call is about money. Shit, I might be able to put ya bull, Myron, on this, too."

"Nah, let's not move too fast. Everything's not for everybody. Y'ah mean? I'ma keep this hook-up to my damn self."

"Aiight. I feel you. Look, make sure Felice gets back to me real quick."

"I gotchu, mami," Big Boy assured her.

"Don't embarrass me when I introduce you to Smash. You better be as big and burly as you were the last time I saw your ass."

"Shit, if anything…I'm bigger!" he promptly responded with uproarious laughter.

Misty laughed with him. "Okay, Big Boy. I'll see you tomorrow." She disconnected the call.

"Damn, I'ma playa! Did y'all hear all that game I just kicked!" Misty shouted.

When no one answered, her gaze drifted over her shoulder. Sailor was engrossed in CNN news. Troy was nowhere in sight. Probably in the bathroom.

"Hey, Sailor. Did you hear what I was saying on the phone?" Misty asked, puffed up with pride.

"No, I didn't. I don't eavesdrop on personal conversations."

"Stop being a hater, Sailor. You know you need to give me my props."

"Seriously. I wasn't paying any attention."

"Whatever."

The jangle of her phone pulled her attention away from Sailor. She didn't recognize the number on the screen.

"Hello." *Please be Felice!*

"'Sup, Misty?"

"Felice?"

"Yeah, girl. How you been?" Felice went through the pleasantries.

"I'm doing fabulous, Felice. I just got in from Miami, girl. I'm working with Smash Hitz."

"Get out of here!"

"Girl, you know how I do. So look. I need for you and a couple of your stripper friends to put on a private show."

"You want us to dance for Smash Hitz?"

"Chill, girl. You gotta work your way up the ranks before you dance for Smash. I need y'all to shake your asses for his protégé, a young bull from Miami. Underground rapper called D.B. Spydah."

Felice screamed, "I love Spydah!"

"You heard of him?" Misty was shocked.

"Yeah. They always play him where I work at."

"Well, get your girls together and meet me at the Sheraton Suites parking lot. The one on Island Avenue."

"Okay. So…um, Misty, how much is Spydah paying?"

"That's the thing. This gig ain't totally about money. Know what I mean?"

Felice didn't respond.

"Y'all gon get free tickets to the show at the Wachovia Center and backstage passes."

"That's all good, but I gotta tell the girls how much they getting paid."

"I'm paying *you* a flat rate. Five hundred for the night. You can break your friends off any way you want to. Look, if you're not feeling this, let me know. I got some other strippers lined up; big fans who are thrilled to party with Spydah."

"I'ma fan, too. I'm just saying…"

"Take it or leave it. I was lookin' out for you. Getting you in with the hottest new rapper out of Miami because…you know…we had previous business dealings."

"Alright. I'll get the girls together. What time should we be there?"

As Misty expected, Felice caved.

The story she'd given Felice was a lie. *Free tickets and a backstage pass, my ass. The only thing that hooker is gon' get is a sore pussy and some memories.*

CHAPTER 25

Misty, Lennox, and Troy arrived at the hotel a half-hour earlier than she was scheduled to meet Felice. Sailor had been left home. She couldn't pass him off as a thug.

With Lennox on her left and Troy on the right, she waited for Larry to come down and escort them up to the suites. She wanted to get a feel for the situation… check out Spydah and get a feel for his generosity before she let the strippers run amok throughout the various suites that Spydah hooked up.

Rocking a pair of cut-out platform boots, and a curve-clinging white dress, Misty turned heads in the hotel lobby.

Larry got off of the elevator and took one look at Misty. "Damn, shawty," he mumbled. Lust was evident in his eyes and also in his husky vocal tone.

Times like this, Misty really appreciated being blessed with stunning beauty. She had a plan, and her looks, along with her brains and cunning, were going to get her everything she wanted.

Unlike his cousin, Izell, Larry was not tall and had no bulk. He was a short, light-skinned bull. Kind of chubby. No sex appeal that Misty could discern. He was no tough guy, either. She wondered what role he played when Spydah's entourage engaged in a brawl. Did he join in the kicking and stomping or was he the calming force in an unruly entourage?

"I'm Misty," she said. She nodded to her left. "This is my bodyguard, Lennox." With his mean grille on, Lennox gave a head nod.

With a slight head tilt to the right, she introduced Troy as her personal assistant.

"Whassup," Troy said, wearing a poker face.

"I'm expecting the girls to arrive in about a half-hour."

"What about you?" Larry licked his lips unconsciously. "You in da business. I know Spydah's gon' want you for hisself."

Shaking her head, Misty smiled. "Nah, that's not possible. I'm the procuress."

"The pro-what-ess?"

"The middle man," Misty said with laughter. "I don't get involved in playtime. My role is to provide the girls."

"So who you bringing…a bunch of hookers? Spydah don't believe in paying for pussy."

"The girls are exotic dancers. Their services are on me. I'm trying to extend a little brotherly love as a courtesy to your cousin, Izell."

"Aw, damn. I like Philly. Let's go up to the floor."

Inside the elevator, Larry swiped his card and pushed a button. As the elevator ascended, he looked at Misty again. "I don't know, man...Spydah gon' definitely want to get with you."

She smiled politely, but her eyes were on Troy's face, watching him like a hawk. Her stern eyes informed him that he'd better keep a straight face. Like Felice, Troy dug Spydah's underground music. Misty had given Troy a strict order to keep it professional and not to act like a freaking star-struck fan.

So far, he was holding it together. Lennox was on point with the bodyguard role...staying close to Misty like she was precious cargo.

They got off on the top floor. Larry rapped on a door. "Open up, Mustafa."

As though he didn't trust that it was really Larry on the other side of the door, Mustafa opened up slowly, beady bloodshot eyes taking in Misty and the two men accompanying her.

Swiping at his nostrils with the knuckle of his index finger, he was acting like he was on some shit. He frowned at Troy and Lennox. "What these niggas doin' here?" His bloodshot gaze shifted to Misty. "She a fly lil' shawty, but where the rest of the bitches?"

"They coming in a few," Larry informed.

Inside the suite, the three members of the entourage milled about. Spydah had a tricked-up-looking squad. None of them were easy on the eyes. They all looked crazy…like they'd been recruited straight out of jail or from a halfway house.

One of the goons stepped to Misty. "They call me Tragic." His mouth twisted into a snarl as he pointed at her. "I wanna hit that when the party starts." He backed away, biting down hard on his bottom lip, his body jerking like he was doing an angry dance. Then he started rhyming…freestyling about the many ways he planned on penetrating.

"You crazy, Tragic," a goon in the back of the room said.

"I ain't gon' show her no mercy, Jru. She gon' have to work hard to keep up with me. And if she slow down… I'ma pop, pop, pop that lil' ass." Tragic thrust his pelvis hard and fast…smacking the air in rapid succession, giving a demonstration of stroking and ass-smacking.

The fourth member of the so-called entourage, named Jru, wore an idiotic smile as he watched Tragic now extending his tongue, darting it in and out…and even rolling it. Misty would have loved to experience the feeling of a tongue rolling into her coochie, but not Tragic's. His rolling tongue would give her coochie the creeps.

Jru picked up a bottle of Grey Goose and started sipping from the bottle. Between sips, his eyes flicked from Tragic's antics to sneakily roaming up and down Misty's body.

Ew, Tragic is disgusting. And the bull, Jru, looks like a rapist. This has to be the worst-looking entourage in the music industry. I hate all of them, but especially Tragic.

Misty clapped her hands to get everyone's attention. "Listen up. My name is Misty—"

Tragic started making crying sounds, wiping his eyes. His shoulders shuddered as he acted a fool, pretending to be weeping. "Ahhh," he whined with his stupid, ugly self. "You got me misty-eyed, Misty."

Though she wanted to slap the shit out of his silly ass, Misty gave Tragic a patient smile. "So…I put together a party for y'all. I got three girls scheduled to arrive in about fifteen minutes."

"Three! We axed for ten bitches." Mustafa was livid.

"Sorry about that. Anyway, they're coming to party with y'all and they want to give you a good time."

Lots of grumbles about there being only three bitches coming.

Misty held up her hand, requesting silence. The level of noise decreased.

"Ain't gon' be no rough stuff." She pointed to Lennox. "My man over here…his name is Lennox and he's gonna pull the girls out if shit gets out of hand."

"We don't need no overseer," Tragic jeered. And then commenced to dancing and rapping about slavery, masters, and bed wenches. Misty rolled her eyes. She couldn't help herself. She really hated Tragic.

"Chill, Tragic," Larry scolded. "Misty's the manager for the girls; show her some respect."

"So what if she da manager? Whatchu saying, man? We ain't allowed to smash her?" Mustafa sounded angry and offended.

Tragic stopped dancing. Jru's smile slipped from his face. He folded his arms, as he leaned to the side and gritted on Misty. Tragic and Jru waited for Larry to respond to Mustafa's question.

Larry shook his head at the three buffoons. "No, she's not here for—" He paused, his words interrupted by his ringing cell.

Unperturbed by the entourage's blatant disrespect and the disregard of her beauty, Misty took over the question-and-answer session while Larry spoke on the phone.

"I'm the party planner, slash manager. Sorry to disappoint you, but I'm not on the menu." Misty smiled and gave an unapologetic shoulder shrug.

Her announcement was met with grumbles of discontent and hostile stares.

Mustafa gripped his dick and grimaced. "I bet you got some good yams, Misty. Come over here and let me find out," Mustafa said, his voice thickened and lustful.

She shook her head. The nasty and disrespectful comments were irking the hell out of her. She wanted to hurl obscenities at everyone in the room and roll out, but being about her business, she stood there, surrounded by anti-social maniacs, waiting for Larry to get off of the phone.

"Damn, now my dick is feenin' for Misty," Jru muttered. She didn't get his name and didn't care to know it.

"Yo!" Lennox swung around in Jru's direction. "Watch your fuckin' mouth, man. That's enough."

"Ain't nobody scared of you," Jru snarled.

Misty grabbed Lennox's arm. "Let it go." Though she was ready to join Lennox and roll on these morons, she maintained her composure, refusing to be provoked by slurs that came from the mouths of a trio of ex-con-looking morons.

Larry returned his cell to his pocket. "Spydah wants to meet you, but your bodyguard…and the young blood…" He nodded at Troy. "They gotta fall back."

Lennox questioned Misty with his eyes.

"It's cool," Misty responded and followed Larry out of the suite that had become stifling with male testosterone raging out of control.

💋

Spydah was a lot cuter than Misty expected. None of the photos she'd seen had done him justice. He looked to be around five-nine or ten, slim with a slightly muscular build. Faint mustache, smooth brown skin. His gear was fresh. Expensive jeans, designer T-shirt, and a hoodie vest. He had a cleaner-cut look than the average rap artist, and he definitely looked more polished than his squad of ugly goons. *Fucking morons.*

Larry made the introductions and Misty extended her hand. Suave as shit, Spydah brushed his lips across the top of her hand.

"Aw, nigga, don't go soft on me now," Larry kidded the young rapper.

"She's so gorgeous, I'm getting misty, man." Playing around, Spydah dabbed at his eyes.

There was instant chemistry between Misty and Spydah. He couldn't take his eyes off of her.

"My phone is vibrating in my purse. I'm sure the girls have arrived. I brought my bodyguard to make sure they're safe."

"Ain't nobody gon' get hurt."

"You never know."

"Anyway, I wanted to say welcome to Philly and good luck with the new CD."

"Thanks. But um…that ish you said sounds like a farewell speech," Spydah said, frowning worriedly.

Misty laughed. "I didn't plan on staying for the party. But don't worry. My girls will hold it down. They real bitches. Guaranteed to show you and your boys a good time."

Spydah reached for Misty's wrist. "Eff them girls," he said, respectfully refraining from using profanity. "I don't even wanna meet those strippers. For real. I can get with a stripper in Miami…or anywhere else in the world. I'm not feeling that. I'm on some other ish right now. I'm tryna get to know you, Misty."

Misty tossed back her heavy black hair. "I'm flattered, but this is a…a really awkward moment." She withdrew her hand.

Larry coughed and gave Spydah a curious look that said, *Man, what the fuck is wrong with you?*

When Misty's phone vibrated, she quickly retrieved it

from her purse. "Hey, Felice. I'm coming down now. Meet me in the lobby."

Avoiding Spydah's eyes, she looked at Larry. "The girls are getting impatient. You ready to bring 'em up?"

"Yeah, I'm waiting for the boss to give me the heads-up. Whatchu wanna do, Spydah?"

"Go down and kick it with the girls. I want a few minutes of privacy. Is that all right with you, Misty?"

She gave a reluctant head nod. "Lemme call my man and put his mind at ease." Misty turned her back to Larry and Spydah as she whispered in her cell, assuring Lennox that she was okay.

"What man is she calling?" Spydah asked, uncomprehending.

"She brought a bodyguard with her. And a lanky nigga she called her personal assistant."

"Bodyguard? What she into? She gangsta like that?" Spydah sounded intrigued.

Misty was enjoying all the attention from the up-and-coming star, and if she continued to play her cards right, she'd be standing right by his side when his cash flow improved. She hoped his rise to stardom wouldn't take too long.

Larry left to go get the girls.

Spydah eyed Misty from head to toe. "I like what I see. Why you gotta bounce? Why can't you and me chill together…right here in my private suite?"

"Sorry." She gave him an apologetic smile.

"Oh, you're not that kind of girl?"

"No, I'm not."

"You manage a bunch of strippers, so why you frontin' like you Miss Innocent?"

"You rap about blowing up shit and putting niggas in the ground, but I don't take it literally. That's you expressing yourself. It's art. Not your lifestyle." She spoke from knowledge. She'd listened to some of his music on *YouTube*.

"I can't even say nothing. You got me with that."

"Seriously, Spydah...I only came through to make sure everything was copasetic. This was a favor for a friend. I'm on some business right now."

"I feel you," Spydah said sadly.

"If it's meant to be...we'll meet up again," she promised, wearing a smile that told Spydah she was feeling him, too.

"I'm not happy about this. After you leave, I'm locking my door and drowning my sorrows in a couple bottles of vodka." Spydah gave Misty a lingering look.

She threw up her hands helplessly. "I have to go and pay the girls. On some real shit, I'm handling all their expenses. You might as well join your friends. Have yourself some fun. This party is on me."

Spydah looked shocked. "Yo, I told Larry to invite some groupies. How much you gotta pay the strippers?"

"They top-notch. I'm paying 'em three stacks for the whole night." The lie rolled off her tongue with ease.

"I ain't even got that kind of cake on me. But I can get it...after the show tomorrow night."

"Don't worry about it. Tonight is my treat."

"Nah, I gotta make this up to you. I'ma tell Larry to get you and your people good seats at the show tomorrow night. You coming, right?"

"Oh! Are you inviting me to your show?"

"Hell yeah. I want you to be my guest at the after-party, too."

She had Spydah right where she wanted him. "That sounds real good. So...I guess I'll see you tomorrow night."

With those words, she pressed her lips gently against his and then rolled out. Strolling down the corridor, she met up with Larry, Felice, and the other two hookers.

Felice looked the same. Big tits and big ass. Cute...if you were into the trashy, stripper look.

Misty pulled Felice to the side, told her that Lennox would be looking out for her and the other dancers. "I want you to keep an eye on my assistant. His name is Troy. He can have fun, but he's on my payroll. I don't want him leaving here with a drippy dick."

"I gotchu," Felice replied. "You look nice, Misty. You ain't changed at all. Still as fly as ever." Though Felice was smiling, Misty could see the envy in her eyes.

"Thanks." Misty peeled off five bills.

Felice grabbed the money. Pulling a stunt that would have impressed Houdini, Felice made the money disappear...beneath her clothes, somewhere.

Misty smiled. Five hundred dollars was a small sacrifice for a lifestyle change.

CHAPTER 26

"You missed it, Sailor. Last night was off the chain," Troy bragged as he shook Captain Crunch Berries into a bowl. "Titties and ass up for grabs."

Sailor shrugged nonchalantly as he browsed through a University of Wisconsin catalog.

"I hope you ain't smash nothing with the naked dick," Misty said gruffly.

"Nah, man."

"Lemme find out you ain't strap up. I told Felice to keep an eye out. She'll tell me the truth."

"I ain't got no reason to lie. I don't stick my joint up in no strange nookie without covering it up." Troy crunched cereal with a pissed-off look on his face.

"So what about the niggas?"

"What about 'em?"

"Any of 'em working with a broke wrist?"

"I wouldn't know."

"Stop playing, Troy. You recognize the signs to look for. Was anybody staring at your dick while you was stroking?"

"Oh, yeah. That beady-eyed bull was watching me.

What was his name…Mustafa? Yeah, seemed like he had a homo side to hisself."

"I'm not even surprised. That nut-ass was acting all pressed…talkin' 'bout he wanted ten bitches, knowing all along that what he really wanted was some dick."

Troy and Misty laughed together. Sailor turned the pages of the catalog, paying no attention to the discussion.

"You wanna go to a concert tonight, Sailor?" Misty asked.

"A rap concert?"

"Uh-huh. I got free tickets to Smash's show."

"No. I'm good."

"You got tickets?" Troy asked.

"Yeah, Spydah said Larry is gon' hook us up. By the way, how many women went to Spydah's room?"

"None that I know of. He came through the suite where we were. Signed some autographs…joked around for a minute, but that's as far as it went. He went back to his own suite…by hisself."

Good boy!

Misty stared at her cell as it vibrated on the table. "That damn Felice is blowing up my phone." She served her purpose; now she needs to get a life and leave me the hell alone." *I ain't got no show tickets for her dumb ass.*

"Man, Felice's coochie is crazy."

"You fucked her?"

"Nah, I ain't get a chance. I seen it when she pulled

her thong to the side. She got a swollen jawn…big juicy lips!"

"She's too stupid to know what to do with her assets. It'll be a hot day in December before I give that slimy bitch any more work."

"Y'all got beef?" Troy asked.

"She was fucking Dane behind my back."

"Oh." Troy knew better than to dig deeper. Talking about Dane brought out Misty's evil side.

The phone vibrated so hard, it spun around on the table. Misty fell out laughing.

"Felice is really tryna get some work."

"Fuck her."

"That's what I was tryna do." A grin covered Troy's face.

"Don't make me hit you with this phone, boy."

Misty picked up the phone and peered at the screen. "Two calls from Felice. Two from Big Boy."

"Who's Big Boy?"

"Some nut-ass bouncer that thinks I owe him a favor." She turned her screen toward Troy. "Look…"

Troy squinted as he looked at the screen. "*You got three calls from Larry!*"

Misty nodded proudly.

"Call that bull back. He probably tryna finalize some details about the show. I wonder if they gon' send a limo for us?"

"It don't matter to me because I'm not going."

Troy choked. "You not what?"

"I'm not going. That Spydah mufucka can't buy me with a ticket and a backstage pass."

"What about me? I wanna go." Troy had a desperate look in his eyes.

"Chill, Troy. I'm sending you and Lennox. But I'm not going."

"Why not?"

"I'ma let Spydah sweat. Trust. If my plans work, we gon' be out of this dump."

❧

Misty dropped Troy and Lennox off at the Wachovia Center in South Philly. Izell was already there with his cousin.

During the drive home, Larry's calls came in quick succession. She listened to his most recent messages and was surprised to hear Spydah's voice instead of Larry's.

"Why you not answering my man's calls? I'm hoping to see you tonight. Hit Larry back. I'm gettin' ready to go on stage." He paused and then added, "Don't disappoint me."

She had never imagined that someone who seemed so hardcore was actually softer than a marshmallow when it came to matters of the heart.

Damn, that young bull, Spydah, might have some stalker tendencies.

On the home front, Sailor had gone out and bought himself a new Xbox and was in front of the TV playing Guitar Hero. All his white blood was evident as he moved around jerkily, throwing his head around, and grimacing like a rock star.

"Whassup, Sailor?" she yelled over the loud music.

He stopped. Looked embarrassed. "I didn't hear you come in."

"You were caught-up."

He blushed.

"What are you gonna major in when you start college?"

"Economics."

"Oh, you on some high-finance shit."

"I have an aptitude for numbers."

"And your skills are going to come in handy in my business. Tell you what…I realize you're not feeling being in the trenches…you like working behind the scenes, right?"

"Honestly…I hate dealing with those sick dudes that like men."

"I know…so I'm going to give you the new passwords and let you handle the money aspect of things."

"Really?"

"Uh-huh. But I want you to continue dealing with the creative end…filming and whatnot. Also, I want you to help me manage the fellas. Book their jobs and whatnot. Can you handle all that?"

"Yes." Sailor nodded emphatically. "Thank you, Misty!"

He put the guitar down. Took giant steps toward Misty, bear-hugging her, he picked her up and planted an appreciative kiss on her lips.

She hated the feeling of her legs dangling in the air. Squirming, she demanded, "Put me down, fool."

Sailor set her back on the floor. "Thank you for trusting me again, Misty. You won't regret it."

"Show me," she said, licking the pad of her middle finger, and then touching the hard seam in the crotch of her jeans...the area where wet heat was suddenly accumulating. What was stirring her sexual desire? The big payday that was coming her way? Or maybe it was Sailor's guitar performance when he didn't know anyone was watching? There was something unrestrained and primal in the way he moved when he didn't know someone was watching.

I don't know why my coochie is on fire, but it's a good thing Sailor is right here on hand to blow out the flames.

"I've been missing you, Misty." This time Sailor picked her up gently. Cradling her as he moved toward the bed.

CHAPTER 27

T roy came home, causing rattling and clatter as he put the lock in place on the front door. Startled from sleep, Misty sat up, staring into the dark at Troy's stumbling silhouette as he bumped into furniture, and kicked over a wastebasket.

"What's wrong with you, Troy?"

"Nothing. I'm cool," he said in a slurred voice. He staggered to the bathroom. The sound of his piss stream was loud and furious.

"You better not be splashing piss against the wall. And there better not be a drop on the damn toilet seat, either," Misty ranted. "Can't hold no liquor…drunk-ass mufucka." She looked at Sailor, who was sleeping next to her. Knocked out from good coochie, his sleep uninterrupted by the disturbance.

Zipping his pants, Troy stumbled back into the main room that served as bedroom, living room, and kitchen.

"You didn't even flush the damn toilet…or wash your nasty-ass hands."

"My bad." Satisfying Misty, he turned around and went back into the bathroom.

She wanted to hear all the events of the night, and was particularly interested in learning how Spydah behaved. "Troy! I know you ain't fall asleep in there." Misty jumped out of bed and rushed into the bathroom. As suspected, Troy was passed out. Snoring, he was curled in a ball on the soft, oval rug.

"Worthless fucker." She kicked him and left him on the floor.

She couldn't call Lennox for information. Uncle Freaky would have a fit. She'd be so glad when she could get all her workers together with her under one damn roof.

Misty checked the time. Three in the morning. She wondered if Spydah was still at the after-party. She couldn't get any information out of Troy so she figured she might as well go straight to the source.

She called Larry.

He answered on the first ring. "Whassup, Misty?" His voice was raised. Loud music pumped in the background.

"Hi, Larry. I'm sorry I couldn't make it."

"What did you say?" Larry asked. The music was so loud, he couldn't hear her.

"Is Spydah available?" she yelled.

"Yeah, his show was fyah, but he's a lil' down right now. Hearing your voice might cheer my man up. Hold on for a minute."

With the phone to her ear, she listened as the sounds of boisterous voices and thumping music grew distant.

"Hello." It was Spydah. Apparently he'd gone to a quiet spot. There was no loud music and no party atmosphere sounds.

"Hey, baby," Misty purred.

"What happened to you?" She heard the disappointment in his voice.

"I'm really sorry that I missed your show…and the party. But I wasn't feeling good."

"What's wrong?"

"Cramps. But I feel much better now."

"The party ain't over. You can still slide through if you want to."

"No, I'm not in the mood for a lot of people. I'd rather be alone with you." Misty used a pouting tone that was always to her advantage when she engaged in the art of seduction.

"I feel the same way. Fuck this party. You wanna meet me back at the hotel? I can hop in the limo. What's your address?"

A limo ride would be on point, but she couldn't risk Spydah glimpsing her run-down neighborhood.

"I'll meet you at your hotel in forty-five minutes," she offered.

A quick shower would wash away Sailor's scent. Lipstick and a little blush was the only makeup required for a booty call. At this hour of the night, there'd be hardly any traffic on I-76.

"I'll be there in thirty," Spydah boasted. Misty could

picture him smiling…grinning like a happy little boy.

Her breathing increased by the thrill of seduction. She was a tigress. And Spydah was her prey. Without a doubt, Misty was that bitch. She could melt the hardest heart…had always had that effect on niggas.

Her conceited smile faded. *Except for that frontin'-ass Brick.* Since her mother had entered the picture, she couldn't do shit with Brick. But that all would change once she had her money right. It was simply a matter of time.

❧

Two bottles of champagne were chilling. Spydah lifted a bottle from the confining chips of ice. Never taking his eyes off of Misty, he popped the cork and filled two flutes.

"You look good in red." Admiringly, Spydah's eyes moved over Misty's clingy dress.

I look good in every color, mufucka, she thought, but whispered, "Thanks," as she accepted the drink.

"This is delicious," she said after swallowing. "But…"

"But what?"

"I bet you taste a lot better."

Charmed and taken off guard, Spydah glanced away. He bit his bottom lip; a faint frown flitted across his face as if he was somewhat troubled by the way Misty had flipped the script.

"You gon' let me find out?" she pressed breathily.

Flattered and stunned, he muttered, "Hell, yeah. But… uh…you fuckin' with my head right now. I'm a lil' tipsy from the party, yo. This ain't how I handle mine."

"I know. But tonight, I want you to relax. Let me take care of you? Can you do that?"

"Aw, damn. You on some other shit. I ain't have no idea that this whack-ass night was gon' end on a sweet note."

I got this nigga going. Misty took a couple more swigs of champagne, but kept a watchful eye on Spydah's every move and his expression. Thrown off balance by the speed of her seduction, he fidgeted under the spotlight of her gaze.

Misty realized her game was tight. She had an advantage and refused to give Spydah a chance to regain his composure.

A few steps across the room and she was standing in front of him. Her delicate hand removed the flute from his grasp.

Speechless, he stood helplessly while she roughly unsnapped and unzipped his pants.

He stepped out of the denim that pooled around his ankles. Kicked off his sneakers. His hardening dick sliced through the slit of his boxers, twitching with desire.

"Take your shirt off." Her raspy tone was persuasive.

In split-seconds, the T-shirt was over his head and tossed on top of his jeans and sneakers.

CHAPTER 28

Misty pulled on the elastic waistband of his boxers and let it snap back, giving a sting to his flesh. Spydah squeezed his eyes closed, as if savoring the sharp sensation.

She did it again. Harder.

He moaned. "Damn, girl. What kind of shit is you into?"

"Take 'em off," she whispered. "Get naked for me."

If there was any part of him that resisted being told what to do, it wasn't apparent. Giving into the moment, Spydah came out of his boxers and stood naked, waiting for the next command. His tightly closed eyes were the only indication that he might be somewhat embarrassed.

She brushed her palm down the soft hair on the center of his chest. He flinched as if her touch was electricity.

Next, she rubbed the diamond on her pinky ring over each nipple, making his nipples tighten, making his dick flex, and causing him to tremble. Spydah's eyelids fluttered open.

"Keep your eyes closed," she softly urged. With her hands gripping his forearms, she turned him around.

He peered over his shoulder. "Whatchu doing?" His voice was faint and thin. And without much fight.

"Shh. I wanna admire your whole body. Front and back."

Spydah's back was narrow but defined with youthful muscles that didn't require putting in time at the gym. He had a small, but perfectly formed ass.

She touched his skin. Sexual heat emanated from his flesh.

Misty reached in the ice bucket and picked up a chunk of ice, and ran a chilly trail down the center of his back.

Fiercely determined to withstand the frozen caress, Spydah stood erect, fists balled at his sides.

Without warning, she licked the water that trickled down his spine.

"Ah," he groaned, arching his back when her tongue swiped against his skin.

Then she delivered teasing little licks from his back down to the crack of his butt.

He clenched up. "Yo, I ain't into all that," he mumbled, though his tone was weak, lacking strength and authority.

Ignoring his weak objection, Misty guided him toward the table where the champagne was chilling. With her palm flattened against the center of his back, she eased him down until his forehead rested upon the oak table.

From her purse, she extracted a container of gel, and moistened a finger.

Spydah gasped; his body jerked as she caressed the ridged flesh of his asshole. Gritted teeth, clenched butt cheeks trapping her searching finger.

"Relax, baby," she encouraged in a satiny tone.

"I can't."

"Trust me, Spydah. I don't want any barriers between us." Her voice was a caress.

"Yeah, but—"

"Let's explore our sexuality…together." Lowering herself down to her knees, she pressed her lips against his naked buttocks; each kiss made him jerk and moan as if she was burning the image of her lips onto his skin.

She kissed a hot trail toward the seam of his ass. Gently, cooing softly, she separated his butt cheeks and inserted her tongue.

Beneath the quick flicks of her tongue, his body twisted and writhed. His groans were anguished cries and he succumbed to passion. Now his hips moved in slow circles of bliss. As he accepted the pleasure of her sucking kisses, and hot, licking strokes, the sound of his moans were a mixture of agony and ecstasy.

With a sleight of hand, her middle finger replaced her tongue and eased into the slippery but tight entrance, determinedly seeking the walnut-shaped, male pleasure spot. Using the pad of her finger, she massaged his prostate gland until he panted with pleasure.

A smile formed on her sensual lips. *You mine, nigga. You might as well get used to it.*

Continuing her dominant role, she gave him head, but stopped before he busted a nut.

She sauntered over to the bed, wriggled her tight dress up, sat down, and spread her legs.

Spydah's hard dick pulled him in Misty's direction. She shook her head.

"What?" A frown flitted across his face.

She patted her pussy. "You want this?"

"Yeah." He steadied his throbbing dick by gripping it at the head.

"Crawl."

"Huh. You buggin'?"

"If you really wanted it, you'd get it any way you could. Run...climb...or crawl."

"Come on with that crawling shit. You taking this too far."

She pressed her knees together. "You performed tonight. You gave it your all but now it's only you and me. You can be yourself with me. Forget about that hardcore nigga you portray when you cussing and stomping around on stage. Let's get lost in a fantasy. Crawl for this pussy. Ain't nobody here but you and me."

Misty locked eyes with Spydah. She parted her thighs a little. She slid a finger between her legs. She withdrew it, taunting him with sticky moisture before tasting her flavor.

"Umph." That one note spoke volumes. A throaty admission that he'd do anything to please her.

"Come on, baby. Come and get this."

As if he'd collapsed, Spydah dropped. For a few seconds, his body was still.

"Crawl for me, baby," Misty insisted.

He moved into a crouching position. Then...like a stalking lion, he crawled across the floor.

His journey complete, he buried his head between her legs, gasping desperately as he licked and sucked.

With a smirk shaping her lips, Misty pushed his head away.

"I wanna ride you."

Spydah didn't protest. He lay flat on his back, his arousal intense as his arms reached for her, and then gripped her slender hips as she straddled him.

Expertly, Misty grasped the base of Spydah's shaft and guided his iron hardness into her pussy that was drenched from his lapping tongue.

Feeling powerful, Misty looked down at Spydah. He looked tortured as he battled against an orgasm with every thrust.

She bent over, cupping his cute face, calming him with kisses. "Don't fight it, Spydah. I wanna feel your hot seed splashing inside me."

"Nah, I'm staying in this. Gotta kill this pussy." Sweating, veins popping, temples throbbing, Spydah buried his manhood inside her, pumping dick...desperately...as if each stroke had the potential to save his life.

She nibbled along his earlobe.

"That feels good," he whispered.

Another weak spot. Determined to conquer him, she grazed his neck with her teeth and then licked the salty skin. All the while, her pussy became more heated… sputtering and slippery…driving Spydah out of his mind.

"Let it go," she coaxed.

He tensed. Growled in defeat. Grasping hands braced her hips as he discharged with the force of a tidal wave.

CHAPTER 29

Having traveled by limo, Misty joined Spydah as he celebrated the release of his CD at the new Pink Elephant Club in New York. Chilling at their VIP table, Misty basked in the joy of being in the posh, upscale environment that she so deserved.

Tomorrow night, he was scheduled to perform at Madison Square Garden, continuing as an opening act for Smash Hitz. But now that his CD was out and climbing the charts, Spydah's fan base was quickly growing. It was merely a matter of time before he became a headline act.

The celebrity-packed venue was large and luxurious. She recognized the familiar faces that she'd only seen on film or on TV. There were tons of people from the music industry milling about.

Spydah was meeting many of the celebrities for the very first time. Courteously, he introduced Misty to all of his high-profile guests.

Excluding Larry, Spydah's goon squad looked out of

place in the high-class Pink Elephant. They must have felt like the outcasts that they were because they were guzzling liquor like there was no tomorrow. Tragic glared at Misty…looking jealous…like he should have been cozied up next to Spydah. His resentment was so strong, she swore she could smell it. His hot funk was stinking up the place.

Fuck you, Tragic! She sent the angry minion a beaming smile.

Angrily, he wiped liquid from his lips and smirked as he gripped his crotch, mouthing, "I got something for you."

Bring it, nigga. Misty taunted Tragic with a fluttery finger wave. And a wink. Pissed off, Tragic's lips moved rapidly as he muttered obscenities or perhaps he was working on one of his whack rhymes. Who knew and who the fuck cared? Sneering, she gave Tragic her middle finger.

"Misty, I want you to meet somebody." She turned away from Tragic's contorted mug, expecting to finally meet Smash Hitz. Instead of seeing Smash's famous face, she found herself face-to-face with a mature man who was wearing glasses and a suit. The phoniness of his reptilian smile informed her that he was no friend of Spydah's. Nor was he a friend of hers.

"Meet Adam Sorrell…my business manager," Spydah said proudly. "Adam, this is my girl, Misty."

Misty and Adam read each other well. The handshake

they shared was more like an agreement to play nice just for tonight. Misty fully intended to get all up in Spydah's financial affairs and find out what the fuck was what. This fucking crook of a manager might be able to get over on Spydah, but he was going to have to show her some paperwork. Explain to her how one and one equals three, goddamnit.

"I was telling Spydah that I'm about to finalize a deal…Spydah's going to be the face of Banana Republic's new urban clothing line," Adam boasted.

"Spydah's going to have to give that endorsement some serious thought before he signs on the dotted line," Misty asserted.

"Yo, whatchu saying?" Spydah was shocked by Misty's forwardness.

"This is quite an achievement for an artist whose debut album recently dropped."

"What would be better, Spydah…hawking someone else's clothing line or starting your own?"

"Uh…I'll take it whatever way it comes," Spydah said, laughing.

"You have your own unique way of dressing. I think you should consider starting your own fashion line."

Though Adam smiled and nodded indulgently, Misty could tell he didn't appreciate her interference. Judging by the way his glasses were fogging up, the mufucka was steaming.

And he had good reason to be upset. She'd given the

arrogant business manager a glimpse into the inner workings of her mind. He was lucky she'd given him a heads-up that her petite frame and pretty face was merely a façade. She could have given him a sneak attack. Could have concealed her hard-as-nails interior before he had a chance to defend himself.

But Misty loved a good fight. Appreciated a worthy opponent.

It's on, slime ball.

Growing antsy, the goon squad couldn't hold back any longer. Mustafa, Jru, and Tragic began popping bottles of champagne. Celebrities were spared, but they sprayed anyone who didn't have a recognizable face.

When Spydah began his performance, the girls who were still outside waiting to get beyond the velvet rope started screaming, yelling to be allowed admittance inside the club.

Attracted to chaos and mayhem, Tragic went outside, taking it upon himself to speak on Spydah's behalf, selecting girls who could come inside. Most of the girls who were allowed admission had big, protrusive butts, Misty noticed.

Tragic pulled in one wild heathen, who really showed her ass when she got inside the club. Somehow, she managed to swerve her big ass past the security team that was busy inspecting purses. Wearing a dark-colored weave that hung to her waistline, she elbowed her way in front of a cluster of the girls who had made it inside before her. Stomping on their fresh pedicures, she caused a chorus of yelps and screams.

Then, adding insult to injury, the brazen, weave-wearing barracuda pulled a Lil' Mama, and jumped on stage with Spydah.

Misty and Adam gasped. In agreement, they were equally outraged at the audacity of the groupie.

Adam frantically waved for security to do something, but Spydah looked like he was having fun.

The groupie could dance exactly like Spydah…was in sync with all his moves…she knew every word to his new song…rapping with him and throwing her own animated flow that complemented his rhymes. Then she twirled away, dancing solo…dropping it low, enticing Spydah with big booty shaking…inviting him to get up on it.

Shank hoe! Misty was livid.

Looking around at the guests, Adam's expression conveyed shock and embarrassment. But he breathed a sigh of relief when, to his surprise, he saw smiles of approval directed toward the stage.

Misty was beside herself with absolute disgust. She could not give a shit that the crowd approved of that duet bullshit that had unfolded before her eyes. The only reason she didn't demand that security pull out their weapons, open fire, and blast that bitch off the stage was the fact that Spydah was performing his third and final song, which was thankfully coming to an end.

When the song concluded, Spydah hugged the big butt barracuda. The bitch had the nerve to take a bow. The applause was deafening. People thought she was part of Spydah's performance.

Holding the heifer's hand, Spydah led her back to their table.

"Yo, Larry. This is Baad B. We gotta do something with her, man. Talk to Smash…see if we can feature her on the remix of that track we just did."

Misty was seething. Breathing fire. She couldn't roll her eyes hard enough at the big butt, groupie bitch, plugging herself…tryna get a free ride on her man's coattails.

Never in her life had she felt so upstaged, disrespected, and outshined.

Spydah was about as young and dumb as they come. She couldn't wait to get back to the hotel. She'd reveal the magnitude of her displeasure once she got Spydah's ass in bed.

CHAPTER 30

Before having a glass of water, a cup of juice, or even going to the bathroom, Misty powered on her laptop. She had to check on her business. Find out how much money the videos and photos had brought in.

Spydah had yet to put a dollar in her hand, but it was only a matter of time before she took him for all he was worth.

She smiled at Spydah as he slept soundly. Worn out from the wild sex Misty had put him through the night before.

Securing her position in his life, Misty had introduced him to an array of sex tricks, had his body humming from things he'd never done before. Last night Spydah thought he was in heaven...he got so emotional, tears rolled from his eyes.

I had that nigga weeping. He's mine! And he better not even think about ever mentioning that groupie hoe's name again. Dumb-ass mufucka!

Before she went to her own site, she decided to check

the black gossip pages. She looked hot last night, wearing a barely there slip of black and gold beaded mesh across her breasts and gold satin trousers.

The image on the first site made her gasp. Spydah and the groupie bitch were hugged up on stage. The caption read: *D.B. Spydah introduces hot as fire new female rapper.*

What the fuck? She couldn't even bring herself to read the article. She clicked to other gossip pages. Each and every site had an image of Spydah with that bitch. There were quotes from her, explaining why she named herself Baad B.

Ugh! That groupie got the media spelling her name the way she wants, like she really is somebody. Goddamn!

Misty searched and searched for images of her and Spydah, but came up with zip. She didn't know whom she hated more…Spydah, Tragic (for letting the hoe in) or Baad B.

One thing was for certain, that so-called Baad B was messing with the wrong bitch.

❧

There was so much buzz inside Spydah's dressing room, Misty could hardly hear her own thoughts.

Mustafa, Tragic, and Jru were whooping and hollering and poppin' bottles, as usual. Tragic's wannabe rapper-ass was wearing some extra-gaudy bullshit and some outrageously ugly jewelry. Possessing an overabundance of youthful vigor, Tragic was alternately dancing around and freestyling. Every now and then, he stopped to preen in front of Spydah's full-size mirror.

Tragic was foul. Gut-bucket ignorant. Misty couldn't see what purpose he served. She couldn't wait until she had enough power to give Tragic his walking papers back to the 'hood. Or back to jail. Didn't matter as long he got out of Spydah's life.

Larry was in and out of the dressing room, looking worried as he wrapped up last-minute details before Spydah went on stage.

Spydah was expecting to switch positions with the R&B crooner who was scheduled to perform right before Smash Hitz came on.

Refusing to get dressed until he received word of the schedule change, Spydah was sitting around in his robe, sulking.

His expression grave, Larry stepped to Spydah. He lowered his voice and spoke words intended for only Spydah to hear.

But didn't much get past Misty. She heard Larry clearly when he said, "The crooning bull's people are giving me grief. I'm waiting for Smash to say the word."

Spydah was wearing a robe, refusing to get dressed until it was time to hit the stage...and that wouldn't be anytime soon as far as he was concerned.

"I ain't no opening act, man!" he yelled at Larry. "My CD is steadily climbing! It's number four on the charts, man! What I gotta do to get some respect, man? Do I gotta contact Adam to handle this shit?"

"Nah, I got it. I'm waiting on Smash. Calm down. I got it." But Larry was sweating bullets. He was out of his depth in this situation. Misty could tell that he was a nervous wreck by the way he trekked over to the hospitality table and started downing the complimentary Ed Hardy Vodka that nobody else had bothered to touch.

Misty hid her smirk behind her hand. After rearranging her features into a look of caring concern, she said to Spydah, "Baby, this is your night. Can't nobody take this from you. But tonight is not about your ego."

Spydah frowned.

"Seriously…you got fans that have been with you throughout your underground career. How you think they'll feel if you pull out of this show? Huh, baby?" She stroked his hair. "You gotta always remember that it's your fans that got you here."

Spydah smiled for the first time since they'd arrived in the stadium. "That's a good reason why I'm falling in love with you. You keep me focused."

Misty beamed.

Larry's cell went off. He started pacing with the cell to his ear. His worried expression morphed into relief… his lips spread into a wide grin.

"You're on before Smash, man." Larry returned his cell to his pocket and pumped his fist in the air. Victory cheers boomed from the paid leeches. Those idiots didn't even know what they were happy for. For them, what-ever Larry was talking about was another reason to pop champagne.

In a panic, Misty hurried from offstage where she'd stood watching most of Spydah's performance from the wings of the stage. During the commotion of accompa-nying Spydah to the stage, she'd forgotten her purse in the dressing room. Her cute little beaded purse was filled with cash and credit cards.

A few of the goons had never left the dressing room… too busy snorting blow, drinking, and getting their own party on.

Shit! If one of those mufuckas clipped me…I'm gon' make sure security does a cavity search on every one of the bastards.

In the corridor, behind-the-scenes personnel walked back and forth hastily. Some scowled at clipboards. Others shouted into headsets as they hustled along, doing their duties. Misty felt fortunate that she didn't have to rush around trying to make shit work out. All she had to do was stay beautiful and stay on top of her bedroom skills. Keep Spydah depending on her for his sexual needs.

Walking quickly in too-high stilettos, she began strategizing a way to ensure that she was photographed in every picture taken of Spydah tonight at the after-party. Click-clacking happily down the hallway, she suddenly noticed people beginning to scurry and scatter, as if in fear. They appeared to be almost throwing themselves up against the walls on either side of the hallway. Watching this shit was like viewing the parting of the Red Sea.

What the fuck is going on?

Down the center of the hallway, she saw four bare-chested muscular men approaching. The men formed four black glistening pillars around a smaller male that was in the center.

The human pillars walked in military precision with the smaller man. They were following his every move, while managing to keep their protective pillars intact.

Misty was mesmerized. As the five men grew closer, she could feel the power emanating from the man in the center. It was palpable, electrical.

Damn, that's Smash Hitz.

Spydah was off stage by now. But being on Smash's tour, he probably knew the drill, and wouldn't dare come down the corridor until the coast was clear. He and Larry were probably cowering in a corner or hiding under the stage somewhere.

The audience must have sensed Smash's approach because they began chanting his name.

Misty forced herself to shake off the spell. In a panic, she struggled to collect her thoughts. She had to meet Smash Hitz and no time was better than now.

Realizing that she had to make a memorable first impression, Misty's mind raced. *I can't let this opportunity go by.*

The column of men was gaining on her. From the

glare of their angry dark eyes, she could imagine them saying, "Bitch, who you think you is? Move out of the fuckin' way."

Anxiety couldn't possibly describe the swirl of frenzied emotions that overtook her. It was do-or-die time.

Faint, she decided. Before she could punk out and change her mind, she was lying on the floor, in front of the approaching black pillars.

The two leading pillars didn't break stride. They stepped right over her, like a fallen leaf had blown in their path.

Aw, shit. This ain't working. Maybe I should roll out of the way before these other buff mufuckas start to happily trample my lil' ass.

But Smash stopped. Cocking his head from one side to the other, he frowned as he surveyed Misty's inert body.

This is going to be very embarrassing for me and for Spydah if I don't come up with something, quick.

Smash squatted down. Misty met his eyes. Surprisingly, instead of annoyance, she saw concern in his gaze.

She was briefly bedazzled by his twinkling, signature medallion. She'd never seen so many diamonds, or any with such clarity.

Pulling her eyes from the mesmerizing diamonds, she bestowed upon him her most dazzling smile, and then whispered, "Would you mind helping me up, Mr. Hitz? After all, your magnificent presence is the cause of this fainting spell."

After what felt like an eternity, Misty saw the beginning of a smile starting to form on his face. Smash laughed. "Girl, you a trip."

Misty replied, "I know."

Smash pulled her to her feet. "I seen you back here with Spydah. What's your name?"

"Misty."

"Misty, huh?" He gripped his chin.

Before she could come up with any clever or flirtatious words, Smash turned and continued his march to the stage.

CHAPTER 31

The after-party for the New York leg of the Smash Hitz tour was a pricey soiree that was thrown at one of the hottest clubs in New York. Product logos were on display everywhere. Ciroc Vodka, the leading sponsor for the bash, boasted a gigantic vinyl banner.

Despite all of the free-flowing alcohol, and the big-named celebrities in attendance, Misty wasn't having fun.

Spydah had her joined at his damn hip, preventing her from mingling like she wanted to. And if that wasn't bad enough, they were seated in some dinky VIP area, while Smash Hitz was holding court in the Gold Room—a VIP area that was designated exclusively for his twelve-man entourage and the other elite members of his party.

Misty didn't like playing second fiddle. She should be with the number one man. Being relegated to this dinky area with Spydah and his moron-crew was insulting.

"What's wrong, baby?" Spydah asked.

Misty pouted. "Nothing."

"Yes, it is."

"I'm good," she said, poking her lips out, clearly sulking.

"You don't like that vodka? You want something else to drink?"

"I thought it was mandatory that we drink this bull-shit—being that they sponsoring the party."

"You can drink whatever you want," Spydah told her.

"What you want, some champagne?" Tragic butted in.

Misty sucked her teeth. *Ain't nobody ask fucking Tragic to be minding my damn business.*

Itching to get into some devilment, Tragic ventured over to a silver bucket where three champagne bottles were embedded in ice.

But it wasn't Tragic's call.

It was up to Spydah to decide when they were ready to pop some bottles. Misty hated the way Spydah let his crew run all over him.

The instant that Tragic put his hands on one of the bottles, Misty snarled, "If you spray any of that shit in my direction, I'ma put these four inches all the way up your fuckin' ass." Grilling him, she stuck out her stiletto, showing off the jewel-encrusted four-inch heel, which was stunningly beautiful, yet deadly.

There was a hush at the table.

Tragic blinked his eyes in shock and indignation.

Spydah looked down in embarrassment. Gripping his chin, he dragged his fingers down his skin.

Larry cleared his throat.

The groupies at the table snickered, which made Tragic start swiping at his nose like he was trying to restrain himself from punching Misty's lights out.

Mustafa shot a look at Spydah. "You gon' let her dis your man like that?"

All eyes were on Spydah, waiting for him to choose sides. He moved closer to Misty, cracked a smile. "If the shoe fits..."

Bursts of laughter erupted at the table. The groupies looked at Misty with admiration. Mustafa quickly adjusted his attitude and regarded Misty with a faint smile that requested a truce.

She gave Spydah a quick peck on the lips. "Excuse me, baby. I have to go to the ladies room." She grabbed her handbag.

The moment she stood up, the groupies at the table stood up, muttering that they had to go to the restroom, too.

With a corner of her top lip jutted upward, Misty looked the girls up and down in disgust.

"I don't travel in a pack. And I don't need any escorts," she informed. She glared at them, completing the reprimand with a disgusted, "Ew!"

At first the groupies looked around in confusion. Then their expressions changed to hostile and indignant.

The moment one of the girls planted a hostile hand on her hip, Spydah asserted his authority. "Yo, she don't want a bunch of y'all following behind her. Can't she take a piss by herself?"

"Oh, okay," the hand-on-the-hip groupie said, letting the defiant balled hand fall limply at her side.

"We didn't know," another groupie said, using an

apologetic tone. She threw in a dimpled smile to express her sincerity.

None of the groupie girls wanted to be cast out into the street. They liked hanging with a celebrity. Would kiss his ass…Misty's ass…and the ass of every member of the entourage if it was required of them.

Spydah had won some points for defending her honor. She had something special for him when they got back to the hotel.

Her mind was on money right now, though. She needed to call Sailor and find out what was up with the apartment she was dying to rent. All this running around with Spydah wasn't putting one thin dime in her bank account. She was going to have to do something about that.

A few feet short of the ladies room, she looked up. Though he was short in stature, Smash Hitz' presence was bigger than life.

Oh my God, it's him!

From the Gold Room, he stared down at her, sending her strong, sensual vibes.

She wanted to acknowledge his presence, but didn't know what would be the right move to make. *Should I wave at him or something? What the fuck does he want me to do?*

Looking up, she stood paralyzed, waiting for some direction. After a few seconds, he turned around, moved away from the glass enclosure, leaving Misty both relieved and disappointed.

As if she'd been released from a magic spell, she shook

her heavy, long hair. Then she took slow, hesitant steps, still looking upward as she moved toward the ladies room.

Inside the pleasantly fragrant restroom, she sank into a red velvet chair and collected her thoughts.

What the fuck was that about? Why is Smash fucking with my head? I don't like the way he acting. Me and Spydah need to get up out of this whack after-party.

Before going inside a stall, Misty called Sailor. "Did you hear anything about the apartment?" Her tone was gloomy, like she expected bad news. Her credit was jacked-up. Trying to get a fly crib in her own name was asking for the moon.

"We got it!" Sailor told her.

"For real? Are you serious?" Misty was elated.

"All you have to do is sign the lease."

"That's incredible. It's like magic. I can't believe they accepted my application. My credit is atrocious."

Sailor laughed. "Not anymore."

"What changed?"

"I'm good with numbers. I played around on the computer, did a little bit of hacking…juggled some numbers and changed your credit score."

"Ooo, Sailor. I love you. I really do. Call Izell and Lennox. Tell them to start packing. Tell them we have room for three extra niggas, so they should bring a couple of friends. Smart niggas who are ready to jump Uncle Freaky's sinking ship."

"Do I have to say that word?"

"What word?"

"The N word that you're always using."

"No, you don't have to. Tell 'em to bring a couple extra dudes. You comfortable saying that?"

Sailor laughed. "Yeah."

Misty laughed with him. "You're my man, Sailor. You got mad computer skills."

"Thanks."

She could picture him blushing. "Tell Izell and Lennox it's time for them to get tatted. Take them to see Zelgore at the tattoo salon." Misty paused in thought. "Umph. I sure hope my brand can show up on Izell's black-ass arm."

Sailor laughed again. Heartily.

"Oh, you like to hear me talking about somebody's black ass, but you can't stand hearing the N word?"

"We don't talk like that in Wisconsin," he said.

"I feel you...I guess. Whatchu consider yourself, Sailor? Caucasian or what?"

"I usually check the box that says 'other.'"

"Oh, yeah. I can dig it." Misty wasn't even mentally involved in the conversation. She was saying anything, while her mind pleasantly wandered.

The world suddenly seemed right. Things were starting to work in her favor. Sailor had her back, and she was ready to show him some appreciation.

"When are you coming home?" he asked. "I miss you."

"I miss you, too. I'll be home soon. Real soon. But I gotta go. I'ma talk to you tomorrow. Aiight, Sailor?"

"Alright."

Misty hung up.

She was seriously ready to roll out of New York. Sick of Spydah's needy ass and she was totally over his imbecilic crew.

Getting approved for a big-ass, luxury apartment had her feeling real haughty when she left the ladies room.

Standing in front of the ladies room was one of the dark-skinned brothers that had marched Smash onto the stage at the Garden.

"Misty, right?" he said in a deep, baritone voice, his expression all business.

She swallowed. His deep voice made her nervous and shaky, and being nervous felt like crap. "Yes, I'm Misty." Oh God, she hated the shrillness of her voice. *Damn, why my voice gotta be sounding all squeaky? I ain't no pussy, mufucka. Nah, it ain't even like that. I'm a real bitch. Nigga, you don't know?*

"Smash asked me to extend an invitation. He wants you to join him upstairs in the Gold Room."

Smash Hitz was regarded as a king. It was an honor to be summoned by him.

But what I'ma do about Spydah? Misty frowned. Then shrugged. *Fuck Spydah, he gon' have to deal with this. He ain't paying my bills. I'd be as big of a moron as Spydah if I turned Smash Hitz' invitation down.*

"Of course," Misty said, giving the attendant a dazzling smile. "It's my pleasure to join Mr. Hitz."

CHAPTER 32

In the Gold Room, a few of Smash's people were pouring cognac for all the guests.

Ugh! Misty held her glass, but didn't dare try to take a sip. She'd never get the bitter liquid past her tongue and down her throat.

I'ma puke if I try to swallow this nasty crap.

Smiling at Smash, Misty swirled the brown liquid around in her glass. Acting like she was on some fly shit, she swirled a few more times, trying to give the impression that a certain amount of swirls would put the liquor at the right temperature...make it taste better. Or something. She really wished she had something good to drink.

Smash noticed that she wasn't drinking. "You're not happy with your drink?"

"No, not really." She hated to admit it, but she would be so much more pleased if she had a drink with an umbrella and some fruit on a stick.

Smash snapped his fingers. Twice. Two men instantly appeared, flanking Smash.

Aw, now see. This is some fly-ass shit. Wait 'til I get my ass back to Philly…I'ma be snapping my fingers all day long. I ain't gon' have to say a mufuckin' word to get my point across.

"Whatchu drinking, lil' lady?" Smash smiled at her.

"Pure Paradise."

"Oh, yeah? That sounds sexy…like you. So what goes into it?"

"The bartender should know the ingredients, but for your information, it's mixed with coconut rum, exotic fruit juice, and some other erotic stuff."

"Erotic, huh?"

"Mmm-hmm." Misty was finally starting to have a good time. Being in the presence of power was seductive. And addictive. She wanted to start rolling with Smash Hitz. Spydah's feelings would be crushed when she left his young ass for Smash Hitz. But fuck it. She had to do what she had to do.

This time Smash didn't snap his fingers. Without taking his eyes off Misty's face, he uttered in a low, but stern voice, "Handle that."

One of the men promptly removed the glass from her hand, and then both men hurried away.

Smash's eyes were all over her body. He kept moistening his lips and running his hand down the side of his face, like he was feenin' for her.

Being as petite as she was, standing next to her made short to average height men feel ten feet tall. Smash was much shorter in person than she had ever imagined, so she assumed he had the short man's complex. Misty made it a point to look way up, like Smash was as tall as Shaquille O'Neal.

When the two men returned...one carrying her pastel-colored drink, the other carrying a napkin, Smash Hitz walked Misty near the glass enclosure, making sure that Spydah could see him and Misty sharing a drink. Kicking it. Laughing and having fun.

The men treaded softly behind them. Misty supposed they were Smash's bodyguards.

"Why there ain't no tables where we standing at?"

Misty wasn't sure if she was supposed to have an answer to that question, but before she could even come up with a clever response, one of the men slowly lowered himself down, and assumed a position that gave the impression that he was now a table.

Smash set his glass of cognac on the man's strong, unyielding back.

Misty was beyond impressed. *That's some freaky shit, right there. I'ma try that as soon as I get home. Troy better watch it. Better stop playing and getting on my nerves all the time. I know how to fix him now. I'ma turn his ass into a mufuckin' table. Think I won't?*

"Put your drink down. Wouldn't want your pretty lil' fingers to get frostbite."

Acting like she'd been setting drinks on niggas all her life, she placed her glass on the man's back. She set her handbag next to it. She looked around at Smash's guests and noticed that Smash was being given privacy. No one looked in their direction. People were laughing and talking. Obviously having a good time, while being careful to mind their own business.

"Tell me something about yourself, Misty."

"I'm from Philly."

"That where you met my man, Spydah?"

"Yeah, but I'm not a groupie."

"Didn't say you was."

"You insinuated."

"Nah, I don't pass judgment."

"I'm a businesswoman. A people pleaser. I bring individuals together."

"Whatchu running…Black Hook-up, Dot Com?"

"Something like that. I get money."

"I bet you do."

Misty laughed. Feeling more relaxed, she picked up her drink.

"But you ain't getting enough," he said, his vocal quality changing to a taunt.

Wondering why the conversation had gone in another direction, she took a sip of her drink to calm herself down.

"I got fifty stacks for you. Right now. If you get under that table, unzip him, and suck my man's dick right now."

Choking from shock, she almost spit the pink-colored liquid out. She forced it down her throat and said, "Huh?"

"You like money. I got plenty of it. Suck his dick like I said and I'll throw some cake your way."

The man who was pretending to be a table didn't budge. But when Smash snapped his fingers, the man widened his legs, as if giving Misty the space she needed to perform fellatio.

Misty saw red. "You must be crazy, mufucka. How you gon' come out ya mouth like that? I ain't sucking nothin'. Kiss my ass. I ain't no goddamn hoe."

Smash snapped his fucking fingers again. The table nigga jumped up, grabbed her arm and disrespectfully escorted her out of the Gold Room.

Spydah was waiting for her at the bottom of the stairs. Her hair was all over the place, her clothes disheveled. "I'm ready to go," Misty spat.

"What the hell happened?"

"I hate that black bastard. Take me back to the hotel."

"Misty, what happened?"

"Smash tried to disrespect me."

"Why'd you go up there without me?"

"He invited me. He got us drinking what the fuck he wants us to drink. He snapping his fingers and shit, making niggas do everything he wants them to. You wasn't around to say nothing, so I thought I *had* to go."

"Nah, you ain't have to do shit. I'm your man. You do what I tell you to do."

Ha! That's a damn lie and you know it. You don't tell me what to do.

"Man, Smash be on some other shit. Did he put his hands on you?"

"No! But he tried to play me. Tried to make me look like a skank hoe."

Looking troubled, Spydah gazed up at the Gold Room. "How you want me to handle this?"

"Look for another label, nigga."

Spydah flinched. "I can't do that. I signed a contract with Smash. I gotta give him two more albums before we renegotiate my record deal."

"So whatchu gon' do? You gotta do something, Spydah. He was really foul."

"What can I do?"

"Go upstairs…act like a man with some balls, nigga. Take your crew if you have to. But you need to be putting your fist in Smash's grille."

"Man, that's my boss, Misty."

Misty shook her head. "Damn, Spydah, you on some real bitch-assness. You know that, right?"

"Nah, it ain't like that. This is business."

She looked at Spydah with revulsion.

"I'm sorry, Misty. But I'm just getting out the gate. Whatchu expect me to do…ruin my career before it gets started?"

"I said, I'm ready to go!"

CHAPTER 33

Spydah was trying his damndest to make Misty feel better, massaging her satin-smooth naked skin while soft music played in the background.

"Relax, baby," he whispered.

She lifted her head from the pillow, flung her hair out of her face. "I'm trying."

"No, you're not. You acting all tense and stiff. Let yourself go." He picked up a candle from the nightstand. "Mmm, smell that, Misty? That's one of them aromatherapy candles. It's supposed to put you in a good mood."

She sighed in exasperation, took a sniff...scowled... and then pushed her face back into the pillow. As Spydah straddled her back, she could feel his dangling ball sac brushing against her skin.

"Ew, Spydah. That shit feels all kinds of nasty. Will you put some goddamn drawers on? I don't need your smelly balls rubbing all over my ass. You seem to be getting all the enjoyment. Is this massage bullshit supposed to be for my pleasure or yours?"

"This is for you."

"Don't seem like it. You're so fuckin' selfish, Spydah!"

"Damn, you been pissed with me ever since you had that run-in with Smash."

"How you expect me to act...after the way that sawed-off bastard treated me?"

"The shit that went down wasn't my fault!" he yelled, getting angry. "Ain't nobody tell you to take your ass up to the Gold Room!"

She rolled over, forcing him off of her. She sat up and squinted an eye. "I fuckin' hate you," she said in a tone that was filled with emotion.

"Come on with that. You don't hate me."

"Oh, yes, I do. And I hate Smash, too."

"I can't do nothing about how you feel about Smash. But saying you hate me...that ain't right. It ain't cool, Misty."

A wicked idea worked itself into her mind.

"I might be able to forgive you, Spydah...if you play out one of my fantasies with me."

"Here we go." He shook his head, laughing. "How many fantasies can one lil' woman have inside her head?"

"They're unlimited," she bragged.

"You a freak." Spydah smiled. Licked his lips, as if expecting to be introduced to yet another freakish pleasure.

Somebody had to pay for the public humiliation she'd experienced tonight. And it might as well be Spydah.

She looked around the room.

"Whatchu looking for?" Spydah's eyes were alit with anticipation, wondering what type of sex play Misty had in store for him.

"I see your pants on the chair…"

"Yeah? And…"

"Where your boxers at?"

Spydah frowned. "My boxers? Whatchu want them for?"

"I have my reasons."

He pointed to a puddle of white cotton imprinted with red stripes. "There they go…over there on the floor."

"Oh! I didn't even see 'em." Misty sounded delighted. She got out of the bed and pranced over to Spydah's boxer shorts. Picked them up. And, to his amazement, she stepped into them.

She looked at herself in the mirror. The fit around the waist was a little loose, so she pulled the waistband into a knot on the side. Now she smiled at her image.

Turning around, she asked Spydah, "How do I look?" She put both hands on her hips for effect.

"Crazy. In a cute sort of way."

She wagged her finger beckoning him to her.

"What?" He smiled bashfully, but couldn't conceal the lust in his eyes.

"You been a bad boy, Spydah," she teased.

"I know, baby." The smile disappeared.

"You let Smash disrespect me."

"I know. I'm sorry."

"Wanna know how you can make me happy?"

His head was hung low. "Yeah, man. I wanna get past this."

"If we gon' move forward, you gotta come out your comfort zone. You need to experience what your mentor put me through."

"Aiight." He still wouldn't look up.

Smiling devilishly, Misty took retreating steps until she backed into a wall.

Using the wall for support, she rested against it.

"Come on, Spydah, you know what I what."

Spydah took long strides across the room. When he reached Misty, he was panting. Desperately, he kissed her lips. Breathing hard as he lathered her neck with his tongue. Dipped his head down, taking in a mouthful of titty.

"No, baby, that ain't it."

"Whatchu want?" he whispered, his voice rough with desire.

As she shoved him off of her, his hungry lips were puckered, yearning to recapture her aroused peaks.

Misty reached down and spread open the fly of the boxers, revealing her nest of curly, dark pubic hair.

"Suck it, baby. Suck my clit. But I need you to suck it like it's a big hard black dick." She spread her cunt lips; her pink, moist clit surfaced and throbbed in expectancy.

Spydah obliged, stretching his tongue past her slick petal softness and into a bubbling pool of wet heat.

His mouth moved upward toward the achingly swollen flesh. She gripped his head, guiding him, keeping his mouth trapped between the slit of the male boxers. Humping his face, she thrust like a man.

"Suck it, suck my big dick, pussy," she demanded. Her words provoked a low guttural moan from Spydah as he reached down to stroke his own swollen member.

"Oh hell naw, nigga," Misty snarled, smacking the side of his head. "You're gonna need both those hands to hold my dick while you play with my balls."

Confused, but daring not to question Misty, Spydah improvised. Reaching into the boxer's open slit, he used one hand to spread her slippery swollen pussy lips. The other hand searched and found the base of her now elongated clit. As Spydah began to gently and rhythmically pull on it, Misty's knees buckled.

"Oh shit…oh shit…now put my dick in your mouth, bitch!"

Spydah flicked the tip of Misty's "dick" with his tongue. Then, still massaging the base, wrapped his thick lips around Misty's "female dick" and sucked.

Misty screamed, undulated, gyrated, her body went into spasms. She cussed Spydah out, babbling in an unknown tongue until that blinding cataclysmic moment of ultimate release.

Misty and Spydah lay in bed. Like a normal couple, they kissed and cuddled, the intense, reverse role-playing scene now behind them.

"Oh, yeah…I've been meaning to ask you something."

"What?"

"Wanna go to the BET Awards with me?"

Excited, Misty sat up. "Are you nominated for anything? Your CD just came out."

"No, I'm not a nominee, but I'm scheduled to perform."

"Of course I want to go. But why did you wait so long to invite me?"

"I just found out myself. Someone had to cancel and I'm filling in that spot. Adam sealed the deal today."

"Spydah! I'm so proud of you. You're on your way to the top," she said, while actually thinking, *It won't be long now. I'm on my way!*

CHAPTER 34

One would have thought it was Misty's wedding day. Thomasina was in the kitchen preparing enough food to feed an army. Her daughter was going to be on TV, on the red carpet with her boyfriend, D.B. Spydah, at the BET Awards ceremony. Misty had turned her life around and that was a reason for her mother to celebrate.

"Is it on yet?" she yelled from the kitchen.

"No, baby. Commercial's still on." Brick glanced at the brand-new, fifty-five-inch, 3D TV, a gift from Misty. She had insisted her mother accept the expensive gift, adamant that mere high definition wasn't good enough. She wanted her mother to watch her walk the red carpet in high-tech, 3D.

"Call me the minute the show comes on."

"I will."

It wasn't envy that Brick was feeling, and he certainly didn't wish Misty any ill will. There was some other…indefinable emotion stirring inside him…leaving him feeling torn.

He wanted to be as happy and as proud as Thomasina, but he couldn't. If he really believed that Misty had turned her life around, he'd be sitting here like a proud...well....he didn't feel like her father, but he'd feel like a proud sibling if he could believe that Misty was walking a straight and narrow path. But Brick knew better.

Misty couldn't do right if her life depended on it. She was always doing something foul. And when her foul actions came to light, it would be up to him to comfort her mother. Now that Misty was playing in the big league, her fall from grace would be harder than ever.

"The show's starting!" Brick yelled.

Thomasina hustled into the living room. She set a plate piled up with wing dings on the coffee table in front of Brick.

"Mmm. Smells good." He dipped his finger in the sauce and tasted it. "The sauce is banging, baby."

Thomasina didn't utter a word. She'd tuned Brick out. Staring at the TV screen, waiting for Misty to hit the red carpet.

"Here comes my baby! Look at Misty!" Thomasina yelled when her daughter stepped onto the red carpet.

"Look at lil' Misty, rubbing elbows with the stars," Brick said admiringly. He looked at his wife, who was dabbing at her eyes. "You crying?"

Thomasina nodded. Didn't speak. Brick nodded in understanding, knowing she didn't want to speak. She couldn't. Too choked up. In Thomasina's opinion, this was her daughter's shining moment...the moment Thomasina had been waiting for Misty's entire life.

The host on the pre-BET Awards, red carpet event directed her question and comments to Spydah, asked him questions about his new single, and told him "good luck" on his performance later on.

"She didn't say one word to Misty," Thomasina said angrily.

It wasn't about Misty. She was arm candy, but Brick knew Thomasina wouldn't see it that way.

"She could have asked her about her dress or even said that she looked nice. The heifa acted like Misty wasn't even standing there. Jealous. Women always jealous of my baby."

"Here we go. I thought you said you were going to stop focusing on Misty's looks. You admitted that you helped mess her mind up," Brick said, sucking in a long breath.

"Everyone's focusing on beauty at those award shows. What do you expect me to do...pretend that my daughter is an ugly duckling?"

"No. But you have to understand...Misty was the date of that young rapper. He's the man of the hour. It wasn't about her."

"I don't care. The heifa with the microphone deliberately ignored and disrespected my baby."

"How? Can't nobody ignore Misty. Did you see how

the camera stayed on her the whole time? Did you see how she was smiling and glowing? I think it would have been too much for everybody if Misty would have started talking. She would have straight stole the show from that young bull."

Thomasina perked up. She smiled. "You have a point, Baron. Misty filled the whole screen. I don't know why she doesn't consider going into acting or modeling... you know...she could start a petite line. They have the plus-sized models...why not have someone represent the lil' girls? Misty would be perfect."

CHAPTER 35

After the BET Awards ceremony, Misty was a hot topic on Twitter. She may have been ignored by the host, but America wanted to know more about her. Online gossip columns posted her picture, calling her Spydah's "hot mystery date."

Spydah's people requested a bio from Misty so they could have a handy blurb regarding her identity. But Misty refused to submit a bio.

Let them keep wondering about me. I'm not giving Adam's entertainment agency shit unless they pay me. Ain't nothing free in this world.

So far Spydah hadn't put her on the payroll, but Misty had started hitting him up with monetary requests on a regular basis. Fuck waiting for him to take a hint that his gifts weren't cutting it anymore.

After Spydah had spent money to dress her for the BET Awards, their relationship evolved to the point where it was acceptable for him to continue dressing her. He liked her looking fabulous and didn't seem to have a problem forking over cash toward her wardrobe.

Well...at least that's what she told him she needed the money for. Actually, a great deal of Spydah's money went toward the crazy, high down payment on her new apartment. And the extra things necessary to be comfortable until she hired an interior designer.

The apartment complex was tucked away in the East Falls section of Philadelphia, situated in a historic nineteenth-century former textile mill. Advertised as an oasis in the shadow of Center City, the location was a perfect hideaway from prying eyes that might not appreciate Misty's unconventional lifestyle.

She loved everything about her new luxury apartment. It had three large bedrooms, fourteen-foot-high ceilings, classic oak flooring, built-in desks and bookcases, elegant archways, oversized garden tubs, walk-in closets, side-by-side refrigerators, and a full-sized washer and dryer inside the apartment. There were added amenities, including a pool and a state-of-the-art fitness center.

It was a giant leap from her little ghetto studio apartment. She was back on top and still climbing.

The next thing she had to take care of was her transportation. She needed to turn the X5 over to Sailor and let him tote the boys around from one job to the other. She needed to be wheeling something sleek and sexy. Something fast and exotic. Something crazy expensive.

The boys, her term of endearment for her team of dick slingers, were out buying furniture for the two extra bedrooms. The master bedroom belonged to Misty and whomever she chose to share it with for the night.

For the time being, she was sleeping on an air mattress. She'd get her bedroom together in due time. As long as she had desk space and her laptop, she was a happy camper.

As usual, Troy was getting on her nerves. Chilling at his mom's crib because he didn't want to share a bedroom with the boys.

Misty intended to make good use of the space. At present, she only had a staff of four...Izell, Troy, Sailor, and Lennox. But there was a new dude moving in tomorrow. He'd already been doing a couple jobs here and there. His name was Horatio...big mufucka...built like a damn linebacker.

Eventually, there would be four boys per bedroom. That would require two sets of sturdy-ass bunk beds per bedroom.

She'd already checked it out...loft bunk beds were designed for two full-sized adults. She would pack as many dudes in her apartment as possible. On some real shit, the sleeping arrangements could be extended to the living room.

She hadn't purchased any furniture yet, and if she could get the rest of the male models away from Uncle Freaky, Misty would be stacking for real.

Maybe she could use scare tactics...hint that Uncle Freaky looked a little sickly...it was possible that an old homo like him was carrying the package. An HIV scare might send the rest of those pretty boys scattering like scared mice.

Izell loved to run his mouth. Misty would make it her business to mention that she noticed that Uncle Freaky's complexion had a gray tint to it.

Her cell rang. It was Sailor. "How's it going? You boys finding everything you wanted for the bedrooms?"

"Yeah, it's working out. I called because the clients are still calling my cell to hook up dates. We forgot to reroute the calls back to your phone."

"Oh. Do we have to? I have so much on my mind right now. I'm not in the mood for it. Can't talk to any horny clients. Not right now."

"That's not a problem. But there's a request for Troy. We don't get along, so I figured you could work out the details with Troy."

"Is it one of his regulars?"

"No. It's a woman looking for service. New client."

"I hope you informed her that the fee for couples' fun is double. Clients are always trying to pretend that they don't know that, but I make sure that everything pertaining to money is written in large, bold print." Misty's temper was starting to flare. She didn't want to go there, but cheap-ass, tryna-get-over clients could easily work her nerves.

"I didn't get the impression that she had any money concerns. She wants him to stay overnight."

"Oh!" *This apartment is costing me a grip. I can't be turning no money down.*

"Can you persuade her to take Izell or Lennox? Why

would she choose bony-behind Troy over those big hunks of masculinity? And what about the new bull, Horatio? That big bruiser looks like he could tackle a whole bunch of mufuckas. You got his picture posted, don't you?"

"Yeah, she saw all the photos and the videos, but the lady wants Troy. She mentioned something about liking the ashy aspect of his image."

"Oh, God," Misty groaned. "Okay, I'll get in touch with Troy." Misty hung up and stared into space.

This is so fucked up! Wearily, she ran her fingers through her hair. For a day that had started out with so much promise, Misty was slipping fast into a rotten mood. All she wanted out of this day was to sit and bask in self-appreciation. She had moved herself out a fuckin' shit hole into this beautiful, upscale, new apartment. And she couldn't even enjoy it. More money...more problems. She supposed the saying was true.

Now she had to deal with Troy's temperamental ass. Sweet-talk him into making some money. What kind of insane bullshit was that?

"Hey, Troy," Misty said cheerily when she got Troy on the phone.

"Whassup, Misty?" He sounded stern...like he was determined to stick to his guns.

"I gotta big money date for you."

"I ain't feelin' it right now. I'm on the block...chillin' with my niggas."

Chillin' with my niggas. Misty grimaced as she mimicked him in her head. Ugh! Troy was so stupid. She wished she had him in her clutches, so she could kick him in his damn head.

"How's your money holding up?"

"I'm good."

"What's your version of being good?"

"I got a coupla dollars."

"Umph. I would kill myself if I only had a coupla damn dollars," Misty said sneeringly.

"We don't think the same. Obviously, we don't see eye-to-eye. I been with you all this time, but you tryna throw me in a dormitory with a bunch of smelly niggas. I'm good right here at my mom's house. Least here, I get to have my own room."

Misty counted to ten. Got control of her emotions and kept a level head. "You're right, Troy. I'm going to let you have one of the bedrooms. All to yourself. Okay?"

"Aiight then. Cuz shit…those niggas all know each other. They used to being all piled up on top of each other—"

"Shut the fuck up, Troy. I said you can have your own goddamn room. Why you still complaining?"

"I'm just saying, yo."

"Catch a cab. Damn! I'll pay for it when you get here."

"That'll work," Troy mumbled.

"See you soon." Misty ended the call.

I can see that I'ma have to fuck Troy up. Turn his ass into a mufuckin' table.

CHAPTER 36

Now that she was out of the 'hood and living in a respectable area, Misty decided to give Spydah her actual address, rather than forcing him to continue sending her presents to a post office box.

"I must have done something right for you to finally trust me with the address to ya crib," Spydah had said over the phone.

In less than an hour after talking to him, her apartment was swamped with flowers. Dozens and dozens. The splashes of color added another dimension to the crib.

But Spydah didn't know that she didn't possess one stick of furniture yet. Luckily, there was ample counter space and lots of built-in cabinets to display the beautiful flowers.

Being creative, she and Troy covered some of the moving boxes with expensive linen and luxury bath towels and used the covered boxes as unique pedestals to flaunt the floral arrangements.

As Misty and Troy sat on the floor admiring their decorative touches, Sailor called.

"Bad news," he said.

"What now! Can I be happy for a damn second?"

"The lady cancelled."

"Why?"

"She didn't wanna pay double because she's single."

"That makes sense. Why didn't you tell her she could pay the regular fee?"

"I did. But she didn't know that she had to pay five thousand to have him for the whole night."

"What the fuck? I know that bitch don't think I'm running a charity that gives away free dick at midnight."

Troy was on the hardwood floor, his back resting against a pillar. He bumped his head against the wood and sighed in frustration. "I shoulda stayed in my 'hood."

Misty glanced at Troy. "Shut the fuck up. I'ma come up with something. One bitch can't stop my money flow."

"I'ma call a cab. Roll out 'til you need me," Troy said.

"Wait, Troy. You ain't got nowhere important to be."

Misty spoke into the cell. "Sailor, I have an idea, but I need you and the boys to stop everything you're doing and come home. ASAP!"

❧

Misty amazed her own damn self with her brilliant mind and cunning.

An email blast to VIP customers inviting them to an Exotic Open House Celebration had done the trick.

Sailor looked quite spiffy in the tux that Misty had hurriedly rented for him to wear that evening.

Lennox, Izell, and Horatio were hot as hell, their muscled bodies oiled, each man wearing only a loincloth.

Troy, however, was a skinny, ashy hot mess. But he would still makes lots of paper. Troy had a huge following of men and women that lusted for his ashy, long dick.

The paying guests buzzed with excitement as Sailor worked the vast living room, serving wine that he carried on a silver platter.

Misty had never intended to meet her clients face-to-face. But money issues will take a person out of their comfort zone.

Shunning the spotlight, she tried to downplay her stunning beauty by wearing a simple, Yves Saint Laurent, black sheath dress. Her dark, glossy hair was arranged in a classic chignon style. And she wore pearls…one of Spydah's numerous gifts. A shocking gift because she really couldn't picture a thug nigga picking out any damn pearls.

But at least the corny jewelry was finally coming in handy. Prior to tonight, those stupid pearls had been stuffed inside of a piece of luggage.

Despite all of her effort to look plain, Misty's beauty shone through, and she was still undeniably hot.

As she mingled with her guests, discussing everything from the weather to how the Sixers were doing, she was hit on at least ten times, and was offered a king's ransom for a mere sniff of her exotic coochie.

Some people were never satisfied with what they were offered. Here Misty had allowed these horny mufuckas into her crib for a special erotic extravaganza and they still weren't satisfied. They wanted a piece of her. Fuck no.

Along with the decorated boxes on the floor, Misty had added an assortment of human tables: Lennox, Izell, and Horatio. And sadly…Troy. Troy was the worst-looking, rickety-ass table she'd ever seen.

Izell and the boys were sturdy as statues…unmoving. Their bodies glistened, their strong backs more than capable of supporting anyone who wanted to take a seat.

But Troy. *Oh, my God!* Misty shot him an evil glance. He looked terrible in the loincloth. Making matters worse, he kept twitching and moving. His arms and legs looked spindly and were covered with an extra thick layer of ash. He was the kind of table that required being rubbed down with generous amounts of furniture polish.

Smash Hitz didn't have anything on Misty. She'd taken his idea and run away with it.

There was one problem though; Misty didn't have enough "tables" to go around. Misty had to insist that each guest take a number.

When Happy Hubby's wife picked the first number, she squealed with excitement and raced over to Horatio, slid beneath his strong body, pulled his loincloth to the side and immediately got to sucking.

After everyone received a number, long lines began to form behind all the masculine "tables."

"Sailor," Misty whispered. "Let them get their own wine. You did enough serving. Can't you help out with some of this work?"

Sailor frowned. His bottom lip quivered. "You said I didn't have to do that anymore."

"Look at all this money standing around."

He squirmed. "I know, but…"

"Don't you wanna go to college?"

"Yeah."

"Aiight then. Grab a bitch if that'll make you feel better. Don't you see all those women checking for you?"

"No, I didn't notice."

"Well, I did. Get out of that monkey suit. And go get naked. I'll broker the deal. You be waiting inside one of the bedrooms. You can at least appreciate the fact that I'ma let you do your work in private." Misty gave him a tight smile. "Play with yourself while you're waiting. Do whatever you need to do to get a big boner. Aiight?"

Sailor nodded unhappily.

"Stop looking all sad, Sailor. It's not the end of the world. This shit is bringing in the bucks. I'ma break you off. Put something nice toward your college fund. For real." She nodded her head as she spoke, trying to convince herself to actually be a woman of her word.

So far tonight, she'd collected a quarter of the money that Smash Hitz had offered her. But she had her eye on the dicks that were being sucked, and she was running a tab in her mind. It was obvious that before the night was over, she would make much more than fifty stacks.

CHAPTER 37

Misty couldn't be everywhere at once. Controlling her business while trying to control Spydah took a great deal of effort. She despised Smash Hitz, but in order to keep tabs on Spydah, she had to travel with him sometimes.

Though she really didn't have time to be fucking around with a bunch of assholes on a concert tour, she had to keep her relationship strong. So she flew to Chicago and joined him at the United Center.

Now that she and Smash had beef, Misty was glad that Smash separated himself from the other members of the tour. She didn't linger on stage with Spydah. Hell no, she got the hell off stage well before Spydah's last song. She had no intention of bumping into crazy-ass Smash Hitz and his moving, human pillars.

Thank God this tour would soon be over. She promised herself she'd never listen to, talk about, or even think about Smash Hitz. Not ever again.

In Chicago, Illinois, Misty was racing back to the dressing room, trying to avoid Smash Hitz.

She opened the door and got the shock of her life.

Baad B was chillin' in the dressing room, working her jaws, chewing on gum, and fanning herself with a backstage pass.

Misty wanted to vomit.

"'Sup, Misty?" Baad said, looking slutty in some cheap hooker shoes. The girl had a crazy body. Her waistline looked like it was about eighteen inches, while her hips and butt were large and outrageous. In Misty's opinion, Baad looked like a slut. But most black men wouldn't agree with Misty's opinion.

"Who invited you?" Misty gritted on Baad B.

"Spydah."

"That's a damn lie. How'd you get that pass?" Accusingly, Misty narrowed her eyes at Tragic.

He held his hands up. "Don't look at me."

"Well, which one of y'all gave her that pass?"

"It wasn't me," Jru said.

"Look, heifa…I ain't travel all the way to Chicago to listen to you run your mouth. Me and Spydah got business together. Why you messing with him, anyway? You need to get with somebody your own age."

"Excuse me." Misty found her eyes glued to the hooker's cheap-looking, fake fingernails. *What the hell is wrong with Spydah? Why would he even risk being seen in public with this trick bitch? I'ma cuss him out the minute he gets off stage.*

"Spydah's only twenty-one years old. I heard that you're twenty-five."

"So what."

"You too old for him. You act like you think you're his mother. All in his business, tryna run his life."

"Who said I try to run his life?"

"Don't look at me." Again, Tragic raised his hands in surrender, but this time, he took backward skipping steps, as if he was enjoying the excitement.

"Spydah said it." Baad was way too close in Misty's face.

"Get this bitch out of my face!" Misty demanded, looking around, as if she expected one of Spydah's crew to jump up and beat the snot bubbles out of Baad B. No one made a move in Misty's defense.

"Make me get out your face." Bending down to Misty's height, Baad pushed her face even closer to Misty's...so close Misty could see inside her mouth, could smell the gum she was chomping on.

"I'm not going anywhere," Baad said, her mouth wide open. "Spydah sent for me. He's paying for everything... he paid for my transportation...my hotel bill..." Baad B started counting on her fingers like a little child. "And he told me to add up all my miscellaneous expenses."

"That's bullshit. You're a groupie."

Baad B rotated her neck, chomping down on a piece of gum. "You might think you know what you talking about, but you don't. I ain't no damn groupie. I'm a rapper. In fact, I'm *Spydah's* new artist."

Misty's eyes became wide with horror. Having a verbal dispute with this heathen was demoralizing and totally unexpected. But hearing that she was a signed artist was faint-worthy.

"That's right; his management team signed me up last week."

This pimply faced, ugly-mug hooker…This ghetto bitch with press-on nails and a horrible weave was all in her face talking trash.

Spydah and Larry came in the door. Spydah was drenched in perspiration from working hard on stage.

Baad B trotted toward him, grinning and giggling, with her arms outstretched, hands flapping in the air, acting like Spydah was her long-lost boyfriend, home from Afghanistan or somewhere.

"What the fuck is up with this chick?" Misty said, hand on her hip.

Spydah looked terrified. "Ain't nothing. Adam signed her to a contract. I'm just her mentor."

Still grinning, Baad B threw her arms around Spydah's neck. "Hey, Spydah. I made it."

"I see," he muttered, cutting his eye at Misty and squirming out of the hot-to-trot hooker's embrace.

"Aiight, everybody needs to roll out. Now! Me and Spydah gotta have a private conversation," Misty said.

"Roll out to where?" Tragic wanted to know. "We can't be hanging around in the hallway when Smash comes off stage."

"I don't care where you go. Go back to the hotel. Take a cab cuz me and Spydah ain't sharing the limo."

Misty shook her head. "No…not tonight. We need our privacy." Misty waved her hand. "Go on, y'all. I'm not playing. You too, Little B."

Baad B sneered. "My name ain't no Little B. It's Baad B with two A's—that's the short version of Bad Ass Bitch."

Looking distraught, Spydah covered his face. Larry took control of the situation.

"Go 'head, Baad. Go to the hotel. You and Spydah can talk business later."

"Spydah's not talking about nothing with her…not if I can help it!" Misty shouted.

🙖

In the hotel suite, Misty resorted to shedding tears.

"I thought you loved me," she whined.

"I do. Don't I buy you jewelry and all kinds of shit?"

"Yeah, you're very generous, but it doesn't mean anything if you're going behind my back, cheating on me."

"Ain't nothing but business between me and Baad. You gotta believe me, Misty."

"I don't feel like I can trust you." She shook her head.

"Yes, you can." He cupped her face. Looked deeply into her eyes. "I only invited Baad so we could talk about this track that we're gon' work on together."

"Why are you talking about a new track, when you're still promoting your debut album?"

"It was my manager's idea. When he saw her on stage with me in New York, he saw a lot of potential."

"For who? Adam ain't worried about you. You already have a career…and it's skyrocketing. You don't need any help from that nobody broad."

"Adam has this vision for me and Baad."

Misty sighed. *I hate Adam. I gotta get Spydah to stop listening to his greedy ass.*

"I wouldn't never disrespect you. I didn't realize you were coming to Chicago. You popped up out of no-where."

"I didn't know I needed an invitation. I thought I was making you happy by surprising you with a visit." She cried harder, her face pressed against his chest.

He stroked her hair. "I am happy. Don't cry, Misty. I'm sorry about all this. I hate to see you acting all broken-hearted." Tenderly, he wiped her tears. "Come on with that. Stop crying. Be the strong woman that I fell in love with. What can I do to make this better?"

If Spydah's fans only knew….they'd be shocked to find out that his life doesn't come close to what he perpetrates in his music. The nigga is weak. And all his bitchassness is starting to really get on my fuckin' nerves. What I gotta do to make this dickhead straighten his act up?

"Send that bitch packing. Seriously, I can't stand her." Misty's words were filled with venom. "I can't bear to look at her. I don't want to be in the same hotel with her. It's hard to deal with, knowing that I'm in the same state with her. She's so fucking ugly, Spydah. What's wrong with you? How could you associate yourself with someone who looks like that? She's fuckin' with your image."

"She look aiight."

"No, she doesn't. She looks stank. And triflin'."

"Adam already signed her. What can I do?"

"All you and Adam see is a big ass. She can't even rap worth a damn fuck. You know what, Spydah…if all it takes is a big ass to make you happy, I might as well end our relationship right now."

"I'm not interested in her like that. She's like a sister or a cousin."

"How is she like a sister? You met that bitch at your release party!"

"Her ass is not what I'm interested in. With me and her…I swear, it's strictly business. So this is how I'ma handle this…"

"How?"

"To make sure you don't feel insecure, I'ma send her back to New York. Aiight, baby?"

Misty sniffled, wiped her nose, and nodded her head. *Hallelujah!*

She'd won the battle. But that Baad bitch was forcing her hand. Misty was going to have to make some real slick moves. And very soon.

CHAPTER 38

Spydah's business manager called early in the morning.

Pulled out of a deep sleep, Misty was aggravated. The clock on the bedside table read eight-fourteen. *Damn, Adam is trippin'.*

Now that she was wide awake, she was curious about what Adam wanted at such an unreasonable hour of the morning. Hearing only Spydah's side of the conversation put her at a disadvantage.

"Put him on speaker," Misty urged.

Spydah turned his mouth down. Shook his head.

Misty folded her arms in anger. Spydah ignored her.

She reached over and picked up the receiver of the hotel phone and, in a loud voice, she ordered breakfast.

"Whatchu wanna eat, baby?" Misty said, making sure Spydah's manager heard her.

"I'm good." Spydah blew her off with an irritated hand gesture.

"You gotta eat something," Misty persisted.

"I'm talking business, baby. Come on with that."

By the time her food arrived, Spydah had finished his conversation with Adam and was pinching pieces of bacon off her plate.

"I knew you were gon' be hungry."

"I was too excited to think about food."

"Excited about what?"

"Adam got me the deal. I'ma be the new face for Banana Republic."

Misty frowned.

"What's the frown about? That endorsement is bringing in major paper."

"How much?"

He shifted his gaze. "It's not finalized yet. But it's gon' be crazy."

"I don't trust Adam."

"Whatchu getting at?"

"I'm trying to help you, Spydah. If you keep listening to your greedy business manager, you might as well set your money on fire."

"How you figure?"

"Your manager is getting twenty percent of all your earnings and he doesn't do anything to earn it."

"How can you say that? He reviews all the contracts, makes sure I don't sign nothing bogus."

"You don't need him. You only think you do."

"He got me the cover on *Upscale* magazine."

Misty gave him a look. "Oh, you think he pulled that off? Those *Upscale* people came at him. Know why? Because you're selling tons of records and they want to sell tons of magazines. All that Adam had to do was get you to sign the contract. Ain't like he's working up a sweat on your behalf. He's reading over paperwork that's coming through."

"Seems like you saying I don't need representation."

"I'm saying that a good entertainment lawyer can do what Adam's doing for you. And you get to keep a lot more of your own dough. Besides an entertainment lawyer, all you need is Larry...what's his job title?"

"Personal assistant."

"Okay, well, all you need is Larry and you need to put me on your payroll as a consultant. All those other leeches...Tragic, Mustafa, and Jru...man, they need to get cut. You keep rolling with them and I guarantee that you're going to get embroiled in some kind of lawsuits. Those niggas gon' drag you down. I can feel it."

Spydah frowned. "Man, I don't wanna hear that. I ain't gon' front on my homies."

"I don't like them. They're bad news."

"You don't like nobody associated with me."

"That's not true. I like Larry. And I trust him. He puts your interests ahead of his own. But that Adam... he's a shark. I want you to be careful. Don't believe everything he tells you." Deep in thought, she ran her fingers through her hair and shook it away from her face. "Where's my scrunchie?" She looked under the bedding to find the band to tie her hair back.

"Let your hair stay like that. You look as good in the morning as you do at night." Spydah was changing the subject.

"Tell me something I don't know."

"Stuck up and conceited, too."

"So I've heard."

"I love that about you. Your confidence. Your maturity."

"Oh yeah...you know your girl, Baad, said I was old enough to be your mother."

"She said what?" Spydah looked shocked.

"She said that you told her that I'm too old for you... that I try to act like I'm your mother."

"That's a lie. I ain't nevah say nothing like that. There's only a coupla years between us."

"I know. Tell that to your hoe."

"Come on with that."

"She is a hoe."

"She ain't *my* hoe."

"Whatever."

"How did this conversation change? One minute we were laughing, having fun, planning our future. Now you bring up Baad and look at you...you're burning up."

"I didn't get the memo about me and you planning a future together." She stuck her fork into a pile of scrambled eggs.

"You didn't? I told my assistant to send it." Spydah laughed as he picked up a slice of toast and started munching.

"Nope, I didn't get it. Why don't you tell me about our future together? I hope it includes me being more involved in your career. And by the way, don't stick your hand over here and try to broady my last piece of toast," Misty said, playfully rolling her eyes.

"Broady. You always using those whack, Philly terms." Spydah picked up a spoon from the breakfast tray and helped himself to some of Misty's scrambled eggs.

"Philly slang is better than that country shit y'all be kickin'."

"Who you calling country? Baby, ain't nothing country about Miami."

"I hate Miami."

"How you gon' hate one of the most poppin' places in the country. But I forgot…you hate everything. That's all you ever say."

"I don't hate you," she said sweetly.

"Aw, here we go. What do you want now?"

"I want you to tell me about your plans for our future."

"After all that you said, I don't know if you're gon' like my plans."

"Try me."

"Well, Adam's been looking at some property for me. And I'm about to invest…" He paused. "You ready for this?"

Actually no…since Adam is behind it. She smiled, however, and nodded.

"I'm about to invest in a crib. Ten thousand square feet. Basketball court and indoor pool. I want you to move in with me. I need you to keep my ass grounded."

Misty wrinkled her nose like something smelled bad. She couldn't hide her feelings. This was the worst news he could have given her. She didn't want to live anywhere with him. And she didn't want him blowing his dough on a stupid mansion unless he was buying it for her.

"What's wrong?"

"I'm not ready to pick up and leave Philly. I can't do that. Besides, you should have run it by me before you agreed to buy yourself a mansion."

"Man, you ain't my mother!" He yelled so loud, Misty winced.

"Calm down. Damn, Spydah. Chill."

"Don't fuckin' tell me what to do. I just did the most important thing in my young life. I bought a crib. And you throwing shade like I ain't accomplished nothing." Spydah yanked the breakfast tray from Misty's lap. Tossed it on the floor, kicked the silver lid, and then grabbed his foot, jumping and hollering from stubbing his toe.

Misty's mouth was wide open. Witnessing Spydah in a full-blown tantrum was shocking. And a little scary. Maybe they needed some space.

CHAPTER 39

Spydah walked out of the hotel room, slamming the door behind him.

Misty began packing.

Ten minutes later, he returned, eating a bag of Doritos he'd gotten from a vending machine.

He gawked at Misty's open luggage. "Whatchu doing?"

"What does it look like? I'm packing."

"What for? Don't you wanna go back to Miami with me?"

"You must be crazy."

He glanced at the mess on the floor…the overturned glass of orange juice, the scattered pancakes, potatoes, bacon and eggs. "Yo, I have a short fuse sometimes. I'm sorry."

"You need to call housekeeping," Misty said as she continued packing.

"Baby, come on. Don't leave."

"I'm not going to Miami with you. That short fuse that you have sometimes might get me killed or beaten half to death."

"I would never hurt you. Look…this is the deal. I'm frustrated because Adam said people are asking about you. They wanna know your background, how we met. I'm mad because I realize your background is shady. I can't tell the media that I met you when you sent some hookers to my hotel."

"Make something up."

"You don't get it. I'm 'bout to blow up. Adam is polishing up my image, sending out a message that I'm not your average rapper. I'm a role model."

"A role model? Have the executives of the products that you tryna endorse had a look at your ugly crew?"

"I'm the front man. The way my crew looks isn't the issue."

"So why is my background an issue?"

"You my girl. You the one in the public eye with me."

"So you expect me to stop running my business…drop everything and move to Miami?"

"Yeah."

"That's not going to happen. I'm not going to depend on your kindness, Spydah. I need my own money. I've been asking you for weeks to put me on your payroll. Why don't you tell the bloggers that I work for you? That should satisfy their curiosity."

"Adam is worried that if the media begins to dig into your life, they're going to find out that you're running a hooker business."

Dick slinging business is more accurate, but you don't know shit. "How does Adam know what I do?"

"Larry might have slipped up and told him."

Now I hate Larry, too. "How I get my money shouldn't concern Adam."

"He's looking out for my best interest. Seriously, I can't be associated with something that would ruin the image that Adam's working hard to build."

"So if you weren't the face for Banana Republic, my business wouldn't be an issue? Am I right?"

"Probably wouldn't even have come up. But now that we're getting offers for endorsements overseas...fruit juice, cereal and all kinds of stuff, Adam wants to make sure there aren't any skeletons in the closet that could hurt my image."

"So now, all of a sudden, I'm a problem. I'm in the way. I hate Adam! Hated him on sight. Can Adam do what I do for you?" She gave Spydah a suspicious look. "Hmm. Maybe Adam can. Maybe that's the problem."

"Whatchu saying? Don't even go there. That's real foul, Misty. Why you always throwing that shit up in my face? What we get into behind closed doors wasn't my idea. All of that freaky shit came from your mind, so don't point the finger at me, like I'm on some homo shit. I'm one hundred percent all man!"

"I'm just saying, yo. Adam must want you for hisself. He keeps filling your head with a bunch of bullshit. Nigga's on his grind, working overtime, trying to get me out of the picture."

"It's not even personal. He's looking out for my best interest, that's all. All I'm saying is...if me and you are going to be together, then you're going to have to stop managing those hoes."

"I don't like being told what to do."

"Stop making this harder than it has to be. Move in my new crib with me. I'll take care of you. You won't have to worry about where your next dollar is coming from."

"What about marriage? I wouldn't feel secure unless we were legally married," Misty said, watching his face closely.

"Married? Man, I'm only twenty-one. I'm not ready for that."

"Maybe we need a break from each other," Misty suggested.

"Nah, I don't want that."

"Then I need a break, Spydah. We need a break. You're asking a lot of me, but you're not really giving anything in return. I have to think about whether I want to give up my life in Philly and move to Miami."

Spydah's face lit up. "You're going to think about it?"

"Yes."

"How long is it gon' take?"

"I don't know," she snapped.

"Give me some idea."

Spydah's youth was really showing. And he was getting on Misty's nerves.

"A week or two."

He frowned. "After I handle the business with my house, I'm flying out to L.A."

"For what?"

"Work on some new tracks."

Good, working on music would take his mind off me. Give me some breathing room.

CHAPTER 40

Misty gasped and her eyes nearly bugged out of her head. She could feel the steam rising as she read that no-rappin' bitch's tweet again:

"Me and Spydah chillin' at poolside. Having lunch. Discussing upcoming tour."

Chillin' at poolside? What the fuck! He's supposed to be at the studio working on his album.

Spydah's number was programmed on speed dial. She pushed a button. Her call went straight to voice mail. *Oh! So, it's like that, nigga?*

Furious, she called Spydah's main man, Larry. Larry's phone rang and rang. He didn't pick up either. Pissed, she poked "end call" as hard as she could, wishing she had a receiver to slam down.

Next, she called Spydah's pompous manager. She got his ditzy secretary instead. She called the recording studio. Nobody knew where Spydah was or what time he was expected back.

She even called Spydah's room at the Beverly Hills Hotel. No answer.

This is some real bullshit.

Misty was perspiring, heart beating fast. She needed to take some action…beat that hoe's ass for tweeting about her man. Any fool could read between the lines. Baad B was insinuating that Spydah was eating her box out, munching on the lunch that she was serving between her legs.

Spydah deserved some major retaliation for putting her through this kind of anxiety. Enraged, she wanted to have her henchmen stomp Spydah's ass. She wanted to take a used Maxi pad and bitch-smack that no-rappin' hoe's face.

Who else could she call? Misty paced. His bull, Tragic…nah, she refused to lower herself by calling any of the worthless leeches that hung around Spydah.

She decided to leave him a threatening message. "I saw your bitch's tweet. You need to be tryna see about me. It's seven forty-seven in Philly. You got ten minutes to return my call."

Feeling like she'd accomplished something, Misty waited as time ticked by. At seven fifty-eight, she had no choice but to take action.

She picked up her phone, scrolled to a name. Stared at it. Took a deep breath and hit the CALL button. Pressing that number gave her a thrilling sensation that must be similar to detonating a bomb.

"Who dis?" he said gruffly.

"It's Misty." Her voice was a sweet melody.

"Lemme call you back," he said in his gravelly voice that emanated power.

The line went dead. Misty's heart dropped. That ego maniac bastard was playing mind games with her. But in order to hit Spydah where it really hurt, she would have to play along with Smash Hitz.

Her phone rang. But it wasn't Smash. It was Spydah, finally returning her call.

She unleashed her wrath on him. "Working hard at the studio?" Her voice heavy with sarcasm.

"Oh, I ain't go."

"I know you didn't. You too busy sitting at poolside fucking with that bitch," she snarled.

"That wasn't about nothing. Promotion move. You know the game."

"That bitch is deliberately giving people the impression that you got your tongue imbedded in her funky twat," she snarled at him.

"Come on with that, Misty. She's only doing her part to boost ticket sales."

"That ain't her job. You got promoters that handle that aspect of the business."

"She's overly excited. First big tour—"

"Fuck you, Spydah. And tell that no-rappin' bitch she's lucky that I don't smack the taste outta her dumb-ass mouth."

"It's not that serious."

"Don't fuckin' tell me what's serious. But you know

what, Spydah…if you can't control the behavior of the people on your tour, then you're not man enough to be with me."

"You had to take it there."

Misty knew how to hurt Spydah. Any mention of his masculinity was a low blow to him. "I'm just saying…"

"Why you talking to me all grimy? Ain't nothing going on between me and Baad B. Look, if it'll make you feel better, I'll tell her to call you."

"Fuck outta here. The damage is already done. You and that hoe deserve each other. Tell her I said she can call me if she wants some pointers on how to really keep you satisfied. Never mind, I'll tweet it. Let the whole world know how you like to get down."

"How I get down? You calling me out on some fag shit?"

"If the shoe fits."

"That's a fuckin' lie!" Spydah shouted. "What about all that shit you was kicking about what goes on behind closed doors?"

"Whatever."

"You dirty, Misty."

"Fuck you, pussy." Misty ended the call.

Spydah called back repeatedly, but she hit the IGNORE button on all of his calls.

CHAPTER 41

The next six months had gone from bad to worse. Baad B was always on Spydah's arm. The tabloids had them linked as a couple and it was driving Misty insane.

Spydah claimed that their relationship was some hype... a fake romance that Adam had concocted. A publicity stunt.

But Misty really started getting nervous when the media publicized that Baad's new Mercedes was a gift from Spydah. Of course, he denied it, claimed that Adam had bought the car.

Making matters worse, Baad's new CD had dropped and, overnight, the trampy hooker had a tremendous teenage following.

With her own career taking off, Baad B was getting out of control, tweeting all kinds of shit. Just this morning, Misty read something that made her eyes pop.

Baad B tweeted:

Forgot to take morning after pill. Guess I'll have to piss on a stick. Will keep you posted. Might be nice to have a new addition inside the web. Oops. I meant...inside the crib. ☺

Baad B was a fuckin' attention-seeking, industry whore. Throwing hints to get people talking. Spydah's fans knew that he always referred to his crib as his Spydah Web.

Baad B was putting it out there…insinuating that she was pregnant with Spydah's little insect.

Sailor came into Misty's bedroom slash office, giving her the daily report. His business update fell on deaf ears. Misty was too furious to concentrate on business.

"Stop fucking telling me everything, Sailor. What do I pay you for? Stop running in here every five minutes. You know what I like. Handle it the way I would. Damn! Can I get a fuckin' break?"

"Okay…" Confused, Sailor began backing away.

Sailor had let his hair grow out over the past few months. His reddish curls were now so long, he kept his hair back in a man's ponytail. He looked hot! But not hot enough to take make Misty melt. Maybe later, but definitely not right now.

After Sailor closed the door, Misty narrowed her eyes at the computer monitor. Read the tweet once again, as if perhaps it had changed. Fury caused her vision to blur. She regarded the female rapper's tweet as a personal taunt.

I hate that bitch. I want her dead! Blacking out, Misty began knocking shit off of her desk. She shattered an antique desk lamp. Sent a crystal picture frame crashing into the wall.

Something had to be done. Spydah was putting her through all kinds of hell. Constantly lying about his relationship with that no-rappin' bitch.

Swallowing her pride, she called Smash Hitz again. She got one of his assistants, and left a message.

Shockingly, a few minutes later, Smash Hitz called her back.

"You ready to stop cheering for the pee-wee league? You ready for the majors?" he said. She could imagine the smirk on his face.

She took a chance and released her feisty side. "You should be asking yourself if you're ready to get misty."

Smash Hitz chuckled. "Oh, yeah, that's right. I forgot. According to your name and your reputation, you be leaving niggas weeping."

"Oh, you heard about me, huh?"

"I know you had my artist, D.B. Spydah, sprung like a mufucka."

Had him sprung? If Smash Hitz worded her relationship with Spydah in past tense, then Misty had to accept that Spydah had moved on...with that ugly-mug bitch.

"Weeping and sobbing is for suckas. I'ma big boy. And big boys don't cry. So, bring it, pretty lil' mamacita."

Along with a collection of Louis Vuitton luggage, and a big bruiser named Horatio, Misty accepted Smash Hitz' challenge...and she brought it!

Horatio was there for back-up. Smash had bank, but he also had serious mental issues. After his stunt in the Gold Room, Misty knew that the man was unstable.

She brought a henchman of her own, in case Smash decided to try to get rough.

The first-class flight from Philly to Miami had been extremely pleasant. But she also realized that Smash enjoyed lulling his victims into a sense of security before showing his sinister side. If that bastard wasn't worth billions, Misty wouldn't even be wasting her time.

Inside Miami International Airport, as Misty and Horatio glided down the escalator, she mentally braced herself, wondering what annoying issues lay ahead. Anything could go wrong. Fooling with Smash Hitz was like playing Russian roulette.

Smash said he'd have a car waiting for her. Annoyed, she pulled out her cell, expecting to have to call one of his people to get information about her ride.

But downstairs, there was an assemblage of men wearing black caps holding signs with names on them… like that shit you see in the movies.

What a surprise when she noticed that one of the men was carrying a sign that read: *Misty Delagardo.*

Aiight, Smash. I'm impressed so far. Misty walked jauntily toward the older, Caucasian man. "I'm Misty Delagardo."

A look of surprise glinted in his eyes. She supposed he had expected a blonde-haired, white woman from Spain.

Caucasians aren't the only people with bank, you know.

The driver smiled, and then cut a glance at Horatio. "You're a big guy…you play for the Dolphins?"

Here he go stereotyping us. Why Horatio gotta play football in order to have a limo waiting?

Well-trained by Misty, Horatio didn't respond. He merely grunted, and then put on a mean, intimidating facial expression, refusing to appease the chauffeur's curiosity.

Put in his place, the driver restrained himself from being overly friendly, and assumed a more professional demeanor. He straightened his shoulders and stood erect like he was paid to do. "Ma'am, do you have a lot of luggage?"

"Depends on what you consider to be a lot," Misty responded.

The driver released a nervous chuckle. "There's an awful lot of black suitcases spinning around."

"Mine is Louis Vuitton. Four pieces."

"Oh, that won't be a problem. Your luggage will be easy to locate."

As soon as Horatio's single duffel bag came around, he grabbed it. In Horatio's big hand, the bag looked like a little pocketbook.

The Louis Vuitton luggage appeared, and the driver began tussling, particularly with the trunk.

"Should I help him out?" Horatio asked.

"Yeah, go ahead. Otherwise, we're going to be in this airport for the next three hours."

CHAPTER 42

The driver was perspiring. His face was red. Misty didn't blame him for waving over a skycap to push the heavy luggage. With his burden lifted, the driver led Misty and Horatio to a black Lincoln Town Car.

"Damn, it's hot," Horatio commented, pulling off his leather jacket.

"I told you not to wear that jacket with its thick-ass lining, but you wouldn't listen."

Misty had expected spring-like weather, but the temperature was unseasonably high, forcing her to come out of her lightweight denim shrug.

She hated Miami. Hot as a bitch. Too many different types of bugs. It wasn't hurricane season, but you never knew when a killer hurricane would strike this area. But here she was stepping off a plane in Miami.

As soon as Misty slid into the back seat, she pulled out her cell and began texting Smash, letting him know that she had arrived safely and was on her way to the hotel.

Smash texted back: *I'll get at you later*.

Cool, nigga. Ain't nobody sweatin' you. I'm good. She closed her eyes, trying to strategize. Smash Hitz wasn't your average wealthy mufucka. He had game like nobody she'd ever dealt with before. Just because he had promised to treat her to a few days in the sun here in Miami, and then fly her out to Los Angeles for the Grammys didn't mean a thing. He'd proven in New York that he'd flip on you in a second. Being his date for the Grammys…well, she'd believe it when it happened. Right now…she was taking it moment by moment.

As the Town Car traveled across the bridge into South Beach, Misty could feel the vibe change. There was a different type of energy. One side of the bridge was lined with million-dollar homes, white swaying yachts, and crisp aquamarine water that could be seen in every direction. On the other side of the bridge, there were enormous cruise ships and cargo boats.

"Wow. Look at all those yachts. That shit is crazy." Horatio couldn't contain his enthusiasm, which gave the talkative driver another opening.

"First time in Miami?"

"Yeah, I've been to Orlando, but not Miami," Horatio blathered.

Misty shot Horatio the mean mug. Horatio kept his big mouth shut for the rest of the ride.

When the driver pulled up in front of the Ritz-Carlton on Lincoln Road, Misty whispered to Horatio, "Deal with the baggage and tip the driver." She strutted to the front desk and waited to be checked in.

There were several bouquets of flowers on display...
red and pink roses, compliments of Smash, Misty assumed.
The décor was sophisticated and chic and with every
modern convenience.

"This jawn is about as big as your apartment. How
much something like this run?" Horatio asked.

"I don't know, but I'm sure it costs a grip."

"Smash got deep pockets; I wouldn't be surprised if
he paid a thousand a nut for this dip."

Misty looked at Horatio. "This is living," they both
said at the same time and then fell out laughing.

"Yo, all I know is Smash understands how to treat a
lady. This is some rich shit. I can get used to this."

"Smash got us rolling first-class all the way," Horatio
added.

"The Grammy parties are going to be off the chain. I
don't know if we're going to L.A. Reid's or EMI's after-
party, but I have to be red carpet and paparazzi-ready."

"We?" Horatio said.

"Not you. I'm talking about me and Smash. Damn,
Horatio, fall back with your thirsty-ass self. You got a
free trip to Miami. Ain't that enough?"

"I'm just saying..."

Horatio had a lot of nerve to think he deserved the
same perks she was getting. Rolling her eyes, she picked
up the hotel phone and called the concierge desk.

Before she opened her mouth, she heard a pleasant-
sounding male voice saying, "Hello, Ms. Delagardo, may
I help you?"

"Uh. Yeah. Hi. Um… I need some information. I want to go shopping. Can you tell me…uh…where is the closest mall?"

"I'll be happy to assist you. We're very close to a Macy's, and there are also a few boutiques nearby."

Misty turned up her nose. "I don't wanna go to Macy's. I need to get to a high-end mall. Macy's won't work. I need some real fly gear. You know…designer wear. Something that someone who's going to several Grammy after-parties would wear." Misty winked at Horatio.

"Oh, I see. Yes, ma'am. I can certainly help you with that," the concierge politely replied.

Uh-huh. You don't know nothing about this.

"The Bal Harbour Shops is only a few miles from here."

"The Bal who shops?"

"The Bal Harbour Shops is one of the most exclusive malls in the Miami area. You'll find a Dior store as well as Oscar de la Renta—"

"Now you're talkin' my language," Misty blurted, excitement building. "Dior is hot, but I'm not feeling that other designer. Any other designers at the mall?"

"Absolutely. The women's stores include: Carolina Herrera, Chanel, Chloe, Dior, DVF, Escada, Intermix, Lulu Couture, Max Mara, Miu Miu, Valentino, and Vera Wang…to name a few."

"Okay, I've died and gone to heaven. I have to get to that mall."

The man on the other end of the phone laughed politely. "Are you driving, ma'am? If so I can print out directions for you."

"No, I am not driving," Misty whined.

"That's not a problem. I can arrange for a car to take you to Bal Harbour, if you'd like."

The Bal Harbour mall sounded like the business. Misty experienced a million little tingles as she envisioned the shopping oasis. *All those designer stores under one roof!* Overwhelmed and titilated, Misty became lightheaded. She needed to collect herself.

"Let me think about it. I'll call you back."

"Yes, ma'am. Take your time. We look forward to taking care of your needs," the concierge said before hanging up.

Misty stared at Horatio. "Yo, they serious up in this joint. I dig the way they take care of the guests. Bastard was calling me ma'am, offering to order a car for us... talking to me like I'm Princess Di or somebody. Well, not Princess Di cuz she dead...but you feel what I'm saying?"

"Yeah."

"I'm serious, yo. This how we gon' be rolling from now on. First class. I can't accept less." Misty shook her head emphatically.

"Nah, we can't deal with flying coach no more. Them seats are way too small for me."

"I don't mean simply when we fly. I mean everything... hotels...the works. That damn Spydah kept sticking me in the Sheraton all the time. He act like he had half-price coupons for that dip. I'm through feeling like a second-class citizen. I like all this rich shit."

"Me, too," Horatio agreed.

"Get ready, yo. It's 'bout to pop off. You got to be down for whatever. You feel me?"

"I feel you, Misty." Horatio gave a firm head nod.

"I changed my mind about shopping."

"You got jokes."

"I'm serious. I might need five or six stacks when I run up in Bal Harbour and I'm not tryna dip into my cake. All my expenses should be on Smash."

"I don't know, Misty. You might be pushing it if you expect that man to pay for one of your wild shopping sprees."

"Hmph. After he sniffs this..." She patted her crotch. "He might as well prepare to become my official sponsor. Smash Hitz is gon' start picking up the tab for everything I want," she boasted.

"Aiight, if anybody can pull it off, you can."

"Wanna know what I really want?"

Horatio looked at her.

"A crib. Like a mini-mansion...something with six or seven bedrooms. My business is expanding and I need more space."

"Why don't you let the boys move into their own spots? You breaking everybody off. By now, everybody should be able to afford their own apartment."

"Nah, I like having my dick slingers in close proximity."

"Suppose I wanted my own crib...what would you say?"

"Do you?"

"Nah, I'm just asking. I'm curious."

"I'd let you leave...but you wouldn't get as much work as the boys who are under my roof and who remain loyal to me."

"I ain't going nowhere, Misty. I was just asking."

Hmm. I'ma have to keep an eye on Horatio.

CHAPTER 43

A very pompous member of Smash's organization called Misty's cell. The man identified himself as Mr. Hitz' assistant. He was extremely articulate, with a voice of authority that reminded her of a newscaster's. He enunciated every word, sounding real fake.

The fake-ass assistant told Misty that a car would be sent to pick her up promptly at five o'clock. "Please be punctual. Mr. Hitz is a very busy man."

"I gotchu, boo. Don't even worry about it. I'ma be ready. It's all good. Y'ah mean?" She laughed to herself, hoping that her street talk was as offensive as she'd intended. *Punk-ass*.

Five o'clock was several hours away. With time to kill, Misty told Horatio to order room service. "Get whatever you want."

Horatio perused the menu. "Man! These prices are steep."

"Why you worried about it? Our meals are all on Smash's tab."

While Horatio waited for his feast to arrive, Misty changed into a tube dress. She put on a pair of beaded flip-flops, and took a stroll down to the beach. The sand between her toes irked her. The blue water was pretty, but she didn't want saltwater or any seashells or shit to come into contact with her fresh pedicure. *That's enough beach experience for me!*

After leaving the beach, Misty ended up on Ocean Drive. She was instantly impressed by the lively atmosphere. Restaurants—one after another—with outdoor seating lined the street. The scrumptious aromas that wafted from the cute little cafés made it hard for Misty to ignore that she hadn't eaten all day. But she was too excited to take the time to sit still and actually eat.

Moving along, she noticed that the color scheme of Ocean Drive's art deco architecture seemed to be from a palette of pastels…light yellows, pale pinks, baby blue, and soft peach.

Palm trees were providing shade for everyone eating outside. People of every nationality were milling about, but the Caribbean influence on Ocean Drive was quite distinctive. It seemed like Misty had left the States and had gone to some exotic locale.

People-watching was interesting. She noticed people zipping past on scooters, attractive couples holding hands as they strolled leisurely, taking in the scenery.

The street was jam-packed with expensive cars from Maybachs to Lamborghinis.

Perhaps her last visit to Miami had been in the wrong part of town, but now that she'd experienced ritzy South Beach, Misty was starting to like Miami a lot.

❧

After answering a zillion different questions and even being searched, the Town Car was finally allowed to proceed past the gate.

"Getting inside the White House is probably easier than getting in Smash's house." Misty was hot and in a sour mood, after being ordered to get out of the car so she and Horatio and the driver could be searched.

"I have to tell you in all my years of driving, I've never been put through a search. My God, did you see the way those security people went through my trunk?" the driver said, sounding like he'd enjoyed the excitement.

As the car traveled up a winding road, Horatio let out an audible sigh of relief. Misty closed her eyes.

"Oh, no," the driver said. "Another gate."

Misty's eyes popped open. "You gotta be kidding." She craned her neck. Unbelievably, there it was…another goddamn gate. This one was manned by three bulky men. All looking like they were overdoing the steroids.

"What the fuck is all this? This is getting ridiculous. Man, I should turn my ass around and go back to damn Philly."

"Be cool, Misty," Horatio said.

"No! I'm about to pitch a bitch." Misty stomped out of the car. Horatio followed, walking slowly.

The three men approached. "I need you to open your purse, ma'am?"

"Aw, come on. Not this same shit again." Misty was pissed. "You mean to tell me that we gotta get checked and patted down...again?"

"Yes, ma'am."

"All this 'yes, ma'am' and being polite don't do it for me, if y'all gon' be treating me like I'm some kind of a criminal."

"Just following procedures, ma'am."

"I hate Miami," she told Horatio. "People don't act like this in Philly," she complained, as she unclasped her purse.

Horatio shook his head at the injustice. He stood obediently with his hands behind his head, while enduring different pairs of strange hands traveling up his pants legs, into his pockets, and in and out of his shirt.

"Y'all some molesting mufuckas," Misty snarled as hands began to roam over her body parts.

"All clear," one of the three men said, talking into a mouthpiece.

"They on some Secret Service shit," Horatio muttered.

Intending to let Smash know how much she didn't appreciate the disrespect, Misty strolled up the cobblestone walk that led to the extremely tall set of double doors. Before Misty could reach for either of the enormous ram's head door knockers, the doors opened. A butler dressed in what seemed to be authentic butler gear greeted Misty and Horatio.

Crossing the threshold, they entered a marble-floored foyer area that split into three different directions. Misty looked around in awe. Palm trees and other potted foliage. A flamboyant chandelier dangled from a domed ceiling. Colorful murals decorated the walls.

"Follow me," the butler said. "This way, please."

Misty and Horatio fell in step behind him.

"That butler bull is on top of his game," Horatio whispered.

He took them to a sun-filled room. "We call this the Room of the Ram. Make yourselves comfortable. Mr. Hitz will join you shortly." The butler gave Misty a tight smile, and then left.

"Yo, can we move in?" Horatio chuckled.

Still standing, Misty gazed at the elegant furniture, the interesting rugs, and the drapery that was absolutely regal. She couldn't take her eyes off of the stone fireplace that was carved in the shape of a ram's head. "This room is awesome."

"This crib is serious," Horatio added. He turned in a complete circle. "Yo! This jawn is crazy. Smash is on some Scarface shit."

Misty had never seen such opulence. Not in real life. No wonder Smash thought he could snap his fingers and have mufuckas jumping. Maybe she better act a little more humble. Smash didn't simply have bank...he probably owned a couple of small countries.

"Misty Delagardo."

Her head snapped in the direction of the voice. Smash had quietly entered the room. He was dressed casually in a T-shirt and a pair of jeans.

Misty wanted to say something flippant...like, *Living like this, I expected you to be on some James Bond ish...I would have expected you to enter the room more dramatically, like from a secret tunnel or float down from that high-ass ceiling, wearing some type of cape.*

But instinct told her to tone down her sarcasm. "Good to see you, Smash," she said politely, and offered her best smile.

CHAPTER 44

"You're looking better than ever. My bad about New York. I had too much to drink that night."

"That's in the past," she said graciously. She was proud of herself for coming across as seeming calm and collected, when she was actually freaking out inside.

"Have a seat." Smash made a gesture.

Misty and Horatio sat next to each other. Smash stood in front of them.

"I dig the way you brought your own protection."

Misty looked over at Horatio and shrugged. "Seemed appropriate."

"What's your name, my man?"

"Uh…Horatio." Horatio cleared his throat. Coughed. He was nervous and couldn't conceal it.

"Uh-Horatio," Smash mocked him, laughing. "Nice to meet you, big man." Smash reached out to shake Horatio's hand.

Courteously, Horatio stood up. He towered over Smash Hitz, his giant hand swallowing Smash's.

"Is Uh-Horatio going to check on you while we're in the bedroom?"

Misty's gaze flashed to Horatio. "Does he need to?"

"Not at all. You're safe with me. I don't bite." Smash laughed again. "Only if you want me to."

"Nah, I'm good," Misty said, laughing. Smash had a set of beautiful teeth. Nice and white. Very expensive dental work. His teeth looked healthy and strong. Like they could hurt something.

"Whatchu feel like getting into, Uh-Horatio? You wanna take a swim? Watch a movie? Hang out in the game room?"

Smash is taking that Uh-Horatio business way to the extreme.

Horatio's mouth spread into an uncomfortable smile. "Uh…I'm okay."

Get it together, Horatio. You supposed to be my bodyguard. Stop stuttering; you making me look bad, man.

Smash looked a little irritated. "Whatchu saying, man? You gon' sit in this room and stare at the walls? Is that all you want to do?"

"He wants to hang in the game room," Misty affirmed, helping Horatio out.

"Aiight, my man. Mr. Butler will escort you to the game room in a few."

"Your butler's name is actually Mr. Butler?" Misty asked.

"That's what I call him. Mr. Jerry Butler…a cool crooner from back in the day."

Smash Hitz lost Misty with the cool crooner shit.

Maybe her mom would know who he was talking about.

Like the other rooms she'd seen, Smash's bedroom was like something from a movie. His bed was on some Arabian Nights ish and was centered in the middle of the vast room. The walls on one side of the bedroom were made of overlapping thick sheets of tinted glass with water shooting upward. "Your bedroom is awesome. Those walls with that water—"

"That's my wall fountain, baby. Keeps me calm when I have a lot on my mind."

She nodded like she understood, but she really didn't know what else to say. She'd never seen a wall fountain.

Over top of one of Smash's dressers was a huge, ornate wood carving of a ram's head.

"I like that, too. You're really into rams," she acknowledged.

"I'm an Aries...the sign of the ram," Smash explained. "Being a ram, I go hard. I don't ask for permission...I feel entitled. If I see it and I want...I take that shit." He looked at Misty and chuckled. "Like you. I let Spydah have his fun, but playtime is over. It's time for you to be with a full-grown man."

No wonder Smash had stayed on top of the charts for all of these years. His game was tight on wax and one-on-one, in person.

What he'd said about her needing to be with a grown man was a valid point. She completely agreed. *Absolutely!* she wanted to say, but decided to keep that thought to herself. Maybe she'd get more out of this relationship if she played a little hard to get.

Smash was known to love 'em and leave 'em. Why would he treat her any different? She was gorgeous, for sure, but so were all the women he'd been involved with over the years.

Being realistic, Misty realized she'd be lucky if she got any real money from Smash. He was also notorious for being tight with his dough. She'd simply play her part and take it moment by moment. Spydah was going to be her real cash cow.

As Smash took her on a tour of his personal suite of rooms, Misty couldn't help from making little sounds of admiration at his interior designing skills.

Damn, now she wanted a mansion. Or at least a mini-mansion. No wonder Spydah and everybody else was riding for Smash Hitz. Smash was the man.

"You realize that Grammy date comes with some conditions," Smash said, taking off his shirt. His chest and abs looked alright...like he'd put in a little work.

She was glad she wasn't feeling him all like that. If that were the case, she'd be in a very vulnerable position. Luckily, all she wanted was whatever Smash was willing to come up off of. Having a little of his money, power, and influence was a major come-up.

Misty had never thought she'd play herself like this... give up some coochie for a front seat at an awards ceremony. But it was more than that. She needed to get

Smash into her grips to teach Spydah a lesson. She probably couldn't keep a hold on Smash, but rolling with him for a hot minute would motivate Spydah to leave that ugly trick alone and maybe after the Grammys, Misty would be able to persuade Spydah to put her on his payroll. Make up some shit that he says she does for him. His stupid gifts were getting old. She needed some regular income from him.

Misty went into role-playing. Looking at the big picture…a financially solvent future…she convinced herself that Smash was sexy and desirable as she slowly…seductively…stripped out of her clothes.

"Little and luscious," Smash said, looking at Misty and licking his lips like she was a gourmet delicacy. Smash's dick wasn't erect yet, but even so, it was obvious that he didn't have much of a package. *Damn, Smash Hitz got a lot of nerve snapping at people, knowing he walking around with that little-ass dick.*

But this house is bangin', she told herself as she strolled over to Smash. *This is how I'm supposed to be living. I don't care if he ain't holding.*

Smash sat down on a luxurious white chair. That white fabric against his black-velvet skin was an intriguing sight.

Instead of continuing her sexy swagger, she stopped mid-strut. Like an experienced belly dancer, she used soft, rolling hip patterns as she lowered her body to the floor.

CHAPTER 45

B eing on her hands and knees was not an act of submission. She felt the confidence of a cunning animal—a patient hunter that had spotted prey. Feeling predatory…her senses on high alert, Misty was on all fours. Crouched. Muscles rigid. Unmoving.

Stimulated by this provocative display of undisguised, primal sexuality, Smash adjusted his position, wiping away perspiration from his brow. The aroma of masculine sweat broadcasted his arousal.

Misty went into action—her sleek, naked body crawling confidently as she crept in the direction of his scent. Like a tigress going in for the kill, she stalked the mighty ram, her movements calculatingly slow and sensual.

She felt almost light-headed from the primal heat that ignited and charged through her body.

Smash's breathing became harsh and uneven as Misty drew closer.

But instead of pouncing with savagery…instead of forcibly subduing him, like a ravenous tigress, Misty's aggressive seduction evolved into a performance that was comparable to that of a gentle kitten.

Gently, she lapped at his scrotal sac, felt it tightening...tensing against her lathering tongue.

A low growl rumbled from Smash. "You working that tongue, baby." His fingers grazed through her hair. "Pretty hair," he muttered, his splayed fingertips coursing across her scalp, lifting the silken curtain of her ebony tresses. Then he got rougher...seizing a fistful of hair. Tugging. Yanking roughly, as he guided her mouth to his awakened dick.

"Suck it," he demanded. His voice hoarse and guttural. Caging her head between his hands, he held Misty in place as he rose from the chair.

Her murmured protests were weak. Smash didn't seem to hear her.

It was clear that the tables had turned. The ram had taken control.

Before she could make herself heard, a defiant dick stabbed at her lips. Thrusting hard, he forced her mouth open. Engaged in an oral invasion, his stiff dick poked and probed. Luckily, Smash's dick wasn't bulky enough to do any real damage.

"Suck!" he demanded, standing over her, gripping her cheeks so hard, she was unable to move her jaw.

Too impatient for her to leisurely work her way from his nut sac to his shaft, Smash was going wild, trying to violate her mouth. Misty shouldn't have been surprised; he'd already warned her that he enjoyed taking whatever he wanted.

"Whatchu waitin' for? Show me your oral skills," he said gruffly. "Give me a reason to walk you down the red carpet."

How the hell do you expect me to get a grip on your dick with my mouth wide open? You got me cocked and locked, mufucka.

Impatient and frustrated, Smash released Misty's face. He sank down on the white chair, his defeated dick sagging between his thighs.

"For some reason, I'm not feeling you. Had I known you were all show…no substance, I wouldn't have wasted my time. Hell, I could have called in some big-titty smuts from the porn industry, but I was trying to give you a shot."

Smash's arrogance was maddening. *Ain't nobody tell this deranged bastard to squeeze my jaws so tight, that he had my mouth stuck open like a damn goldfish.*

He was the one that had created the tension, but he was pointing the finger at her.

Smash in on some nut ish, but damn, I'm not tryna waste my time either. I got too much riding on this. I'm too close to the red carpet to slip up now.

She could imagine Grammy night…the excitement of flashing lights, big-money connections, hobnobbing with the rich and famous. Shit, she'd already dropped a knot at the King of Prussia mall before she flew out of Philly. Putting together a wardrobe for the Grammy after-parties wasn't cheap.

Smash's hand was resting lazily on his soft dick. "Damn,

what time is it? I have a meeting with some developers. Have to talk to them about the hotel I'm having built in Vegas."

Smash was getting restless; Misty had to think fast. Since Smash had mentioned hiring a porn star, an idea entered Misty's mind. "Hey, Smash…you said you like watching porn, right? Well, I have a suggestion." She lowered her lashes, and gave him a coy smile.

Unimpressed, Smash looked up at her briefly, then shook his head…glared at Misty like she was a terrible waste of human life.

Smash leaned forward. "You think my eyes gon' pop outta my head over a smut bitch that's trained to fake a loud orgasm?" Smirking, he waved his hand. "Fuck outta here. I'm a majority shareholder in LiveSex TV network. Any porn you brought here was probably made by one of my companies," he said with a sneer.

This nut-ass acts like he owns a piece of every damn thing.

Conscious that gun-toting men were a few finger snaps away, Misty said, "I was thinking me and Horatio could put on a show for you."

"Oh, yeah? You and the bodyguard?"

"Yes, my bodyguard has multiple talents. He not only protects me, but he also serves me."

Looking more interested, he sat back and grinned.

"I'd like to see that." He got up and threw on his pants. Walked over to a table, picked up an expensive-looking pen. He clicked the little tab on the end of the pen.

Not more than five minutes later, the butler walked in.

What the fuck? In New York, Smash was snapping his fingers; at his home he clicked on a pen to get shit poppin'. He could have at least given me a warning, so I could cover my-self up.

Smash walked his butler to an adjoining room. He spoke softly to Mr. Butler, but Misty clearly heard Horatio's name, and presumed that Smash was sending the butler to fetch Horatio and bring him to his bed-room.

Now Misty was nervous. Horatio was well-hung; his bedroom skills were on point. But being around Smash Hitz had him acting nervous…had her worker all wound up and off his game.

She needed a good performance from Horatio to solidify her deal with Smash. She crossed her fingers, hoping that Horatio could relax and perform for the rap icon.

She thought of Chicago, and the way she had ordered Spydah to send Baad B home. *Karma's a bitch. If Horatio doesn't bring his A-game to the bedroom, Smash is gon' send my ass packing.*

"Grab your stuff if you want to…" Smash pointed to Misty's clothes that were in a heap on the floor. "I can't have a lot of traffic and strange niggas up in here. I'ma watch the freak show in another room. Come on." He motioned for her to follow him.

Misty grabbed her skirt, purse, and the rest of her

belongings, figuring if Smash decided to push another button or snap his fingers, she needed to be ready when the clean-up crew swooped down.

🙶

Horatio didn't have a clue why he'd been summoned. His eyes were as big as saucers when he entered the beige and black bedroom.

"I'ma leave you two alone for a few," Smash said and left the bedroom.

Naked and comfortable in her nudity, Misty plopped on a chair. "You're not gon' believe this bullshit."

"What happened?" Horatio scowled, his voice was raised in emotion, as if he expected to hear that some-one had died.

"Smash's dick went soft while I was giving him some oral. Nigga had the nerve to say he ain't feeling me. Can you believe that?"

Horatio didn't utter a sound. It seemed as if his wide-eyed expression wasn't going to change until he found out why he'd been summoned upstairs.

"I had to come up with something quick...or this trip was going to end in a real disaster."

Horatio nodded. His eyes went back to their normal size, but the scowl on his face urged Misty to continue.

"So, I told him that we could put on a freaky sex show for him."

"Who?"

"Keep your voice down," she scolded.

"Who?" he whispered.

"Me and you."

"Doing what?" Horatio managed to pull off a whispered shout.

"Now is not the time for you to go soft on me, Horatio."

"I'm saying…I didn't come down here for nothing like that."

"Shit happens. You promised to be down for whatever, remember?"

"I didn't realize you was talking about putting on a live sex show." He clasped his chin. "For Smash Hitz! That's out of my depth."

"You earn your living doing sex jobs, so stop frontin'."

"I can't deal with this. How do you expect me to switch gears like that? I been a fan of that man's…watching him on TV and on stage since I was in ninth grade. Now all of a sudden, I'm supposed to take my clothes off and put on a freak show for him. I can't do it."

"You have to!"

"Nah, man. I can't."

Misty grabbed Horatio's hand. "This is make or break time. Follow my lead. I'll get us started—"

"Where Smash gon' be at?"

"Probably sitting in that chair." She pointed to a chair that faced the bed.

Horatio dropped his head. Scratched his scalp. "I don't know, man."

"Take your fucking shirt off. I'm not gon' let you screw this deal up."

"Whatchu mean?" Angry now, he threw up his hands. "How you gon' make me do something? Whatchu gon' do...rape me?"

Chuckling, Smash Hitz entered the room. "If I see lil' Misty raping you, big man, this freak show will be turned into a comedy routine. And I didn't bring y'all down here to amuse me."

Misty went into character. "Is that what you want? You want me to take charge and have my way with you?" she asked in a flirty voice.

Smash said he didn't want any comedy, but the sound of his laughter told Misty that he was having a good time.

"Nah, I don't want that," Horatio said miserably. His eyes kept darting toward the open doorway.

Misty wanted to smack Horatio. *This is not a high school football game, and the threshold is not a goddamn finish line.*

She began to unbutton Horatio's shirt. He broke out in a sweat. *This fool is scared to death.* "Don't be scared, big man," she said breathily.

"Aiight." He stood still while she pulled his shirt off. He didn't budge...not even to help pull his arm through the short sleeves. Once she had his shirt off, she kissed her lip print that was tatted on his arm.

"What's that on his arm?" Smash asked, voice raspy.

"My brand," she murmured. Every time she saw her brand, she went into a coochie fit. Having so many pretty boys wearing her signature tat was an ego trip out of this world.

By the time she had Horatio down to his boxer briefs, Smash was behind her, breathing hard…so aroused she could feel the heat that crept over his skin.

Sandwiched between Smash and Horatio, Misty took a shuddering breath. She was down for a ménage, whatever it took to make Smash happy.

Smash's hands clenched her hips, and he moved Misty out of the way.

CHAPTER 46

"Misty called. She's in Miami."

"Oh, yeah," Brick said, feeling tense. He always felt tense when Thomasina brought up Misty. She had a way of upsetting the balance in his household without even being in town.

"Uh-huh. She said she's going to the Grammys."

"I thought the Grammys were in L.A."

"It is. She said she's flying out to Los Angeles from Miami."

"Misty's doing big things," Brick said. "Is she going with the same young cat that took her to the BET Awards last summer?"

"No. I don't think so. Somebody different. Another one of those rappers."

"Which one?" Brick was curious.

Thomasina looked up in thought. "Hitting Something...Breaking Records...I can't remember. It's one of those crazy rapper names."

"Don't tell me Misty's going to the Grammys with Smash Hitz!"

"Yeah, that's his name. Smash Hitz. Is he somebody important?"

"Is he?" Brick reared back like he was offended. "Smash is the man. Ain't nobody in the industry bigger than Smash Hitz. He created the game. And he's still in it. That's why she's in Miami. Smash runs that town."

"Oh, well, I'm glad you're a fan of his. Maybe now you'll go along with this idea that's been running through my head."

"What's that?" Brick looked at Thomasina suspiciously.

"I want to throw a Grammy party next week," Thomasina said.

"Here? At the house?" Brick frowned, shook his head.

"Why not? We need to try and start being a little more neighborly."

Brick laughed. "Neighborly? You want to invite the nosey neighbors to the crib?" He shook his head in disbelief.

"I figured it would break up the tension. Everyone else on the block are real chummy with each other. We're the ones that don't mingle."

"Well, you chose not to be sociable because they always tryna get in your business. Isn't that what you always say?"

Put on the spot, Thomasina squirmed. "I know... but—"

"You're the one that's always complaining that every time FedEx or UPS delivers a big box to the crib, everybody comes out of their houses and stands around watching like they spectators at a sports event."

"It's true. All conversations stop…and they stand as still as statues, watching the delivery people struggling to bring in the giant boxes. I get the impression that they expect a public announcement informing them of what's inside all the boxes."

"Yeah, but that wouldn't even be enough. After you tell 'em, they gon' want to know if we secretly hit the lottery or something. Any fool can see that my salary couldn't pay for all this expensive stuff."

"We have each other and that's enough. But I think it might be human nature for most people to be curious about the lives of others. That's why gossip magazines sell."

"We're not celebrities. So why do they give a shit about us?"

"Because of our age difference. Because you and Misty used to be a couple. And because we keep to ourselves and don't give them anything to talk about."

"So why can't we keep it like that? Seems like inviting people who don't like us into our home is only asking for trouble."

"I didn't say they don't like us. They probably resent us for not allowing them to be in our lives."

"Oh. They feeling some kind of way cuz we don't let 'em get all up in our business."

"You could put it that way."

"Like I said, we need to keep our business to ourselves."

"Baron...it's probably human nature for people to be curious about what they don't understand."

"Oh, now you want to make excuses for the nosey bastards that get on your nerves so bad, you hate to even go out front. If the back wasn't blocked off, you'd come and go through the back to avoid their curious glances. You told me that you can't even say hello without somebody using that as an opening to fire off some questions... 'How's Brick handling fatherhood? How come we never see Misty? Does Misty like being a big sister?' You said that they have no shame in their need to know what's going on in our home."

"I know."

"How about the time you caught that couple from across the street standing around our trash, reading the outside of an empty TV box. Everybody already knows what we get delivered. They make it their business to know."

"Most people probably share information with each other. We're the only ones that don't."

"We don't have to report to these neighbors. What... are we supposed to give everybody a breakdown of how we live our lives?"

"Not a report, Brick. Just mention some aspect of our lives. People feel that you're unfriendly when you don't tell them nothing."

"Let them think whatever they want to. Soon as you start telling people shit, trouble starts."

"You might be right." She shrugged. "I didn't always keep to myself like this, Baron. When I was living here alone, I was very friendly with the neighbors. It wasn't until after all that commotion with Misty…" Thomasina paused, took a harsh breath before she continued. "And after you and I became a couple, tongues really started wagging. Seems like the neighbors' level of inquisitiveness got out of control after you and Misty broke up."

"What's going on between you and me ain't nobody's business. Inviting curious niggas in the crib seems like we asking for all kinds of trouble."

"I know. I know. You're right, but since it's obvious everybody has been itching to see all the new stuff we have, I figured I'd invite them over for a Grammy party. Let them see with their own eyes how well my daughter is doing. Kill two birds with one stone. They get their curiosity satisfied and I get to show off my beautiful child…at the Grammys. How many mothers get to do that?"

Brick didn't like the idea one bit. Breaking bread with a bunch of snooping mufuckas wasn't the way he wanted to spend a special evening at home.

But Thomasina's heart was set on it. She was proud of her daughter and wanted to boast. Hell, he'd feel the same way if Lil' Baron was doing something special.

"Aiight, baby. But I don't want you slaving in the

kitchen. Let's do it up big—give them something to really talk about...call a caterer to cook and serve the food."

Seeing his wife's broad smile was worth putting up with a pack of gossip-mongers. And dipping deep into their savings.

CHAPTER 47

The hotel phone rang. Horatio jumped up, like he thought the call was for him. Getting it in with Smash Hitz had apparently gone straight to his head.

"I got it," Misty said with scorn. For Smash to prefer dick over coochie had been a surprising turn of events.

There'd been tension between Misty and Horatio ever since Smash had pushed Misty to the side so he could get on Horatio's dick. Misty accused Horatio of deliberately tempting Smash. Horatio claimed innocence. He said he was as shocked as Misty was when Smash started slobbering on his jawn.

Smash blamed his sudden desire to suck dick on being overly medicated. He said his muscle relaxants had him trippin'.

Yeah, whatever.

She had no clue if Smash was still taking her to the Grammys or not.

With an image of Smash Hitz on his knees, sucking Horatio's monster-sized dick, Misty angrily yanked the phone off the hook. "Hello?"

"Hello, this is Jules Miata. May I speak to Ms. Delagardo, please?"

"Who is this…Julius who?" Misty didn't recognize the voice but she could tell the man was gay.

"Jules Miata." The man spoke his name with great pride, as though he expected to hear Misty gasp with name recognition.

Who the fuck is Jules Miata? "This is Misty Delagardo. What can I do for you?"

"Mr. Hitz would like me to come over and get you ready for the Grammys. I'll take your exact measurements when I get there, but to get started, I'm going to need your shoe and dress size."

Relief flooded through her. *I'm going to the Grammys!*

"I wear size 4 shoes and a size three dress," she said calmly.

"Oh, you're an itty-bitty lil' thing. It'll be fun dressing you. I'm bringing some fabulous dresses to show you. We'll get your jewelry together after we settle on a dress. I can be at your hotel in an hour. Will that work for you?"

"Hold up! I don't mean any disrespect, but I'm not walking the red carpet in a gown you whipped up in your basement, Mr. whatever you said your name was."

Titters of laughter sounded on the other end of the phone. "Jules Miata," he said, laughing hard. "But call me Jules."

"I'm sorry, Jules, but I can't be seen in any of your

gowns. I need to be flossing something by a top designer. Smash gotta be crazy, tryna put me in front of the paparazzi looking 'hood rich."

Titters of laughter came across the phone. "Ooo, chile. We gon' get along. I like a woman who speaks her mind. Let me worry about which designer you wear to the Grammys, okay?"

"No! I don't want your gear. I want to get something from the Bal Harbour place with all those designer stores."

"Ms. Delagardo…is it okay if I call you Misty?"

"Yeah, I guess so."

"I don't care how glitzy Bal Harbour is, Smash Hitz would not appreciate it if you accompanied him to the Grammy Awards wearing something off the rack. Okaaay?" Jules sounded gay as all hell.

"So whatchu sayin'? I can't make my own decision? I gotta wear your homemade junk?"

"I'm saying that I'm a premier stylist. My clientele includes many A-list celebrities. I don't make clothes… I bring clothes."

"Oh!" Misty got it. Jules was going to bring her clothing from top designers for her to wear and promote. She wondered why Spydah hadn't sent her a stylist when they went to the BET Awards.

"Okay, I understand. I'm starting to feel you, Jules," Misty said with a smile.

"Good. I'll see you in an hour, chica."

"Okay." Misty twirled around like a happy child. *Gay*

boys definitely recognize how to make a bitch look fierce. I'ma be the flyest chick on the red carpet. Now tweet that, ugly-mug Baad bitch!

Smash paid Misty thirty stacks to keep his sudden lust for dick a secret. She broke Horatio off with five thousand. She planned to use most of the hush money to buy something fly from Bal Harbour, but now that she'd talked to Jules, she was happy to keep that money in her purse where it belonged.

"Who was that?" Horatio asked.

"Jules Miata. He's a celebrity stylist. Smash is sending him over to dress me for the Grammys."

"What about me?"

"What about you?" Misty made a face and turned her nose up at Horatio.

"What am I supposed to do while y'all out partying… stay back and chill at the hotel?"

Misty shrugged. *The nerve of this dick-slinging fool, giving me the third damn degree.*

"Can't I meet up with you and Smash somewhere? You know…after the awards."

"No, you cannot. In fact, you're not going to Los Angeles with me. You're going back to Philly. Smash is a client; he's not your boyfriend."

"Yo, I ain't say he was. I'm not gay."

"He's not even your friend, either. So get over it."

"Can't I ask a simple question? Dag," Horatio said, looking dejected.

An hour later, Misty sat in the lobby waiting for Jules Miata. Misty didn't mind waiting in the beautiful Ritz-Carlton lobby, which had large leather sofas and a golden-glow wall of lights.

Jules walked in. He was very tall and very gay. His swagger put Naomi Campbell to shame. But he wasn't cute. Not at all, but you couldn't tell him that.

Misty waved and he rushed over to her.

"Hey, Diva, how are you?" When he opened his mouth, Misty detected an unattractive overbite. *I would be so upset if I had buck teeth. Poor Jules. Shame he got an ugly-mug. His love life must suck. With those teeth, his blowjob must be a disaster.*

Jules was all smiles, revealing more of his overbite. "Your body is fire." He appraised her from head to toe. "Oh, girl, those dresses are going to look fabulous on you. My assistants will be here in a few. They're getting everything out of the truck."

This is exciting. Jules has a team of people to dress my tiny body!

"Lawd, look at all that hair." He stepped forward and quickly ran his fingers through Misty's tresses.

"It's real," she said with a smirk.

"I know! I'm just feeling for the kind of style that'll work with your hair type."

"You do hair, too?"

"Oh, no. I'll hook you up with a hair stylist in L.A."

Clipping his chin, eyes squinted, he studied her frame. "When I get finished with you, you are going to look absolutely stunning."

Though she felt she was already stunning, she smiled anyway.

"You're going to love the dresses I pulled for you."

"You didn't ask me the names of the designers I prefer."

"Names! Please don't tell me you're a label whore." As he shook his head pityingly, two women entered the lobby, carrying tons of bags on a rolling rack.

"Theses are my assistants...Paula and Venus." The two women smiled politely.

"Come on, girls, bring the rack to the elevator," Jules instructed and strutted toward the elevator.

Misty caught up with Jules. "Suppose I don't like the stuff you got on that rack. Then what?"

"I'm not worried about that."

"But you said you didn't bring anything by a well-known designer."

"There are a lot of red-soled shoes in those bags," he said with a chuckle. "And other expensive shoes. But the gowns are designed by up-and-coming designers."

Misty frowned. "Up-and-coming? Ew."

"Sweetie, you have to put your trust in me. I know what I'm doing. And when I dress you, you won't see your twin on the red carpet."

"I would hope not!"

"It happens. But not when you're dressed by Jules Miata."

❧

Jules and his assistants set up the living room area of the suite as if it were his personal studio. Paula busied herself lining up the shoes that Jules wanted Misty to see. Venus began pulling accessories out of one of the bags.

"I thought I was going to get my jewelry in L.A."

"I came across some special pieces that I couldn't resist," he said with a cheesy grin.

Venus set out rows and rows of accessories…necklaces, rings, bracelets, and big sparkly, chandelier earrings. "Most of those pieces are from Jennifer Fisher's line," Jules said with pride.

"Who the hell is Jennifer Fisher?" Misty was getting sick of this so-called stylist. For all she knew, he could have grabbed these trinkets from a thrift store. Nothing screamed Gucci, Fendi, or Louis Vuitton, or any recognizable names. For all Misty knew, Jules could have pocketed Smash's money and was trying to cut corners by sending her to the Grammys in Salvation Army wear.

"Jennifer Fisher provided Sarah Jessica Parker's jewelry for *Sex and the City: The Movie*. I see you in those gold hoops," Jules suggested.

After gazing briefly at the jewelry, Misty's eyes went back to the shoes, which were quite incredible. Looking like they cost a fortune, the shoes were making her lust.

"I want these," she said, picking up a pair of candy-jeweled shoes with a skinny heel. She read and tried to pronounce it.

"Giuseppe Zanotti." Jules enlightened her. "Those are fifteen hundred-dollar shoes."

"I don't need to look at any other shoes," Misty said, hugging the glittery shoes to her chest. "Now let's look at the dresses."

Jules unzipped black garment bags, and pulled out a variety of gowns and dresses. She shook her head at each item of clothing. And she said, "*Hell no*" to a pink sequin dress and a black dress with a big bow.

She began to pout. "You picked out this crap? I'm not impressed at all. In fact, I'm starting to get depressed."

"Now stop sulking, diva. I've dressed everyone from Zoe Saldana to Jada Pinkett Smith. Smash chose me for a reason. He values my opinion. I've personally selected an array of haute couture designs for you to choose from. Now let's not be too snooty, little diva. You're going to have to trust my fashion taste…like Smash does."

"Here, try this on." Jules handed her an aqua dress that had a long split up the side.

Who does this drag queen think he's talking to? Agitated, Misty walked into the bedroom with the gown. Horatio was lounging on one of the beds.

"Can I get some privacy?" Misty barked.

"Where do you want me to go?"

"Take a walk on the beach or something. Go sight-seeing or something. I don't care where you go."

Lazily, Horatio got off the bed. He clicked off the TV and slammed the remote on the dresser.

It's time for Horatio to go back to Philly. He served his purpose and he earned way more than I had originally planned to give him for playing like he was my bodyguard.

After Horatio left the room, Misty tried on the dress, expecting to hate it. Surprisingly, she didn't. The aqua number was extremely form-fitting. Flatteringly, it hugged the enticing curves of her body. She looked down and frowned. The dress was much too long. *Damn, times like this, being a little under five feet tall is a real drawback.*

Holding up several inches of extra fabric, Misty returned to the living room. "I really like this. But look…" She dropped the fabric and let it puddle around her feet on the floor.

Jules waved his hand. "That's nothing. My seamstress can take off those extra inches. Remember, I still have to measure you so that this dress fits you like a glove."

With a hand on his hip, his knuckles pressed against his chin, he studied Misty. "Let me see how the gown looks with those shoes you've become attached to."

Paula helped her try on the jeweled shoes. Misty walked over to a mirror.

Jules clapped his hand. "Work it, diva. Work it like you're on the red carpet, girl."

Misty looked in the mirror. Her eyes lit up. "I look beautiful!" she shouted as she spun around.

Jules wagged a finger. "Be careful with that delicate fabric, sweetheart. Wait until my makeup stylist gets finished with you…" He shook his head. "All those other hoes might as well sit down. Mark my words, Ms. Delagardo…tongues are going to be wagging after Grammy night. You might have to retain me as your personal stylist because you're not going to like the work of any other stylists…not in Philly, not in L.A., and certainly not in Miami…because I run Miami."

CHAPTER 48

Invitations had been extended to only ten neighbors. But everyone took the liberty of bringing along a friend who also brought a friend. Brick and Thomasina's tiny row home was filled up…wall-to-wall… with a pack of strangers.

While Thomasina was busy directing the caterers, Brick caught a shifty-eyed crackhead trying to slip in behind some of the in-vited guests.

"Yo! Beat it," Brick said, blocking the smoker's entry.

The man wore a filthy green Eagles jacket. The once shiny fabric was dull with multiple stains. "Can you spare some change for a hungry brother?" the man asked.

"Nah, man. This ain't the soup kitchen. Go 'head with all that begging." Angry, Brick closed the door in the drug addict's face. *Damn, it's fucked up when the town beggar be tryna squeeze up in yo' crib.*

The caterers were harried and overwhelmed as they tried to squeeze through the throng of loud-ass, ignorant people while carrying trays filled with glasses of white and red wines.

Billy from down the block came in wearing grubby work clothes and a big old, ratty-looking coat. When Thomasina offered to take his coat, he declined, complaining that it was freezing in her house.

"What's to eat?" Billy asked, taking a seat in a newly purchased light-colored suede chair.

It killed her to see Billy squatting in her chair; she wanted to point him over to one of the folding chairs that she'd rented for the occasion, but didn't want to appear to be rude.

Thomasina looked over her shoulder. "The food's coming out now."

"It's gonna take a couple dozen of these lil' things to fill me up," Billy said, laughing. With a big meaty hand, he grabbed as many bite-sized hors d'oeuvres as he could hold.

"What kind of TV is that...plasma?" a neighbor named Sarah asked.

"No, it's 3D." Thomasina tried to keep her voice even-toned; she didn't want to sound boastful.

"Umph. Somebody moving up in the world. A gift from your daughter?" Louisa from two doors down inquired.

"Yes, Misty is very generous."

"What exactly does she do for a living?" Sarah asked, eyebrows squeezed together.

"She works with the stars."

"Doing what?" Louisa, a big drinker, guzzled her wine

and reached for another when one of the caterers inched through the throng.

"Misty does consulting work," Thomasina said, sounding vague because she had no idea what Misty's job actually entailed.

"Uh-huh…" Louisa murmured with a question mark in her voice, expecting Thomasina to provide more details.

"Excuse me," Thomasina said, when she noticed Billy standing up and frowning down at the seat he'd been sitting in.

"I forgot I had my tools in my coat pocket," Billy said.

Thomasina looked like she was about to go into cardiac arrest when she saw the rip in her cushion.

A screwdriver had poked its way out of Billy's coat pocket. With all the twisting movements he'd made as he grabbed food and wine, he'd ripped up her chair. He stood up and shook his head at the damage he'd done. "I know a guy who can patch that up for you," he said and moved to one of the folding chairs.

"I don't think the chair can be patched up," Thomasina whispered to Brick.

"Sure, it can. We paid extra for that wear and tear plan. All we have to do is call the company. They'll come and pick up the chair and fix it. It'll look like new."

Relieved, Thomasina kissed him on the lips as if he had personally repaired the chair.

That one little gesture of affection caused all conversation to stop. All eyes on Brick and Thomasina. So Brick gave his wife a lingering, tongue kiss. Thomasina was very uncomfortable, but didn't pull back.

That intimate, prolonged kiss was more than any nosey neighbor had bargained for. A burst of nervous chatter suddenly erupted.

Misty was a vision on the red carpet, but murmurs from the neighbors about her scandalously revealing dress put a damper on Thomasina's spirits.

The three-hour Grammys show could have been more enjoyable had Thomasina listened to Brick and kept the viewing private.

Still, the camera loved Misty. Throughout the night, her expressions were highlighted. When Smash Hitz won an award for Album of the Year, the camera stayed on Misty's face until Smash climbed on the stage and began his acceptance speech.

One by one, the neighbors finally started trickling out. A few people had broadied the bottles of wine that hadn't been opened.

"How much did you spend on those caterers?" Sarah inquired. "You know, the average person wants to eat some real food when they come to any kind of event."

"I figured that anyone coming somewhere at seven o' clock should have already eaten dinner," Thomasina replied.

"If you took the time to get to know some of us, you'd realize that we work together."

"Mmm-hmm." The dig that she and Brick were not

very sociable with the neighbors didn't go past Thomasina, though she didn't comment.

"I could have headed up a food committee and we would all have been eating good in here tonight. We woulda pitched in and cooked up some fried chicken, pork chops, potato salad, and whatnot. The kind of food that sticks to your ribs. That stuff them caterers served was attractive, but it don't stick to your ribs."

"I'll keep that in mind for the next event," Thomasina said, taking note that Sarah had helped herself to a large heaping of hors d'oeuvres and had foil-wrapped the finger food. Thomasina could see the silver wrapping tucked inside Sarah's gapping pocketbook.

❦

Misty wore an aqua-colored chiffon Elie Saab gown to the Grammys. Being Smash Hitz' date for the event had unexpected perks. Misty's choice of the aqua chiffon number with the crotch high-split was no accident. She'd already envisioned the paparazzi attention she'd get when it "accidentally" revealed her neatly shaven landing strip.

At Misty's request, Spydah didn't get an invitation. It had to be killing Spydah to be sitting at home while Misty got to enjoy the show and all the after-parties she and Smash were planning to attend.

Getting niggas blackballed was an unexpected perk for procuring sex for Smash Hitz.

Spydah is lucky that all I did was suggest that Smash rescind his Grammy invitation. He better pray that I don't whisper in Smash's ear, mention that it seems like Spydah is frontin' like he's bigger than the man that made him. Shit, if Smash Hitz gets mad enough, he's liable to hold back the release date of Spydah's next album. Might not release it at all. Smash could use a tax write-off…couldn't he?

Misty was acting as a decoy on Smash's arm.

She found out that his main squeeze—a hot Latino tranny named Raquel—was stashed away in the same Los Angeles luxury hotel where Misty was staying. Raquel had a body that was crazy sexy and would put most women to shame. Unfortunately, Raquel couldn't control her *caliente* temper.

While Misty was holding on to Smash's arm and smiling for the cameras, Raquel was back laying up in her suite, holding a cold pack up to her jaw.

Bitch wanted to go to the Grammys. Wanted to walk the red carpet with her arm linked proudly through her man's. Smash laughed in her face. Raquel had a tantrum. Started talking reckless…cussing in Spanish, demanding that Smash upgrade her from hidden in the shadows to limelight status.

Raquel had the nerve to come at Smash with her fingers clawed. Berserk bitch was running toward him, scratching the air, growling, with a bunch of spit spraying out of her mouth. Though Smash would never admit it, Misty could tell that Raquel's wild animal behavior had him shook.

Smash ain't have no choice. He had to stop her. Had to make sure she wouldn't get the idea she could be coming at him whenever she got mad. He used a left hook on that unruly tranny.

Raquel was lucky he didn't ship her back to the streets of Argentina. Or Nicaragua. Or wherever the hell she came from.

Now Misty and Smash had an understanding. He liked trannies but had an occasional penchant for buff men.

Horatio thought he was special. Thought he was entitled to some of the perks Misty got from Smash. When she told him that his shot with Smash was a one-time deal, Horatio got angry and quit. Misty didn't care. She warned him that if he ran his mouth about Smash Hitz' personal business, he was gonna come up missing somewhere.

She assumed that Horatio would take heed.

CHAPTER 49

Brick came into the kitchen. "I don't know how he did it, but Little Baron slept through the whole party."

Thomasina wiped the countertops in her newly re-modeled kitchen. "Inviting all those people over was a big mistake. And who told them to bring all their friends and family?"

"That's our people for you. When they hear about some free food and liquor, everybody and their momma gonna show up." He shook his head.

"Well, that will be the last time I get neighborly. I couldn't even enjoy seeing my baby at the Grammys."

"I know. Too many haters sitting around, tryna throw shade on her dress."

"I should've listened to you, Baron."

"Live and learn. Ain't that what you always say?"

"Yeah, you're right. Misty looked gorgeous, didn't she, Baron?"

"Yup. She's a stunner. Don't worry, baby. We gon' watch it again."

"We are?"

"Yeah, I forgot to mention it. That new HD box I picked up from the cable company comes with a DVR. I recorded the Grammys so we can watch it again."

Thomasina's face lit up. "I didn't realize the new box did all that. You know, I leave all the high-tech stuff to you."

"You can watch the show over and over, speed up to all the parts where the camera's panning in on Misty. I recorded it on the living room TV and upstairs in the bedroom."

"I'm married to a genius," she told him with love in her eyes.

"Little Baron is going to get a kick out of seeing his big sister on TV."

"But he's not gonna understand how Misty got inside the TV," Thomasina said, laughing.

Brick pulled out two bottles of wine—one white, the other red—that were hidden beneath a pile of dish towels.

"I thought the neighbors took all the wine."

"Yeah, they broadied us for most of the leftover bottles, but I stashed these two for me and you."

Brick rifled around inside a kitchen drawer and pulled out a corkscrew. Next, he took two wineglasses out of the cabinet.

"Let this mess wait. I'll help you clean up tomorrow."

"I can't sleep with dishes in my sink. You know that."

"Hurry up, baby. Don't stay down here too long. We gon' have our own little private after-party. Upstairs." He gave her a suggestive look.

"Give me a few minutes, and I'll be right up," she said, her eyes blazing with arousal.

Brick took off everything. Got buck naked in seconds. He uncorked a bottle of white wine and filled the two glasses. He looked down. *Damn, my dick is hard.*

"Hey, baby!" he yelled.

"I'm coming!" she hollered back.

"Don't cum yet. Wait 'til you get in bed with me."

He could hear his wife giggling. He loved her with every breath in his body. Time hadn't changed his feelings at all. If anything...these past two years had made him love her more than ever.

Brick turned on the TV. He hit the DVR button on the remote. As the pre-Grammy show came on, he began taking big swallows of wine. Sipping was for chumps. Back in the day, he used to guzzle a forty-ounce bottle of malt liquor like it was water.

Brick killed his glass of wine and then downed the glass he'd poured for Thomasina. Feeling good, he refilled both of their glasses.

Aiming the remote, he fast-forwarded to Misty's entrance. He gulped down another glass of wine and grinned at the TV screen. Seeing Misty in the limelight made him feel like a proud father.

Look at you, Misty. You're right where you belong. On the red carpet, baby. Do ya thing. You in your world, now, Misty baby.

His thoughts took him back to the way they used to

be. He drank more wine. Shook away the images. It was somewhat confusing to be sitting in bed with a hard dick, looking at his ex-girl—his stepdaughter. Brick shook off the disturbing images.

❧

That was then. This is now. I love my wife and I'm happy for you, Misty.

His lustful thoughts about Misty were accidental. But they still made him feel guilty. *I should have helped Thomasina clean up the kitchen.*

Brick picked up his boxers. He tried to stick his foot inside the leg, but was thrown off balance. He laughed at himself. *Damn, I'm acting like a straight sucka that can't hold his liquor. Getting tipsy after a little taste of wine.*

What the hell is taking Thomasina so long? In his intoxicated state, he got the idea to creep up on Thomasina. He grabbed the extra bottle of wine, intending to take the bedroom after-party down to the kitchen.

I'ma pour some wine down her cleavage. Lick it off...do some freaky wine-tasting in the kitchen.

Carrying the bottle of red wine, he crept down the stairs, steadying himself by holding on to the handrail. *I better hold on to something so my drunk ass don't fall down these damn steps and break my damn neck.* He laughed at himself as he took careful steps. Instead of going through the living room, he turned down the short hallway that led into the back of the kitchen, planning to surprise his wife.

He felt a rush, imagining him and Thomasina engaged in hot sex on the cold kitchen floor. In his mind, he envisioned the scene: puddles of spilled wine on the kitchen floor, discarded female lingerie on the counter, and his boxers tossed in a corner.

He saw himself lifting Thomasina's bare ass onto the countertop, spreading her thick thighs, and entering her from the front. Then he was gonna lower her onto the floor and hit it from the back. Then he was gonna…

Brick stopped cold when he reached the entrance to the kitchen. What he saw threw all thoughts of sex out the window.

Thomasina's complexion was a frightful gray. She was shaking all over. Her tear-filled eyes were wide with terror.

Behind her was an amped-up addict. One arm held her in a headlock; the other held a knife to her throat.

"You schitzing, nigga. I know you crazy!" Brick's voice boomed with rage and indignation.

The home invader narrowed his eyes. "I don't want no trouble, man. I thought y'all was sleep. Gimme some money or something. I don't wanna hurt her, but I swear I will." The man with the knife tightened his grip on Thomasina and dragged her helplessly as he moved a safe distance from Brick. Though he was trembling almost as badly as she was, he was steadily poking the knife into the side of her neck, breaking the skin…proving that he meant business.

The first thing Brick recognized was the stained Eagles jacket. It was the crazy-eyed junkie who had tried to slither into his home earlier.

"You acting real reckless with that knife, yo." Brick's voice became low-toned and sinister.

"Gimme some money, man. Or a small flat-screen TV or something I can flip," the knife-wielding smoker demanded, his face tightening in frustration.

Had he been sober, Brick might have attempted to work out a plan in his head. In an intoxicated state, his mind was too fuzzy for logic.

No time for thinking. The woman he loved more than life was being threatened by a fucking dope fiend. The intruder had Thomasina's neck in a vise-like grip, yanking her head back and forth, showing no concern about snapping her neck.

The sound of Thomasina gagging and gasping for air sent Brick into a dark place.

His ears roared. His eyes dimmed. Cold sweat poured over his body. His dark side took control, forcing the rational side of Brick's brain to shut down. Wearing a maniacal grimace, Brick moved with lightning speed across the kitchen, wine bottle raised. His movements were so sudden and so swift, the frightened dope fiend dropped the knife. It hit the floor with a clatter.

"You brought your ass in here with a knife," Brick

bellowed, his voice cracking with emotion. The notion unbelievable to his ears.

Brick broke the wine bottle over the man's head. Red wine spilled down his neck, and poured down the front of Thomasina's sweater.

Dazed, he loosened his grip on Thomasina. She yanked free from her captor, clutching her chest as she gasped for air.

"You wanna cut my wife, nigga?" Holding the neck of the broken bottle, he opened the man's cheek with the jagged edge. "You like how that feels?" Blood poured down the man's face, intermingling with the red wine that had accumulated around his collar.

"You put your dirty hands on my woman, man!" Brick lunged for the intruder and got him into a chokehold. Then Brick went wild…delivering a series of brutal stabs into his face, neck, and through the front of the stained, green jacket.

The intruder's face was a red mask of blood, but Brick kept jabbing him with the broken bottle, until the dope fiend's legs buckled.

Finding her voice, Thomasina let out a horrified squeal.

Brick released him. The man fell to the floor…moaning as he curled into a ball.

Thomasina had her hand pressed against her mouth. Her voice emerged through the spaces between her fingers. "Baron, we have to call the police."

Brick stood panting, still fuming with rage. Not listening to his wife. Keeping his eyes on the man who came into his home to do bodily harm to his family.

Quite suddenly, the injured man rolled in the direction of the discarded knife.

Like he was squashing a bug, Brick stomped his hand with the heel of his bare foot, breaking bones in his fury. Shards of glass met Brick's foot. Blood gushed out, but Brick felt no pain.

Breathing like a beast, Brick crouched down, clenched the man's head between his hands. "Oh, now you tryna stab me?" He slammed the smoker's head against the ceramic tile floor...over and over until the addict became dazed. One arm flailed about defenselessly.

Considering any movement as a threat, Brick seized the intruder by the sleeve of the green jacket and, in a few swift moves, he placed the offending arm over his bent knee and broke it.

The sound of breaking bone had Thomasina gasping and yelping in shock.

"Stop, Baron. Your foot, baby. You might need some stitches." Her attempt to distract Brick failed.

Looking crazy, Brick used his uninjured foot to kick the man in his side.

"Oh, my God. You're going to kill him. This is a matter for the police. Baby, listen to me."

Brick took no heed. Thomasina's voice seemed far-away...her words were nothing more than senseless babble.

"Lemme show you how it feels to be choked, mufuc-ka." He wrapped his large, strong hands around the limp man's bloody neck….applying intense pressure. As the drug addict kicked and thrashed, Brick stared down into the pleading eyes of the man who had threatened to take everything away from him.

"Baron! Baron! Please stop. Please," Thomasina begged.

Her pleas went unheard. Like white noise droning in the background.

Brick slowly squeezed the life out of the doomed intruder as he convulsed and struggled for breath. Deep in that dark place, Brick held the unlucky gatecrasher in a death grip long after the light of life had left his eyes.

Then the sound of Thomasina's body crashing to the floor brought him back from the dark abyss.

CHAPTER 50

"We got troubles." Fearful of being overheard, Brick's voice was barely audible.

"Who got trouble?"

"Me and your mom."

"That's between you and your wife. Nobody told you to marry somebody with all those miles on her," Misty said snippily.

"This is serious, Misty. I hate to ask you, but I really need a loan."

Misty's high-pitched laughter pierced Brick's eardrum. "You're kidding, right? You and my mom love being regular folks...those are your words, Brick. That's what you told me when I came over that day with all those presents for my little brother. Isn't that what you told me? So keep being regular. Personally, I enjoy living a fabulous life."

"Misty, this ain't no joke. I gotta get my hands on some money. I'll pay you back. I swear."

"Damn, you talking like a smoker. You using drugs or something?"

"Nah, man."

"Well, don't be tryna use my ass. I already give you and mom all the material things y'all broke asses can't afford."

"We appreciate it. But we never asked you for anything."

"I'm generous. But I don't like nobody tryna take advantage of me. Just because you see me rolling with Smash Hitz at the Grammys don't mean you supposed to call me the next day asking for a goddamn handout. I'm surprised that you'd show your greedy side so quickly. It's not a good look on you, Brick."

Brick swallowed his pride. He took Misty's insults without comment…he let her have fun at his expense.

He cringed at the image in his mind—saw himself limping through the night, carrying a heavy knapsack filled with tools. Brick had used a crowbar to loosen the manhole cover, and then lifted it with a manhole cover-lift dolly, a tool he used at the construction site where he was currently working.

After he'd lifted the manhole, he went back to his car, popped open the trunk, and lifted out double-bagged, heavy duty, contractor trash bags. Inside the plastic was the dead man's body.

The dead weight was harder to lift than the bag of steel tools, but he had managed. He had to. Had to get rid of the body. Pushing desperately, he had crammed the plastic bag inside the open manhole, and had given it a shove. The body was stuck…wouldn't move. Pressing on the man's shoulders, Brick had thrust harder until he was able to inch the body down farther. Finally, he had heard a splash. The dead man was down in the sewer.

Relieved, Brick had returned the manhole cover, driven home, and helped his wife get rid of the blood spatter and other evidence.

"Quite frankly, I'm embarrassed for you, Brick." Misty's voice snapped him back to reality. "You left me for my mother…so how do you sound hitting me up for some money?"

"I'm in a jam, Misty." Raw pain was evident in his voice.

"So shouldn't my mother be the person you should be asking to get you out of a jam?" Misty laughed bitterly. "I was starting to believe the hype…thought you were a righteous, hard-working family man."

"I am a family man. I can't go into details. But I gotta get my family out of this 'hood. Move to the suburbs or someplace where it's safe."

"So whatchu expect me to do…buy you a damn home? Sell the one you got. My mom's house is paid for."

Brick cleared his throat. "She…uh…she took out another mortgage when we remodeled the kitchen."

"That's the dumbest shit I ever heard. Y'all put a second mortgage on a home that was paid for so you could have a cheap-ass, crappy-looking kitchen. Ain't even no marble or granite nowhere in that kitchen."

Brick didn't have the strength to argue with Misty or to defend his and Thomasina's actions. "We don't want anything major, Misty. Something small. Something in a nice neighborhood."

"Nigga, you done lost your mind. I'm not out here busting my ass so I can take care of you and your family." Misty exhaled disgustedly.

"I wouldn't ask if it wasn't urgent. This is some life-or-death shit. Real talk." He pictured the body being discovered, and bit his lip so hard, he tasted blood.

"You know what, Brick. You're exactly like every other nigga in the street…out for your damn self. I knew you didn't have any real feelings for my mom. All this time… you been putting on a big front…using my mother so you could keep a roof over your head."

"I love your mother, Misty. With all my heart. I swear."

"Uh-huh. Tell that to somebody who don't know your sorry ass. We go way back, Brick. For as far back as I can remember, you always had security issues. Being homeless is your greatest fear. But damn…you ain't have to knock my mom up and marry her ass to keep a roof over your head." Misty's malicious laughter stung…had hurtful potential to put tears in Brick's eyes.

Brick felt more vulnerable than he'd ever felt. He felt worse than he did when he was a child, dumped on a neighbor, waiting for his mom to come back for him. Fending for himself was one thing. But it wasn't all about him now. He had a son—and a wife—a family that he had to protect. Family that depended on him.

"You're a union man; ask your union for a loan," she taunted mercilessly. "Ask them mufuckas that got you breaking up concrete, and eating lunch outside with a bunch of sweaty mufuckas."

"I can't get another loan from the union. I already got a loan when I bought the family car."

"Yo, I peeped the way you threw the word 'family' into the mix," she said mockingly.

Brick wasn't getting anywhere with Misty. She was so busy kicking dirt in his face, she couldn't comprehend the gravity of the situation.

"Something bad went down after the Grammy party. Some rank-ass, crazy shit." He spoke slowly. His voice held a dream-like quality as he still found it hard to believe the nightmarish turn of events that had gone down after the Grammy party.

"What Grammy party?"

"Your mom had a party here at the crib. Wanted the neighbors to see you walking the red carpet."

"So what happened?" There was a tiny trace of concern in her voice.

Brick looked around suspiciously, as if the walls had ears. "Look, I'ma call you back in about ten minutes. I'ma call you from a payphone."

💋

Finding a working payphone took a lot longer than ten minutes. After finding one, he dumped in all the change he had in his pockets.

"This espionage shit is starting to work on my nerves.

Tell me what happened," Misty said, after she picked up his call.

"I murdered somebody," Brick croaked.

"Huh? Repeat that, please."

"This crackhead nigga broke in our house last night. Had a knife up to your mom's throat. I ain't ask a lot of questions. I fucked him up."

"Protected your wife. Mmm. That's gangsta. I'm loving the visuals. I know how you act when you go off. You black out...you get extremely animalistic."

"Why you joking around, Misty? Ain't nothing funny about none of this. Your mom is freaking out. I had to calm her down with some Xanies. Not the generic ones. I got the strong, football jawns. Bought 'em off the street."

"Umph! I bet my mom flipped out when that doped-up nigga crashed into the crib. With all those bars up to all the windows...that home security system y'all got... how did somebody get inside the crib?"

"I don't know," he mumbled, not feeling in the mood to relive how it was his fault...for drinking...for letting his guard down. Forgot to lock up behind the neighbors... didn't set the alarm. Left his house unguarded and allowed a schitzin' lunatic to walk right through the front door.

CHAPTER 51

"I'm not feeling this loan crap. How much money are you requesting?"

"We gotta move from around here, Misty. Gotta buy ourselves another house." Brick spoke quickly. Desperation coated every word that came from his mouth.

"We can't sit around waiting for somebody to buy this one. The property values in this neighborhood are steadily dropping. I figured we'd rent the crib out... Section 8...so we can get the rent on time."

"How much are you asking for?" Misty yelled, growing impatient.

Brick felt his heartbeat start to calm down. His softer tone conveyed a calmer spirit. "Being that my annual pay ain't nothing to brag about...and your mom is on disability. We need to make a down payment of at least... sixty thousand."

Misty started coughing. "You want me to fork over sixty thousand dollars?"

"I'm not asking you to *give* me anything. I need a loan." Desperate, anxious, and distressed, he blurted, "I'll pay you back, Misty. I promise. Please help me out."

Finding himself in a situation so desperate that he was pleading like a beggar on the streets, Brick suddenly felt compassion for the intruder whose life he'd taken.

"How you gon' pay me back if you ain't got no extra money coming in?"

"I'll figure something out."

"You expect me to hand over that large sum of money and then sit on my hands while you try to figure something out? I don't think so."

"Come on, Misty."

"Well...okay...I know how you can pay me back," she said in a sneaky tone of voice.

"H-how?" Dread caused him to stutter.

"Work for me. My mom don't need to know about it."

Brick wiped his hand down his face. Though it was cold outside, he was working up a sweat. "I put that lifestyle behind me. I can't go back."

"Hmph. Desperate times call for desperate measures," she responded coolly. "If you pick up a few clients a week, you can work the loan off real quick. It should only take a couple of months of grindin'. Then you can go back to your 'regular-folk life'...and act like nothing ever happened. It'll be our little secret, Brick."

Between a rock and a hard place, Brick didn't speak. He couldn't. His chest felt tight; breathing wasn't easy. Forming words and making audible sounds was out of the question.

"I take your silence as 'yes.' So look, go find yourself

a house with a little picket fence. I'll foot the bill…but you owe me, Brick. You owe me. Don't forget it."

"I won't. Thanks, Misty." The words came out in a bitter whisper.

He hung up the phone, and then limped across the street. He'd gotten emergency daycare for his son today, but he had to get home and take care of his woman.

After the horrible ordeal last night…having a knife held to her throat, seeing a dead man's body splayed on her kitchen floor…after cleaning up all that broken glass, spilled wine, and blood, Thomasina would go bonkers if she woke up and her husband wasn't at her side.

Brick got in his car and headed home. Sweating, he imagined his house being decorated with that yellow tape the police used to broadcast a crime scene.

Thomasina was awake and frantic when Brick arrived home. "Where have you been, Baron? I was terrified. You can't disappear on me like that."

"You were asleep, baby. You looked so peaceful I didn't want to disturb you."

Thomasina started crying. "I thought they had you locked up. I thought our life together was over." She clutched Brick. He enfolded her in a strong embrace.

"Nah, it's going to be aiight. I promise you, baby."

"Where'd you go? What was so important that you'd leave me here all alone?"

Ashamed, Brick looked away from his wife's face. He didn't want to tell her that he called Misty. "I…uh…"

"Baron, there's always been mutual trust between us. Please don't start lying to me now."

She was right. He had to tell the truth. "I called Misty."

"Why?"

"Asked her for a loan."

"For what?"

"To buy another house. In the suburbs. Somewhere safe."

"You told her about last night?"

"Yeah, she asked me why we needed a loan. I'm not a good liar, baby. I haven't had any sleep at all. My nerves are shattered. So when she started grilling me, I caved. Felt like I had no choice but to come clean. I gotta get my family out of this house. Out of this fucked-up neighborhood."

"We can't move away from here."

Brick looked at Thomasina like she was crazy. "Why not?"

"I watch a lot of crime shows, Baron. Blood evidence is always the thing that ties criminals to the crime. No matter how much cleaning they do…there's always a drop of blood left behind."

"We're not criminals."

"In the eyes of the law we are."

"We cleaned up. With bleach. Shouldn't be any blood stains left behind."

"Baron, I don't want to move. We'll raise suspicions. Suppose, after we leave, someone comes in here snooping around and finds a drop of blood?" Thomasina pulled away from Brick. "We should let this blow over. This tragedy is between me and you and the Lord above." Looking grim, she shook her head. "And now Misty knows."

"I'm sorry, baby. I should have discussed it with you first."

Thomasina rubbed Brick's arm affectionately. "Like you said, you weren't thinking straight. Neither of us are. I don't want a loan from Misty. I want us to try to move forward. Act like this never happened. We have to put it behind us, Baron...as best we can."

"You got a point. We gon' stick it out together. Won't talk about it. Pretend it never happened."

"I wish you hadn't told Misty," she muttered. "This was our secret, Baron."

Brick had mixed feelings about staying in a home where a murder had taken place. Fortunately for him— and his marriage—he wouldn't need a loan from Misty that would have to be paid back with a pound of his flesh.

❧

Every time Smash had a spell: too much to drink... misuse of prescription drugs...a headache...or a bout of restless dick syndrome, he called Misty to utilize her service. He always expected her to join the worker. Not for a threesome, but rather to throw off the gossipers.

"Can't have my name in the headlines on some gay ish."

Raquel apparently didn't satisfy all of his desires. Whenever the mood hit him, it didn't matter where he was…the States or Europe. Even if he was across the globe in fuckin' Japan, it didn't matter; Smash expected Misty to drop everything and bring him a muscle-bound dick slinger for him to slurp on.

Being a beard for Smash Hitz was starting to get old. Smash paid well, but Misty had to look out for her future. Suppose Smash found someone else to provide him with pretty boy dick? Where would that leave her? *Up shit's creek, that's where I'd be.*

Borrowing a word from celebrity stylist, Jules Miata, Misty approached Smash with the idea of putting her on retainer.

"Put you on retainer? What for?" he barked.

"You never know when you gon' have one of your spells," she said in a concerned voice. "I want to make sure you utilize my services exclusively."

"Fuck that. I don't have that many spells."

Now that's a damn lie if I ever heard one. Smash is in denial. Some-times he used her service two or three times in the same week.

"I don't see why I need to put you on the payroll for work you're not even doing."

"But I'm always working for you, Smash. Every dude I hire…I hire with your preferences in mind. I'm fully staffed and able to offer you a variety of unique services."

"I gotta think on this. Don't want none of this to come back and bite me in the ass."

Not too proud to beg, Misty continued, "I promise that you'll have a never-ending supply of fine, young men. I'll never send the same person twice. And if you don't like the product, I'll have back-up. On standby."

"I hope you don't expect me to sign my name on some shit."

"Yes, actually I do. But don't worry; the jargon will be worded in a way that gives the impression that I'm out-sourcing personal assistants."

"I gotta think about all this," Smash said gruffly.

She didn't want Smash to think too long or too hard. She needed to get a mansion and a sexy car. ASAP!

❦

Baad B and Spydah were carrying on in public like crazy. Misty did not like the way their story was unfolding. Baad was pregnant and living in Spydah's web. Her upcoming baby shower was the talk of Miami. Misty really wished the bitch would miscarry or, better yet... she wished Baad would drop dead from pregnancy complications. *Fuckin' bitch!*

If it weren't for the fact that the media believed that Misty and Smash were considered an item, all the gossip about Baad and Spydah would have Misty hiding her head in shame. But Smash was the wealthiest man in the industry. So as far as the public was concerned, Misty had come up.

But her heart knew the truth. And she couldn't understand it. *First I lose Brick to an out-of-shape cougar; now Spydah's been snatched by an ugly-mug hoochie. I'm slippin'. But I'ma be up in a minute. Watch me.*

CHAPTER 52

It was a long time coming, but Misty finally bought her dream home.

It wasn't nearly as opulent as D.B. Spydah's mansion, and couldn't touch Smash Hitz' palatial estate, but at $1.7 million, the six-bedroom property on Hidden Pond Drive in Chadds Ford, Pennsylvania was more than Misty could have afforded without Smash's generous contributions.

Lately, Smash had been putting her on with some of his high-powered friends that had a penchant for dabbling in dick.

Now Misty was unstoppable. Money coming in from multiple big-money sponsors.

No more worries about keeping a roof over her head.

Before hiring an interior decorator, before one stick of furniture was moved in, Misty plastered the walls with her image. Jumbo-sized photographs and several portraits that were painted in oil were hung with utmost care.

Finally able to pay for his college education, Sailor happily accepted the keys and the title to Misty's old X5.

She was sad to see Sailor go back to Wisconsin, but didn't miss him for very long. She had stripped Uncle Freaky of all his boys and kept lifting the new ones that he copped from the Caring Cottage. With so many hunks to handle, she didn't pine for Sailor very long.

More money, more troubles.

Baad B was her biggest headache.

She had Spydah, she'd given birth to his little insect, and she had her own recording career, but she still wasn't satisfied.

Baad kept tweeting about Misty, throwing slurs in her rap songs, and generally bad-mouthing and tossing threats every chance she got.

Misty asked Smash to handle it. He needed to shut Baad down. After all, Baad was signed to his label…and as far as the public was concerned, Misty was his girl. Of course, tranny Raquel hated that she did the dirty work, while Misty got the praise. *Oh well.*

For him to allow Baad to disrespect her had Misty looking bad in the public's eye.

But Smash acted like Baad's beef with Misty was cute. In fact, he was so much about his money, he was capitalizing on the squabble, giving the green light to a video where Baad and a Misty look-alike were engaged in a girl fight. At the end of the video, Baad whooped "Misty's" ass, brushed off her clothes, jumped in a Lambo, and drove off.

Baad didn't actually own a Lamborghini; it was a loaner

for the video. But seeing her driving one sent Misty into a jealous rage.

❧

"Misty?" Smash's voice sounded uncertain.

"Yes."

"What's going on? I ain't seen you in months. Where you been keeping yourself at?"

"I was just in Miami last—" *Oh!* Smash was pretending to be off-balance, over-medicated or drunk...pretending to be caught up in one of his spells. *This mofo is really sick in the head. Why we gotta keep playing these games? Why can't he simply tell me what kind of dude he wants?*

"I miss you, too. I can come to Miami whenever you want."

"Tonight."

Oh shit! I'm starting to hate this needy mufucka.

"I'll bring two new flavors with me."

"Two? Why you gotta bring two?"

"They've been working on a tag-team routine. I thought you might enjoy it."

"Mmm. That sounds interesting. Same price for two?"

Hell no! "Uh...yeah. For you. Of course."

The new flavors were named Ryder and Kingston. The new boys were on top of their game, double-teaming Smash Hitz for hours. While Smash had Kingston's dick in his mouth, Ryder served Smash from behind.

Misty decided to throw herself into the mix. Just for the hell of it, she gave Smash's little dick a vigorous hand job.

The freaky foursome was a first for Smash. He was hooked and wanted more. Turned out, nothing compared to getting all of his erogenous zones catered to at the same time. He immediately put in an order for three men to pleasure him during the next orgy. *Ca-ching, ca-ching*! However, there was a hitch. Smash demanded Misty's presence at the group sex fling.

He told her that she knew all his erotic desires; he shouldn't have to say a word. She needed to communicate his needs to the hired help. *Damn! Now I gotta position mofos and feed them lines, like I'm directing a porn flick. This is some bullshit!*

Smash was a disgusting degenerate, but he and his freaky, down-low cronies kept Misty's pockets fat. If she ever decided to write a book about all the celebrity and rich-ass mufuckas that like swallowing dick—Umph! Put it like this, there were so many powerful down-low mofos who used her services, it wouldn't be surprising if one day, one of them decided to put a hit out on her ass.

Misty's fee for brokering the team-sex transaction for Smash was a Lamborghini. It didn't hurt to ask, goddamnit!

Smash didn't blink and he didn't stutter. "What color you want, mami?"

"Black," she said in a calm tone, but in her mind, she was jumping, shouting, and doing back flips.

Gloating, Misty sent a picture of her standing in front of her brand-new, black Lamborghini to all the gossip pages. She grinned from ear to ear when she saw the caption: *Smash Hitz Surprises Misty Delagardo with a New Lambo.*

How you like me now, Baad B?

❧

That feeling of elation didn't last for long.

Smash was on a new tour...one that included Baad B, Spydah, and other rappin' mofos. They were in the Philadelphia area with two shows scheduled at the Wachovia Center.

Misty wasn't thinking about Baad or Spydah...they could both kiss her ass.

What she hated was the fact that Smash was in such close proximity. His nut-ass was renting a hideaway mansion in the suburbs, about ten miles from Misty's new spot.

The problem with Smash being so close by was that he kept calling Misty, ordering dick like it was Chinese takeout. As soon as he finished with a dude, he was hungry for another. Even with her long list of workers, she was running out of hunks to satisfy Smash's voracious sexual appetite.

Smash preferred well-built, good-looking men, but Misty was running out of options.

"You my last mufucka," she told Troy. "I done sent everybody on my team at some point in time. Smash don't like dealing with the same mofo twice. So I don't have a choice. I have to send you to take care of Smash Hitz."

"For real!" Troy looked excited.

"Believe me, I don't want to. And don't be surprised if Smash returns your skinny butt back to me, demanding a refund."

"That's not gon' happen," Troy said with confidence.

"It better not, or I'ma dock your pay. Now go lotion yourself up. I can't have you representing my company looking all crusty."

Hours later, when Troy returned from Smash's crib, Misty was expecting the worst. But Troy had good news. He assured her that Smash had such a good time licking the ashiness from his dick, the man had fallen asleep, completely spent. Completely satisfied.

"Great!" Misty said with a big grin. "I didn't think you'd pull it off. I'm so proud of you, Troy."

"He said he was only taking a little nap, cuz he has to jet out of here early…around sunrise."

Have a safe trip…but goodbye and good riddance, Smash! As much business as he'd thrown her way, she should have been happy to speak with Smash every day, but goddamnit, that mofo was hard work. She could use a long break from having to listen to his Miami, country-sounding voice.

Misty had always had a soft spot for Troy. He'd hung in there with her when she didn't have anyone else.

She gave Troy a warm smile. "It's been a long time. Wanna sleep in my bed, tonight?"

"Do I? Damn right. I thought you dissed me a long time ago."

"I ain't diss you. But I got so many young bulls to fuck with, it was taking a minute for me to get back around to you."

"You ain't gotta ask me twice." Troy hastily started taking off his clothes.

They hadn't slept together in ages, but Troy's dick had a navigation system that led it to Misty's moist, treasured place. His long, King Cobra dick slithered its way into the depths of Misty's coochie. Writhing and sliding, pressing its head against her hot spot.

Though she preferred sleeping alone, after the sexual workout Troy gave her, Misty was too exhausted to kick his ashy butt out of her bed.

Fuck it! Their bodies entwined together, Troy and Misty slept like lovers.

Until the blaring ring of her phone yanked Misty from sleep.

It was Smash Hitz. He sounded furious. In her state of drowsiness, she thought he was pretending to be in the midst of a "spell."

But he was serious. Smash Hitz accused Misty of masterminding a plot to steal his blinged-out million-dollar medallion.

Misty had no choice but to get to the bottom of the mystery. She had to fix this shit!

After ordering her bodyguards, Nitro and Tank, to stomp the truth out of him, Troy finally fessed up. He'd taken Smash Hitz' medallion as a prank; it was in his bedroom.

And now Misty was in deep shit.

With the medallion inside her Louis Vuitton bag, Misty refused to be driven by anyone on her staff. First of all, she needed privacy. If Smash really required ass-kissing, she didn't want any of her staff to possibly see that shit.

Second, she wanted to get on the road with the Lambo and blow the bitch out.

Damn, she hated having to humble herself to stay in his good graces. *Why that nigga want me to put lip prints on both his ass cheeks?*

As repulsive as the thought was, she didn't think she had any other choice. Not if she wanted to keep rolling in dough.

Looking extremely glamorous, wearing her finest gear, she jumped inside her new Lamborghini. Gliding through the night, momentarily taking her mind off of her troubles, she listened to music as she tried to enjoy the smooth ride. Driving fast and furiously, her thoughts were everywhere. Agitated, she switched up CDs as she engaged in an internal battle.

Then she heard a troubling noise. Pulled over on the shoulder. Fuck! A brand-new Lambo…how did she get a fuckin' flat?

But approaching headlights meant help had arrived. Or so she thought.

One minute she was smiling at the good fortune of being spotted by a motorist in the middle of the night. And the next minute she was struck by the speeding car and thrown into mid-air.

When she hit the ground, she couldn't get a clear understanding of what was happening. Or why? The only thing she knew with certainty was that someone wanted to fuck up her face. And that someone also wanted her dead.

CHAPTER 53
Three Months Later

Gently roused from sleep by the soothing aroma of coffee and breakfast cooking on the stove, Brick opened his eyes and slowly sat up in bed. Cobwebs still in his head, he wondered why Thomasina had let him sleep so late. Remembering that it was Sunday, he smiled…lay back and savored the fact that he didn't have to work today.

He didn't mind working hard all week. He loved being able to provide for his wife and child, but spending quality time on weekends with his family was icing on the cake. The Kennedy family enjoyed a simple life. There was always an abundance of food, their bills were paid on time, and Brick was extra proud that he was able to put aside some money toward their son's college fund.

Brick and Thomasina were satisfied with what they had. Though Brick played the lottery every now and then, it was a harmless pastime. Neither he nor his wife were wasting precious time, worrying about striking it rich or keeping up with the Joneses. And they felt pity for people who did.

Having spent his entire life feeling unloved and afraid, Brick didn't take his happiness for granted. Not a day went by that he didn't count his blessings and thank the man upstairs.

The room was chilled from the noisy air conditioner sitting in the window, blowing at full blast. He snuggled beneath the sheet. Too cold. He thought about getting a blanket from out of the closet.

With a sigh, he threw the top sheet off and sat up. No point in lounging around any longer. Without Thomasina's soft warm body lying next to his, there was no comfort in the cold and lonely bed.

He threw on a pair of sweats. Still feeling a little groggy, he stepped unsteadily toward the hallway, scratching absently as he headed for the bathroom. The aromas that wafted upstairs had given Brick a pretty good idea what Thomasina had whipped up for breakfast. His woman sure could get down in the kitchen.

Patting his empty stomach, Brick smiled. Sunday breakfast was always a feast. Always a real good time.

But as soon as Brick stepped into the hallway, unexpected sadness overtook him. Then he remembered that nothing would ever be the same. The smile vanished from his face.

Misty.

The painful image of Misty's crippled body, her disfigured face, flooded his mind. Heavy sorrow, followed by feelings of utter helplessness, had him gripping his head, thick fingers dragging down the sides of his face.

Frozen in place, he stared down the hallway. Though no sounds emanated from her bedroom, he could sense her despair. His ex-partner in crime, ex-lover, ex-best friend...the daughter of the woman he loved, was in the back bedroom—the same bedroom he'd been relegated to when Misty had kicked him out of her life and replaced him with Dane.

With a heavy heart, Brick went into the bathroom and relieved himself.

Damn, Misty. Damn. She'd done some mean, selfish things in her life, but nothing so bad that she deserved to end up like this. Misty was bad off.

She had retained the ability to speak, but just barely. Like the numerous bones in her body, most of her teeth had been shattered and broken, adding a lisp to speech that was already challenged by her brain injuries. She was able to turn her head, and with great effort she could move her left arm. From time to time, she wiggled her fingers or opened her hand. It depended on if she was up to the task or not.

The rest of her body was left paralyzed. Doctors had compared Misty's condition to that of a severe stroke victim.

After two months, Misty was released from the hospital. She spent the next thirty days at a rehabilitation facility. The exorbitant costs of medical care had completely wiped out her finances.

Thomasina had visited every day. Hoping for a miracle, she had accompanied her daughter to every therapy session, pleading with Misty to work with the staff.

But Misty wouldn't cooperate. Her painful grimaces, constant tears, and pleading words bore witness that she couldn't endure the pain of having her limbs stretched, plied, and manipulated.

When the end of the thirty-day rehabilitation period drew near, it was suggested that Thomasina place her daughter in a long-term care facility. "It would be better for your daughter," said a somber-faced clinician. "Being that she's indigent, the State will cover the cost of your daughter's care."

"I'm not letting my child waste away inside a convalescent home. What kind of mother would I be if I allowed my child be left somewhere lying in urine and feces all day?" Thomasina exploded.

Determinedly, she'd brought her daughter home. During Misty's discharge process, Thomasina had been approached by another well-meaning hospital employee who'd hoped to change her mind about providing Misty's care at home.

Thomasina impatiently interrupted the woman's spiel with, "Let me tell y'all something for once and for all…" She scanned the room for anyone else who needed to get a piece of her mind. "There ain't no long-term care, no short-term care, no hospital, no convalescent home, no rehab, no hospice, no nothin' in this whole wide world that can take better care of my chile than me—her momma. But I can show you better than I can tell you." Tears streaming down her face, Thomasina snarled through clenched teeth, "Now gimme those gotdamn discharge papers so I can take my baby home!"

Misty had been living in the house she grew up in for two weeks now. The doctors had given up on her, but her mother hadn't.

Five days a week, for four hours a day, a nurse provided care for Misty. Each day, at the end of the nurse's shift, Thomasina asked the same question: "She's doing better, don't you think?"

The severity of Misty's injuries gave little hope for recovery. The nurse merely provided personal care and administered medication to keep her comfortable. Still, the nurse gave the heartbroken mother a ray of hope. "Your baby has a long way to go. Give her some time."

A tortured man, Brick stood in the hallway. Couldn't move. He felt as paralyzed as Misty. His poor wife wasn't thinking straight. Wasn't being realistic about the magnitude of her daughter's injuries. Thomasina hoped that she could love Misty back to good health.

Brick knew better.

He forced himself to move. Took steps toward Misty's bedroom to tell her good morning…find out if maybe she wanted to watch a DVD later.

Nah, not right now.

Brick switched direction. He couldn't face Misty yet. Needed to set eyes on his wife and his son…get centered. Buying time, he bounded down the stairs.

Little Baron was in his high chair, toying with his food. "Whassup, big man?"

The baby grinned at his father, then anxiously reached for him.

"Nah, it ain't sweet like that. You gotta stop playing around and eat some of that grub your mother made for you."

Solemn, Thomasina poured Brick a cup of coffee. Absently, he tousled his son's hair, his eyes latched to his wife's. He sent her a weak smile. Trying to encourage her. Giving her a silent message that they'd get through this difficult time, somehow.

Selecting a seat that faced his son, Brick sat down at the kitchen table.

Thomasina put a steaming mug of coffee in front of Brick.

"Morning, baby," he said in as cheerful a tone as he could manage, trying his best to slice through the thick cloud of anguish and despair that had invaded their once happy home.

"Morning," she replied in a tone dripping with sorrow.

"Daddy!" Little Baron called out, wiggling in his high chair, informing his father that he was desperate to get out of that high chair. "Daddee!" the child wailed.

"You win, man. Hush that fuss. I'ma let you eat with me."

Comforted by his father's promise, the baby quieted down.

"I made you a cheese omelet. Steak and grits." Despondency had stolen the joy from Thomasina's voice. Sorrow had dulled her eyes.

His cries ignored, Little Baron beat the plastic tray connected to his chair. He beat a steady rhythm, amusing himself.

"Thanks, baby. The food smells real good." Brick picked up the hot coffee mug.

Noticing that his father hadn't made a move to rescue him yet, the child became aggravated and tossed his plastic bowl to the floor. "Somebody's throwing a fit." Brick chuckled and stood up.

"Did you check in on Misty?" Thomasina's voice was a whisper.

The question made him pause. "No, not yet. I was going to sit with her after breakfast. I bought a couple DVDs I think she might like. Thought I'd sit and watch them with her."

"I turned the TV on for her and I tried to feed her some applesauce. She didn't want the TV on and she refused to eat." Thomasina squeezed her eyes closed, forcing back tears. "What am I going to do, Baron? My child is suffering and I don't know how to help her."

Brick shot up from his seat. Put a bear hug around the woman he loved. "It's going to be all right, baby. Like you always say, ain't nothing love can't heal."

Her tears wet his T-shirt. "I'm trying to believe that. But she's wasting away. Giving up on herself. Those people at the support group I joined…they said that Misty was going through the first phase. Over time, she'll learn to accept her condition and find meaning in her new way of life."

Brick nodded. "Uh-huh, that makes sense." He was trying to be positive for his wife's sake.

"The police aren't trying to get any justice for my baby. They're chalking it up to a hit and run, putting Misty's case on the back burner." Thomasina lowered her head and paused, attempting to halt the sobs that were forcing their way to the surface. "I just want to see my little girl smile again. That's all I ask, Lord." Thomasina let go and wept bitter tears.

Brick consoled her, squeezing her tighter, as though trying to transfer some of his strength to her.

One hand patted Thomasina on the back. The other doubled into a fist. Brick had been trying to keep it together for his family's sake, but the anger he'd been trying to contain was reaching critical mass. If he didn't get some kind of release, there was going to be a devastating explosion.

CHAPTER 54

Thomasina wanted Brick to get Misty to eat something—anything. She was also counting on Brick to finally put a smile on her daughter's face. But Brick's heart was too heavy to pull off any of his routines that used to have Misty howling with laughter. It was hard enough keeping from totally breaking down in front of her.

It didn't seem right to force a smile out of someone who was doomed to being bedridden for the rest of their life.

Her petite body was broken and useless, her pretty face had been brutally disfigured. But that wasn't the worst of it. It hurt Brick to the core to see feisty little Misty without any struggle in her. Fuck the smiling and grinning. It wasn't like Misty to surrender to the hand she was dealt and not put up some kind of fight.

He took a deep breath. With a DVD in one hand, and a spoon and a container of vanilla pudding in the other, Brick stepped across the threshold into the despair of Misty's bedroom.

She was asleep.

Brick set the pudding on the dresser, balancing the spoon on the top.

He took careful steps over to her bed.

Staring down at what was left of Misty, he shook his head. *This is so fucked up.*

Misty was emaciated. Losing weight every day. Her withered left arm lay limp at her side. Her hair, no longer her crowning glory, was entwined into a French braid… not as a fashion statement, but for the practical purpose of keeping it out of her face. The doctors at the hospital had patched up her right cheek, but hadn't reconstructed the crushed bone.

She didn't have insurance coverage, and the state didn't pay for cosmetic surgery or any vanity-related procedures. The dreadful state of Misty's misshapen face caused Brick's breakfast to lurch in his stomach. Overwhelmed and shamed by his response to his ex-lover's pitiable appearance, he dropped to his knees and began to caress Misty's shriveled hand. Silently, Brick wept.

The merciless blows delivered that fateful night had transformed Misty's million-dollar smile into a crumbled ruin of broken shards and fragments. Misty was in desperate need of oral reconstruction, but there was a long waiting list for indigent people who needed dental care.

Misty's mouth was a source of constant pain. She couldn't chew solid food and refused to make any more attempts at it. The one time she'd tried, her ragged teeth had torn at her cheek and tongue. The end result had been additional pain and a mouth full of blood.

Needing to provide Misty with sustenance in a form that she could manage, her mother religiously pureed meats and vegetables in the blender. But Misty wasn't taking any more chances with food; she flat-out refused to eat the mushy slop.

Looking at Misty all beat up and broken, Brick's mind took flight and escaped to a better time—the day he had first laid eyes on Misty. He dried his eyes. Bravely, he allowed himself to remember.

They were in the school yard. She left the group of kids she was playing with and approached Brick, who was all alone. To Brick's youthful eyes, Misty looked like a storybook princess.

She was dressed to perfection. Socks, little shoulder bag, and hair accessories were colorfully coordinated with her clothes. A well-cared for and vibrant child.

Brick was the complete opposite. Worn-out shoes. Tight-fitting shirt and high-water pants. Clothes that had been passed down to him from a stepbrother that was shorter and thinner than Brick.

When Misty asked his name, Brick found himself tongue-tied. Too stunned to speak. By the time he re-membered his name, he was already hopelessly smitten.

In Brick, Misty had found more than a faithful friend. She had found someone who idolized and worshipped her. Until she'd forced him to reach his breaking point.

No matter what her motives had been back when they were kids, Misty had taken him under her wing and made him her friend. It was Misty who had encouraged him to stand up for himself. Convinced him that he could beat all those kids who picked on him. Bolstered his ego until he became the boy that everyone feared.

Yeah, she used and abused me. But I only have myself to blame. She couldn't do no more than I allowed her to do.

Scenes from the life he'd shared with Misty played inside his mind. Bottled up emotions were stinging his eyes; tears threatened to spill again. Brick rose from his knees and then collapsed into the rattan chair next to Misty's bed.

Misty's eyelids fluttered open. She smiled.

❧

"Hey, Misty." Brick struggled to keep his emotions in check. He wished Thomasina could see her daughter smile. Oh, well. It wouldn't be her last smile. Misty was in it to win it now; there would be more smiles to spread around.

"You hungry?" Brick shot a glance at the dresser.

Frowning a little, Misty shook her head. Then she gave Brick another smile…this one had a dreamy quality.

"You gotta put something in your stomach. Look at you…all skinny and everything. You wasting away."

"Not hungry," she whispered and turned her head away

from Brick, smiling dreamily as if she had an amusing secret.

"You aiight? Something on your mind?"

She gazed at Brick. "Yeah."

Brick had been aching for some information. Now that Misty was talking, it was time to cut to the chase. "Who did this to you, Misty?"

"What?"

"Who was the coward who fucked you up like this? Was it one of them punks who was tricking for you?" His face contorted as contained rage bubbled to the surface.

"I don't know who sent her."

"Whatchu mean *her*? You think a woman did all this to you?"

"Let it go."

Brick reared back so hard, he almost toppled over the chair. "No, I ain't lettin' nothin' go. Somebody's gonna pay for this. And that somebody is gonna end up with body parts scattered all over this damn city. That's a promise…not a threat."

"Let it go, Brick," Misty implored wearily.

"Hell, no. You ain't been no saint, Misty, but you sure as hell ain't deserve to go out like this. Who do you suspect? Give me a name. Give me something to work with."

Misty closed her eyes and winced as if in pain.

"You okay?"

"I'm hungry."

Without a moment's hesitation, Brick leapt up and grabbed the pudding.

Sensing that pressing for information about the person who had left her for dead on the side of the road was off limits, Brick made small talk.

"Your mom is real worried about you. She wants you to start eating something that'll put some meat on your bones, but this is a good start." He scooted the chair closer to the bed, and pulled off the pudding's sealed lid.

Brick aimed a spoonful of the vanilla dessert toward Misty's mouth. She barely parted her lips.

"Come on, Misty. It's not that bad. You gotta eat something."

She opened her mouth wide enough for him to get half a spoonful of pudding inside.

"Now we getting somewhere." Brick sounded pleased.

He had no qualms about spoon-feeding Misty. He'd taken care of her in one way or another for so many years, it was practically second nature.

After eating half the container, Misty shook her head when Brick aimed for her mouth with another heaping teaspoon.

"Had enough?"

She nodded. Brick yanked a tissue out of a box on the nightstand and gently wiped her mouth.

"Yo, what's with the head nods and whatnot? I notice you tryna kick it like speaking too many words might put some stress on your vocal chords."

Misty released a single note of amusement.

Brick didn't need to know that air hitting the exposed nerves of her broken teeth made them ache like hell.

"Oh, you think that's funny?" Brick was starting to enjoy his visit with Misty. This was the best mood he'd seen her in since the brutal assault. Brick wanted to call Thomasina upstairs so she could share in this moment but he didn't. Misty might clam up on her mother. And that would hurt Thomasina to the core.

In due time, Thomasina and Misty gon' be conversatin' like girlfriends.

CHAPTER 55

"I bought a comedy for us to watch. The bootleg dude said this jawn is hilarious. Real clear, too." He pulled out the DVD that he'd tucked inside the chair, held it up so Misty could see the cover. "Wanna check it out?"

"No."

"Whatchu wanna do, then? You gotta do something. You gon' lose your mind if you lay up in this room day and night, staring at the walls."

"I do stuff."

"Git outta here. Like what, Misty?" Her comment was so absurd, Brick couldn't keep the smirk from forming on his face.

"Hangin' with Shane."

Speechless, he gawked at her.

"I have fun with Shane."

"Oh, you been dreaming about Shane?" He spoke in a tone of voice that one would reserve for the feeble-minded.

"Not dreaming. I know how to slip into his world.

We hang out together. So much fun," she said, looking dreamy-eyed again.

Brick was dumbfounded. The doctors had assured them that Misty's cognitive mind was intact. Now he realized those white coats were wrong. That bump she took on the head had jumbled her brain cells around. Or maybe it was the mixture of meds that she took regularly.

Yeah, that's what it is. That medicine is messin' with Misty's mind.

"I'm not crazy, Brick."

Had she read his mind? He scrutinized her face, as though searching for an indication that she possessed psychic powers.

"I got big plans." She used a boastful tone that was reminiscent of Misty's attitude before the assault. Only now, her speech impediment took most of the swagger out of her bragging words.

"Oh, yeah," he said doubtfully.

"Mmm-hmm."

Both wearing serious expressions, Brick and Misty stared at each other, striving to come to an understanding.

What the hell is she talkin' about?

Trying to read between the lines, Brick said, "You ain't even gotta ask me to handle the bitch-ass nigga who did this to you."

She shook her head impatiently. "That's not important anymore."

"Hell if it ain't. Tell me who did it. Was it one of those faggot-ass faggots that was working for you?"

Exasperated, she shook her head again.

"Give me a name and that nigga's days is in the single digits. Trust me on that. After I make that muthafucka lay down, I'ma cut that nigga up in real little pieces. I'ma put his dead ass through a meat grinder. Shit, I should put that nigga's ass through a meat grinder while he's still alive and screamin'," Brick fumed, breathing hard. There was little sanity in his words but a great deal of venom in his voice.

"I don't know who attacked me, but I already told you it wasn't a man."

Brick's brows furrowed in confusion. "You sure?"

Misty nodded. Her face darkened at the memory, a combination of pain and sorrow.

"Damn," he spat, his hands gripping the back of his head. Frowning, Brick mulled over the possibility of having to put a female through a meat grinder.

"You had beef with the broad?"

"Never saw her a day in my life."

"You telling me that some random female did all this to you…tried to kill you? That don't make no sense at all, Misty."

"Maybe she had beef with me…could have been some-body all booed up with one of my workers. Or the jealous wife of one of my clients. Who knows?"

"I can sure find out when you give me the names of

those pussies that worked for you." Bricked scanned the room for a pen and paper.

"At first, I thought one my clients had paid her to put me down."

"Oh yeah? Which fuckin' client was that?"

"I had a lot of high-profile clients. A lot of enemies, too."

"Name the punk-asses," Brick spat.

"Baad B was one of my enemies."

"The rapper that's with your ex...that bull, Spydah?"

Misty nodded. "And there's this tranny chick named Raquel. She hated me over my relationship with Smash. But I was frontin' with Smash. He's a down-low brotha."

"Fuck outta here!"

"Brick, I done crossed so many people..." She paused. "This stripper named Juicy. I scammed her, had her thinking she was going to get paid to lap dance for the stars." Misty sighed. "It could be anybody."

"Whoever did it better start saying prayers."

"It doesn't matter. I don't want revenge."

"Why the hell not? That don't even sound like you, Misty."

"I want to be with Shane."

"You really fuckin' with my head. One minute you sound like your old self and the next minute, you talkin' like a nut-case."

"I'm in my right mind, Brick."

"Don't seem like it."

"Shane told me something only you and he would know."

"What's that?" Brick tried not to smirk.

"Shane said he knows that you used to hear him while you two were locked up in juvy."

"Heard what?"

"He said he used to cry for his mother late at night. He said he knows that you heard him."

Momentarily stunned, Brick swallowed. "You startin' to freak me out."

Misty smiled.

"I ain't never tell Shane that I heard him crying."

She nodded. "Well, he knows now. He said that you think about him and those nights at Barney Hills a lot. You're still trying to figure out why he took his own life."

Brick felt goose bumps popping up all over his skin. "That's true, Misty. I heard him, but I never said nothin' to him about it. Figured that a dude as hard-core as Shane would be embarrassed if he knew that I heard him crying for his dead mother every night."

"Shane can hear your thoughts, Brick. He wants you to know that he was in emotional pain back then. He took his own life because he wasn't in his right frame of mind. Mental illness. Like his mother. But it's all good now. He's well and happy now."

Unnerved, Brick looked around the dim room. Creepy shadows propelled him to his feet. He clicked on the ceiling light, brightening up the spooky bedroom.

Misty laughed softly. "Don't tell me you're afraid of Shane?"

"Yo, I need some extra light. Too many shadows darting around in here."

She giggled. Then she assumed a serious expression. "I'm way beyond depressed. And I'm so over all of this." Her eyes traveled the four walls. "The only joy I have is when I can get out of this room and get to be with Shane. It's not easy to do. Takes a lot of concentration."

"Whatchu saying, Misty?"

"I need you to help me. I can't live like this anymore, Brick." Her eyes filled with tears.

"C'mon, Misty. Stop talking like that." Overcome with emotion, his voice trailed off.

"Please forgive me, Brick. For my selfish ways. For every cruel thing I ever did to you. Shane has helped me to see things clearly. How hurtful I've been to the people who love me. I'm so sorry, Brick. Can you forgive me?"

He waved his hand, brushing off her apology. "That's behind us now. I found what I needed with your mother. Never thought I could have that kind of love. Marriage and a family…that wasn't in the cards for me. I'm so blessed it scares me. In a weird way, I feel like I owe all these blessings to you, Misty."

"Don't give me too much praise. Think about it, Brick. You know me. If this assault hadn't stopped me, I'd still be hell-bent on ruining your marriage."

"I forgive you for that." He shrugged. "So, we're even. Right?"

"No, Brick. We'll never be even. If I lived a thousand years, I couldn't undo all the damage I've done. That's why I have no right to ask anything more of you."

"Whatchu need, Misty? Ask me and I'll do it. But you know that already."

"I'm not asking for a small thing, Brick. It's something that won't be easy for you."

"You kiddin'? You talkin' to Brick, yo. I'll move a mountain to git you straight. So why you stressin 'bout asking me for something? Look, whatever it is, it's already done. I'll put my family's lives on that."

"Damn, Brick. I wish you hadn't swore on my mom and my little brother. You're gonna be mad you put your family on the line like that. Especially when you find out exactly what I need from you."

"C'mon, Misty. What's with all the suspense? Spill it so we can get this thing done and move on to more important things. Like gettin' you outta that bed. Outta this room and—"

Brick's litany of hopes and dreams for Misty was halted by Misty's moan of anguish.

"Stop it! Just stop it, Brick. I'm never going to leave this bed or this room. Not alive anyway."

"Don't talk like that, Misty. If your mother heard you sayin' stuff like that she'd—"

"It's the truth. And it's about time all of you faced it. I have."

"You're still young and have a long life ahead of you, girl. With more therapy to get you movin' and some surgery to get your pretty face back, you'll be your old self in no time at all."

"I don't want any more therapy or surgeries. My *pretty face* is never coming back. I don't even want it back. What I want is...I want to be with Shane again. I wouldn't even ask for your help if I could do it myself. But this fucked-up useless body of mine won't let me do shit. Brick, I need you to help me die. There, I've said it."

Brick was stunned speechless and stood motionless beside her bed.

For Misty, his silence lasted an eternity. Searching his face for some indication of an answer, she pleaded with her eyes.

"There's no one else who can help me. I wouldn't put you in this position if I didn't have to. But I can't live like this anymore. I can't take another minute, another second of being trapped in this foreign body. It's disgusting to *me* and I don't have to look at myself. I don't know how you and my mom can take it. I really don't."

"There you go talkin' crazy shit again, Misty. Why you so hard on yourself? You don't look that bad," Brick lied. "Me and your mom was just sayin' how you're lookin' more like yourself every day."

"I'm so miserable, Brick." Misty was sobbing now. "Put me out of my misery. Please. I'm begging you."

"Beggin' for what? Something like a mercy killing?"

She nodded. "I don't want to be here anymore. There's a better life waiting for me."

CHAPTER 56

Brick's heart was pounding and he felt dizzy. He'd never had a panic attack before but this must be what one felt like.

Is this who she thinks I am? Some kind of gangsta killer?

Angry and scowling, Brick leaned close. "I see. So you think I don't have no conscience anymore? Just because I had to stop that nigga from threatening your mother? That was a kill or be killed situation. It was self-defense! I didn't wanna take that smoker out, but he ain't give me no choice. Think about it…your mom, your little brother and me—your whole family could have been wiped out if I hadn't done what I had to do."

"I don't think you're cold-blooded."

"Then what makes you think that I can kill on command? That's not me. Nah, that's not what I'm about."

"Well, a few minutes ago, you were talking about murdering whoever did this to me."

A shadow fell over Brick's face. "That's different. That's about getting justice."

"And what I'm asking is about getting mercy. From you." Her words came out in a halting whisper.

Brick stood up. "I can't talk about this, Misty. Uh, do you want me to put this movie on for you?"

"What good would that do?"

He gazed at her thoughtfully. "It might cheer you up. Get rid of those crazy thoughts you got swimming around in your head."

"Crazy? It's crazy to be in here pissing and shitting on myself. Can't move shit. Oh, excuse me. I forgot. I can move my head and one arm. Wanna see, Brick?" Misty slowly and painfully demonstrated her limited capacity. Panting as she struggled to move her head, Misty was able to make a barely perceptible turn away from Brick's somber visage. Resting before attempting her next feat, she glared at Brick.

"Look, I get it. It's hard for you, but if you do your therapy, it might get better."

Misty gave him a long look. "Don't insult me, Brick. My life is over. We both know it."

"That's not true, but you have to want to live. You have to make some effort to be happy. If not for yourself, then do it for your mother." A sound of distress caught in his throat.

"You and my mom have each other. And your son. I'm trapped in a mangled-up body. I'm helpless. Do you really think I'm going to find any happiness?"

"You can try, Misty. Try to make the best of it." His voice held a pleading tone.

"Make the best of what, Brick—this living hell I'm in?

Well, that's asking too much. Especially now that I know a blissful life is a few pills away."

"Come again?"

"I've been planning this for the past two weeks. Waiting for you to come in here without my mother."

Uncomfortable with the direction of the conversation, Brick swallowed hard. He could feel sweat accumulating on his forehead. "You want me to give you some extra pills? To overdose you with your medication?"

She nodded.

"Fuck outta here, Misty. You might as well get those thoughts out your head. You got a spot right here." He touched his heart. "Ain't no way in the world I could ever hurt you."

Tears spilled from her eyes. Brick watched as Misty struggled to bring her good arm up to her face. It was very hard to watch as she tried and failed to accomplish an act that he took for granted. He silently swore that he'd never take the small things for granted again. Ever.

With pain etched in his face, Brick grabbed a tissue and dabbed at her eyes, but the tears continued to fall.

"See, I can't do it myself," Misty said between soft sobs. "You gotta help me out."

He gave a long, woeful sigh as he wiped the bitter tears that slid down her face.

"I'm dying anyway, Brick. But it's a slow, torturous death. I've done some messed-up shit…still, I don't deserve to have to live like this. Pissing and shitting all over myself like a fuckin' baby. Then waiting for somebody to clean my pathetic ass. Would you want to live like this?" Her eyes, dry now, were riveted to his. Pleading with him to put himself in her place. To understand her desperation.

He looked away from her beseeching gaze. "What you're asking is murder, Misty. Plain and simple. You of all people should realize I ain't built like that."

As he spoke, he realized that his wife would beg to differ. She had witnessed him transform into something inhuman when he had taken that intruder's life. He could tell by the way she looked at him that she realized that there was a part of her husband that was dark—capable of killing. Without hesitation.

"I'd do it for you, Brick. In a heartbeat."

"I believe you, Misty. I believe you would. But you're not me. I couldn't live with myself if I was responsible for…your death."

"You won't really be responsible. It's all my idea, my plan, and I've already done my part. Been spitting out my meds, dropping them on the floor," she said, sharing information as if Brick had agreed.

"Why you telling me that?" he asked, his gaze sweeping the floor.

She ignored his question. "My nurse has to switch me from one side of the bed to the other. My mom has to move me when the nurse has off. I'll get pressure sores if I stay in one place all the time," she explained. "And my limbs have to get stretched out. You know, so they don't start contracting," she added with a sigh.

That last bit of information made Brick cringe. Though he'd never personally witnessed the stretching procedure, he'd heard Misty's heartbreaking cries and moans. Sounds that made him shudder and often brought his wife to tears.

Misty went on, "When I'm near the edge of the bed, I drop the pills I've been saving. Antidepressants, sleeping pills, and I even gave up my pain killers…my Vicodin."

"What you been taking for pain?"

"Nothing. Been enduring the pain. That's gangsta, right?"

"Damn, Misty. Ain't no reason for this. Why you hurting yourself?"

"Gotta do what I gotta do." Misty was on some serious shit. And all he could do was shake his head.

"My meds are scattered around on the floor. Can you pick 'em up for me, Brick?" Misty sounded exhausted, like she'd expended all her energy.

I'll pick 'em up. But that's it. That's all I'm gonna do, he told himself.

Feeling like he was moving through quicksand, he made his way around the bed.

On his knees, he began collecting the tablets and capsules that had been strewn about the carpet. Most had rolled out of sight and were hidden beneath the bed. Brick stood up, his fist balled tight around the deadly combination of pills.

"How many did you find?"

"Thirteen."

"Lucky number." She gave a sardonic laugh.

"Ain't nothing funny," Brick mumbled. "This is crazy."

"You're right. It's crazy that there aren't any laws that will allow me to choose whether or not I want to live in this condition."

"I realize it's not easy, Misty, but—"

"But nothing. It's fucked-up."

"I know it is."

"Does that mean you're going to help me?"

Brick went silent. He looked around the room, frowning...looking tormented. "What about your mother? She don't wanna lose you. You're not even considering what something like this will do to your mom."

"I love my mom, but seriously, this isn't about her. It's about the quality of my life and my right to decide to live or die. My mom isn't the one who's condemned to a fucking lifetime of staring at these four walls. It's gonna hurt her, but in time, she'll get past it and move on. She'll realize that I'm at peace and in a much better place."

Brick stuffed the pills inside the pocket of his jeans. "I can't deal with this. Not right now. I need some time by myself. I can't think straight with you pressuring me."

"Come on, Brick, please don't leave me like this."

Stubbornly, he crossed his arms over his chest. "Not right now, Misty." Overwhelmed by deep anguish, Brick bit down on his trembling bottom lip. "I can't make a snap decision. I gotta think on this."

He snatched a tissue…then one more from the box. These were used to wipe the tears that were sliding down his face. It took another handful of tissues to muffle the hoarse cries that escaped his throat as he turned his back to Misty and left the room.

CHAPTER 57

Brick went out for a few hours. Drove around aimlessly for the first hour, and then wandered into a random, hole-in-the-wall bar. A place like this was the perfect spot for a tortured soul like Brick. Sitting alone at the bar, shoulders hunched, Brick was forlorn as he nursed a cold beer.

After guzzling down the second bottle, Brick decided it was time to go home.

Thomasina was already in bed when he entered their comfortable bedroom. Using the bluish light of the TV, Brick undressed quickly and slid into bed beside of the soft, fleshy warmth of the woman he loved.

Reaching for her, Brick thought, *Never had to make important decisions by myself before. I always ran it past you first, baby. But I'm on my own with this one.*

Thomasina sat up. "I don't know what you and Misty talked about today but you sure lifted her spirits."

Brick arched a brow.

"She was real talkative tonight. We had the nicest conversation."

"About what?" Brick was hopeful. Maybe Misty had changed her mind about dying.

"She talked about her condition. Said that being paralyzed and having so much time on her hands is forcing her to give thought to what's really important in life."

"Oh yeah? What's important to her?" Brick probed.

"Love. She said that being loved is all that matters." Wearing a soft smile, Thomasina nodded. "Shame it took my baby getting all mangled and paralyzed before she figured that out."

Brick pulled Thomasina closer.

Resting her head on his chest, she stretched an arm across his body. He stroked her cheek consolingly. Kissed her forehead.

"Everything's gonna be alright," he said in a confident whisper.

"I keep telling myself that Misty's always been a fighter. No way she's going to give up on herself."

"You're right," Brick said in a soothing tone.

"Brick?"

"Yeah, baby."

"You believe in karma?"

"Whatchu mean?"

"Well, it's like the sayings, 'what goes around comes around' and 'you reap what you sow,' 'chickens coming home to roost'…"

"Oh, yeah, I get it. I can see the truth in all that. Yeah, I do believe in karma."

"I've been thinking. Maybe what happened to Misty is because of what happened to that man. You know, on Grammy night. In the kitchen," she whispered.

Thomasina was very still as she waited for Brick's response. They both knew his response would determine their future together. She'd never be able to forgive him. Her love for him would turn to hatred. She would be forced to leave him if she thought for one second that he was in any way responsible for her daughter's condition.

Brick gave the only verdict a sane man could give.

"C'mon, baby. Please don't do that to yourself. What happened to Misty was nobody's fault except the mutha-fucka who did it. It was horrible. The worst day of our lives. But some things you just can't make no sense out of. That was a terrible thing that happened to Misty, to our family. It tore us up real bad, but we're gonna get through this. We're not perfect by no means, Thomasina. We made some mistakes but you and me, we're good people, regardless of what happened. Don't you ever forget that. Hear me?"

"Yes. Thank you, Baron."

He massaged Thomasina's neck until her breathing pattern told him that she was in a deep sleep.

Then he eased away from her. Crept to the closet. He threw on a bathrobe and went to Misty.

He entered her darkened bedroom and softly closed the door.

"Brick?" she murmured.

"Yeah, Misty. It's me."

"Did you bring the pills?"

"Yeah, I got 'em."

Her sigh of relief was audible.

"How you wanna do this?" Choked up, his voice cracked.

"Turn the light on."

Brick paced across the room and clicked on the bedside lamp. The light cast a soft glow on Misty's poor, disfigured face.

He eased into the chair next to the bed, anxiety dampening his palms, sweat trickling down his face. Too hot and anxious to be worried about modesty, he whipped off his bathrobe.

Stripped down to his boxers and wife beater, he leaned forward in his seat. "Your mom said you were talking about love," he said, making nervous small talk.

She smiled. "I realize that nothing matters except love. You have my mom and I have Shane."

Brick didn't know what to make of Misty's claim that she and Shane had established an other-worldly relationship. It was clear that she believed it. And her belief made her happy. Now it was up to him to give her what she so desperately wanted. A one-way ticket to join Shane on the other side.

Whether it made any sense or not, whether it was right or wrong. He didn't have a choice. He had to do it. For Misty.

He stood up and began filling a glass with water from a pitcher that was kept at her bedside. The sounds of flowing water and Brick's drumming heartbeat interrupted the quiet of the night.

"I don't wanna do this." His voice was an agonized whisper. "But I realize it's the right thing," he said as he picked up the glass.

Misty nodded. "It's what I want, Brick."

"Despite everything…" His words caught in his throat. "Everything you put me through…don't none of that matter now."

He hovered over her briefly, and then very gently clutched the back of her neck. His fingers stroked the curls at the nape of her neck as he lifted her head from the pillow.

Bitter tears streamed down his face. "I love you, Misty. Unconditionally. I never stopped. You and me…we're family, girl. We go way back. We been connected so long…it's like you're my blood."

"I know, Brick."

From a shaky hand, Brick fed Misty the lethal cocktail. One by one, she swallowed the pills, taking a sip of water after each one rested upon her tongue.

Brick clutched the last pill to his chest as he looked down lovingly into eyes that he'd never be able to look into again. The gravity of the moment rocked him.

Unlike the intruder whose life he'd willfully and purposefully extinguished, Brick didn't want the light of life to go out of Misty's eyes. He wanted to put a stop to this madness. But it was too late. This light would soon disappear and he would be the person responsible. The person who would have to console her mother.

Though tears clouded his vision, Brick carefully placed the last pill on Misty's tongue. She took a last sip of water and then blissfully closed her eyes.

Brick's heart hammered so hard, his chest ached.

She opened her eyes. "I can feel it working."

He grasped her hand. "Are you in pain?" Brick wouldn't be able to bear it if he'd caused Misty to suffer further.

She gave his hand a light squeeze and whispered, "No, I feel good. Real nice. Getting real sleepy though." She closed her eyes again. "Feel better than I've felt for a long time."

"Oh, God, Misty..." Brick gasped. "I can't believe this shit is really happening. How could you be going out like this? It ain't fair. It just ain't fair, man." He sniffled, his broad shoulders heaving as he quietly cried.

Brokenhearted, he lowered himself onto Misty's bed and lay down beside her dying body. As he wrapped his arms around her tiny frame, he saw her open her eyes and smile up at him. He held her tighter, hoping he could stop her transition. Trying to keep life within her by sheer will alone.

Misty buried her head into Brick's muscular chest as she descended into her final sleep.

Sinking into oblivion, her awareness of this world began to recede. It was replaced by a glorious celestial landscape, and Misty was able to discern a shape. A hauntingly beautiful and familiar shape. A man. Walking toward her.

Oh, Shane!

ABOUT THE AUTHOR

Allison Hobbs is the national bestselling author of twenty novels. She resides in Philadelphia and is working on her next novel.